EBURY PRESS

THE RIGHT GUY

Tarun Vikash hails from Patna. He is the bestselling author of *She Stood by Me* and is currently working as a technical lead for a reputed IT firm.

T0294326

THE
RIGHT
GUY

LOVE IS NOT A CHOICE

TARUN VIKASH

Bestselling author of
SHE STOOD BY ME

EBURY
PRESS

An imprint of Penguin Random House

EBURY PRESS

Ebury Press is an imprint of the Penguin Random House group of companies
whose addresses can be found at global.penguinrandomhouse.com

Published by Penguin Random House India Pvt. Ltd
4th Floor, Capital Tower 1, MG Road,
Gurugram 122 002, Haryana, India

Penguin
Random House
India

First published in Ebury Press by Penguin Random House India 2024

Copyright © Tarun Vikash 2024

ISBN 9780143468448

Typeset in Adobe Caslon Pro by Manipal Technologies Limited, Manipal

www.penguin.co.in

Prologue

'Would you like to ride the bike?' Dheeraj asked.

I looked at him and his chubby cheeks. He had gained weight and his hair was cut shorter. He still managed to look cute. If I was his weight and had chubby cheeks like him, my uncles and cousins would have called me 'Teddy Bear'. I was slim. Thank god.

'No. You ride the bike, I'll sit behind you,' I replied.

I was in Patna. The last time I had met Dheeraj was four years ago, in Bangalore. Back then, he had finished his engineering from Vinayaka College in Chennai and I had finished my engineering from MVIT, Bangalore.

Dheeraj twisted the key and started the bike, kicking it hard.

'Where are we going now?' I asked.

'Where we spent our childhood.'

'The zoo?' I asked.

'No monkey-face, we are going to the ghat.'

'Ganga Ghat, you mean?'

'Yes,' he said and accelerated. We spoke about everything—the locality, the hawkers, the old buildings—all unchanged. In the middle of this reminiscing, we slipped in conversations about our childhood friends. Everything was still so recognizable except that they had grown older with time and I had grown younger.

Dheeraj parked at the Ganga Ghat entrance and looked around to see if there were any traffic police. He had not carried his driving licence. While coming here, he'd said that the rules had gotten strict lately.

We sat on the shore of the Ganga, my childhood memories flooding back to me with each soaring wave. Suddenly, Dheeraj nudged me.

'How is Santosh Bhaiya, your idol?' I asked.

'He is fine, living in Raipur. Sanjay Bhaiya, Pramod Bhaiya, Vinod Bhaiya are fine.'

'That's nice to hear.'

'She is beautiful,' Dheeraj remarked as he looked at a girl passing by—the reason he nudged me.

Boys can never ignore beautiful girls—it is disrespectful to their beauty.

'Yes, and I think you are married,' I sniggered.

'That is fine. There is nothing wrong in admiring nature.'

'She is not nature. She is a girl.'

'I am not hitting on her, Dhruv. I am just reminding you of how we used to be, back when we were younger,' he said.

'Dheeraj, we have known each other for a long time now. You don't have to remind me how we were back then. And I know that you still don't stare at girls.'

'Oh, you remember how I was?' he asked.

'Oh, yes. You were the shy one.'

'But you were shyer than me! You'd literally run if any girl in the colony came to talk to you.'

'Hahahaha,' I laughed and just kept looking at the waves.

'Remember, the girl who used to hit on you?' Dheeraj suddenly asked, his tone teasing.

'Who?'

'You forgot her or are you just pretending?'

'Hrithik's sister?'

'Yes, your best friend, Hrithik. His sister used to hit on you. She was beautiful.'

'Okay, okay, fine . . . but we were kids back then.'

'Love was so easy back then. Wasn't it?'

'Yes, and pure too. Those teenage hormones changed everything,' I remarked dryly.

'True that.'

'So, tell me,' I asked, 'what do you think of that girl who just passed by?'

'Oh, come on. I am in love with someone,' Dheeraj said.

'What? With whom?' I sputtered.

'Your *bhabhi*, idiot. Who else?'

'Love, in an arranged marriage? Interesting.'

'Love is love,' Dheeraj laughed and continued. 'You tell me about yourself. Did you tell her your feelings?'

'Who?'

'That girl you told me about. I am forgetting her name . . . oh yes! Avni, right?'

I smiled.

'Come on, Dhruv. You loved her for four years in college and still never told her. Now, it is almost nine years since you have known her. Where is she? Did you meet her again?'

I looked at Dheeraj. His eyes were shining with childlike excitement. True friends always want you to have a successful love story.

'Tell me, Dhruv, please!'

'Yes, I met Avni again.'

'Oh my god. When? How? Where? Did you tell her that you've been in love with her for so many years? Did she accept it? Is she still the same?'

'Dheeraj, you look more excited than me,' I said, ruffling his hair.

'You're my friend, of course I am excited. Love stories are so rare these days. Please tell me,' Dheeraj said, eager to know more about Avni.

'Which answer shall I give first?'

'Everything, Dhruv.'

'Everything?'

'From the beginning. How did you both meet again?'

'Hahaha. That was a funny incident.'

'You've got to tell me now. Even though I've never met her, I know she would be someone no guy can ever forget.'

I sighed. 'That's true.'

'So, tell me your story!'

Taking a deep breath, I said, 'Okay. Listen carefully. This girl has my heart.'

1

I came running back to my hotel room, closed the door and sat on the bed. I'd just seen her downstairs. She still looked the same, just a little more beautiful.

'Was it really her?' the inner me asked.

'Yes, it was her. I cannot forget that face. How can I?'

'Damn it. How did she become so beautiful? In college, she looked just okay, but look at her now!'

'I don't care about her looks. She is still the same Avni to me. I missed her so much in the last four years. But what if she was someone else? What if she was not Avni?'

'Then your last chance to tell her your feelings is gone, Dhruv Mehta.'

'Please don't say that.'

'She was a good friend of yours. You were the only guy she spoke to but you never told her your feelings. And on top of that, just last night you told Maa that you are ready for an arranged marriage. How can you do this?'

'What option does a guy like me have? Should I go down to the reception and check if that's really her?'

'As though she'll still be waiting for you. You think she'll still be there?'

'Let me check once at least.'

I ran down to the reception of the four-star hotel where I had arrived with my family last night. I looked for Avni near the reception but she wasn't there.

'Oh no. Now, how will I find her?'

'I have one suggestion. But only if you have the guts to take it,' the inner me said.

'What?'

'You have her number. She has yours. That too, since college! Message her and ask her. I know you don't have the guts to call her anyway.'

'Dude, I can't message her until I am sure it's her. And it is four years since we last saw each other after college. What if she is already married? What if she is in love with someone else?'

'Dhruv Mehta, this is what you have done all your life, and today because of your ifs and buts, you are ready to have an arranged marriage.'

'But Avni never felt the same way for me.'

'How do you know?'

'She never told me.'

'Did you tell her your feelings in college, you fool?'

'No. But even she never messaged me in the last four years.'

'Will you stop talking and message her please?'

'No way. I can't message her. I have to be sure if she is really Avni. I can't message her.'

'Even after that, you won't message her. I know you.'

'You are right.'

'Loser. Okay, at least go and have a clean shave. With this look, Avni will never recognize you if you see her again. I can assure you that.'

'Okay, fine. I can do that.'

I came back to my hotel room and had a clean shave, which I hadn't done for a month. I heard a message ping and immediately grabbed the phone with my soapy hands. It was from Shreya Didi. Damn it. I thought it was from Avni.

'Maa's waiting for you for breakfast. Come here', the message read.

I immediately ran down and checked the hotel reception again. Avni wasn't there. I missed her. I missed that mole on her chin.

'We are waiting Dhruv', another message from Didi popped up on my mobile screen. I ran immediately to my family seated in the dining area.

'Morning, Maa,' I said as I sat at the dining table and looked around.

'Morning, *beta*,' Maa said and looked at me with a smile, staring at my clean-shaven look.

'My son is looking so cute,' she said. Every mother wants their kid to look like a newborn baby.

'Dhruv, you look so handsome,' Anjali Mami said, moving both her hands over my head—a gesture to save me from the evil eye.

I checked again for Avni. I turned to my left and then to my right but she was nowhere.

'Oh god, please bring Avni back to my life. She is my only hope.'
'Then message her,' the inner me said.
'No way. What if she is married already?'

Maa looked happy seeing my clean-shaven face. She'd forgotten all about screaming at me last night in the hotel room. I'd screamed back; I didn't want an arranged marriage.

'Why did you bring all of them here with you, Maa? You know I don't like them,' I said, looking at all my relatives.

'They love you so much. Why can't you see that, Dhruv? They are all here only for you,' Maa said.

'I know how much they love me. They are here for the free stay and free food. How much money have you spent on booking rooms for them?' I asked, wondering how she managed to book so many rooms on her own.

In a four-star resort, you don't get rooms for free.

She looked at Shreya Didi and shushed me.

So, she was the one who had made all these arrangements. Her US dollars were finally getting used to screw my life.

Shreya Didi married the love of her life six years ago. She used to tell me, 'For god's sake, don't ever go for an arranged marriage. Love marriage is so, so wonderful.' But since last night, she has started convincing me to go in for an arranged marriage.

Last night she told me, 'Love marriages are boring. In an arranged marriage, there is so much to explore about each other.'

I mean, how could she?

If you checked her Instagram and Facebook pics, you would get to know how boring her life is. In her Facebook DP, she's holding her husband's hand somewhere on Miami Beach, and in her Instagram Profile, she's flaunting her love for weekend shopping. And then she says love marriages are boring.

Shreya Didi married Jiju, rejecting marriage proposals from NRIs and green card holders just because she knew getting settled didn't mean having all the money in the world. She knew the meaning of marrying someone you love. And I was the idiot who supported her. Dad was strictly against her love marriage; I convinced him to let her do that. These relatives did not even come for their marriage. They said love marriages were ruining our society. But once they knew that Shreya Didi and Jiju got settled in the US, they were all apologetic. For my relatives, moving to the US means you married the right person.

Last night, I saw my family after six months. Didi and Jiju had arrived from Texas after a year. Bhaiya and Bhabhi had come from Delhi. Maa and Dad had come from Patna. And my parents had invited all my relatives to surprise me. I met them all after a decade. We had only interacted on cell phones in the last ten years.

Suddenly, a message popped up on my phone.

'Dhruv, is that you in a pink T-shirt?' the message read. I saw the name of the sender. It was Avni. A smile spread across my face as I read that name again, Avni.

'Oh god, you listened to me,' I mumbled.

Okay, so I forgot to tell you all about Avni. What could I say about her? Back in college, we were good friends. She was in my theatre group and she had a mole on her chin below her lower lip which was my centre of attention and attraction. Avni used to be one of the most reserved girls I had ever met. Maybe that is why I could never tell her how much I liked her. I did not want to spoil our friendship. I desperately wanted to be romantic, like Jiju is, but I couldn't.

But Avni was very comfortable with me. She told me everything about herself—what she did, when she was busy, when she had mood swings, and everything else. Many times, I felt she liked me too but I was never sure. I had never been sure about anything that was related to girls. They are so confusing. They say something, but they want us to understand something else. And I guess that is the second reason why I am still single. Oh, I didn't tell you the first reason. Every time I spoke to Avni after I started liking her, my throat started drying up, my hands started shivering and my words got stuck in my mouth. I think, if a boy stays single for a long time, he gets these symptoms. Maybe. Maybe not. I don't know.

'What are you doing here?' I typed and looked around to see where Avni was. My phone beeped and I had to look down.

'Leave all that. Tell me first, what are you doing here with so many old people? 😊' she messaged.

The problem with Avni is that she is too direct. She thinks after she speaks. She sent a winking smiley a second later. People mostly come to Goa with college friends and my family doesn't look like college friends at all. Avni might be thinking, my life is still as boring as it was in college.

'They are my relatives, Avni. Where are you?'

'To your right', she messaged.

'You look so different from college days'. Another message popped up in a fraction of a second. I don't understand how girls type so fast.

If I type fast, Bhatinda would become Bhangra and Mahindra would become Miranda. I need to learn so much. I turned to my right and then a little left. Avni faked a smile at me. She was wearing a sleeveless embroidered top and a lehenga. But there was a guy sitting opposite her—a handsome, tall guy.

'Is that guy her husband? Oh god, please don't give me a shock,' I mumbled.

'Whose husband, Dhruv?' Maa asked. I suddenly realized that I wasn't mumbling very softly for Maa's ultrasonic ears.

'No one,' I lied.

'Huh,' Maa said.

Of course, she was pissed off at her son for not listening to her about anything since she had arrived here. If I told Maa about Avni, she and Dad would beg Avni's parents for her hand right now. I knew my parents' mental condition. So, it was crucial to keep things secret from them.

'What happened, Didi?' Amit Mama asked Maa, his right hand marinating his idli in that green chutney.

'He is murmuring about someone's husband but not telling me,' Maa said in a low-pitched voice.

'Dhruv, you know why you are here, right?' Amit Mama said, as he gestured with his eyes.

It felt as though he wanted to say something. There was a message on my phone the next second.

'They want you to get married to Nidhi', the message read. It was from Amit Mama.

He was the only person who understood that I didn't want to get married this way. I had no idea how he could be so cool, unlike my other relatives. He understood me. But my own family had started treating me like every Indian girl gets treated when she turns twenty-five.

'Manohar ji's daughter Nidhi is here. She is back from the US,' Alok Mama said, looking at me.

'Manohar?' I mumbled. I had heard this name before. Oh yes, Nidhi's father, I recalled.

'They are still looking for a guy,' Alok Mama added.

I wanted to leave all of them and sit beside Avni. Her sleeveless top was drawing too much attention from every other table. At Avni's table, there were two older people. Her parents, probably. I looked at her mother. Avni looked just like her. Once, she had shown me her dad's photo, and I had wondered how a man like him could have such a beautiful daughter. I have noticed one thing about marriages in India. I don't know how all ugly men in our country have married beautiful women. I haven't got any answer yet.

'Shall we talk about Dhruv to Nidhi's parents then?' Alok Mama asked Maa.

'Oh god, please save me from Nidhi. She is not my type. Please god, please.'

I thought I would enjoy my first visit to Goa. Even my college friends used to say that Goa means beautiful girls and beautiful beaches. But ever since I came here, I haven't liked the girls I've seen. I can't call them beautiful in the least. To be truthful, I have not seen even one nice girl. It simply means, my friends lied to me about Goa for all these years.

'But Nidhi is too modern. I have seen her wear skirts— really short skirts,' Anjali Mami, Alok Mama's wife, said.

I had never liked Anjali Mami but today I felt like hugging her. After all, she was on my side.

'Nidhi wore skirts when her parents went to the US to meet her. It's fine,' Maa dismissed her.

'But Didi—' Anjali Mami started, but her husband interrupted her.

It felt like my entire family was stalking Nidhi somewhere and I had no clue. I checked my phone and searched for Nidhi on Instagram, but it was a private account. I immediately opened Facebook and typed her name. I couldn't believe what I saw. My entire family was on her friends list. They were all our mutual friends. I was in shock.

'Oh my god, my family members are getting more dangerous by the day,' I told myself.

Is that the level they have gone down to? Hunting girls on Facebook now? If I don't find a girl for myself soon, they might start tagging me on a girl's photo on Facebook and ask my opinion in the comments section. They have no idea how

*fast Facebook really works. In no time, my entire friends circle
would get to know that my family is hunting for girls for me
and they would laugh at me.*

I cursed myself for introducing Maa to Facebook. She
used to complain that she hardly got to see me most of the
year. And the fool that I am, I created a Facebook account
for her, so that she could see the photos of my office trips.

Meanwhile, the discussions had come to a point where
I was finally asked about my opinion of Nidhi. I looked
down as if I hadn't heard, but I knew Maa would react.
She slid her phone closer to me, to show me Nidhi's
photo. Nidhi wore a green silk saree; it seemed like she
didn't wear sarees a lot. Just now I had seen her in a skirt
on Facebook. My brain was divided—does she look better
in a skirt or a saree? Some girls look good in everything.
And then I looked at Avni. She looked really beautiful but
I didn't know who was the guy opposite her. Sigh. She's
so beautiful.

*'If I say no to Nidhi and if Avni is already married, I am
dead both ways,' I thought.*

*'Dhruv, love is all about taking risks. Say no to Nidhi for
now.'*

'What if Avni is already married?'

'Dhruv, do you like Nidhi?' Maa persisted.

'Yes, she is nice,' I said, just to make Maa feel good.

'Let me arrange a meeting with Nidhi then,' Alok
Mama said.

'But I don't like her.'

'But just now you said she is nice,' Maa said.

'Yes, but I don't want a girl like her. I want a decent girl,' I said.

'She is too decent for you, Dhruv,' said Maa.

'Wasn't I supposed to give my opinion, Maa?' I asked.

'Yes, but we don't see the point in your refusing such a nice girl!'

'Sugandha Didi, don't force him. Give him some time to think,' Amit Mama piped up.

'Don't worry, I will marry soon,' I added, looking at Maa.

'Do you have a girl in mind?' Alok Mama asked. He wants to know everything about my life or else his gastric issues will never get over.

'Not yet,' I said.

'I will meet you in some time', a message popped up on my phone. It was from Avni. I smiled, looking down.

'I'm just coming,' I said and left the table. I had told them my decision, so there was no point in entertaining anyone. I got up, walked past Avni's table and sneaked her a mini wave. She waved back, unseen by the others at the table.

'Now you are behaving like a romantic guy,' the inner me said.

'Thanks, dude.'

Avni looked really cute; her haircut was different from our college days. I came down to the washroom area.

'Are you mad?' a lady screamed as her eyes met mine.

I was about to say that she was in the wrong washroom when she pointed at the door. I turned around and looked at the door—it was the ladies washroom. I looked back at her.

'Sorry, aunty,' I said.

'Aunty? Do I look like an aunty to you?'

I did not know what to reply. Some questions are better left unanswered. It would hurt her if I told her the truth. And I had no doubt if I said yes, she would kill me. Every aunty in Goa wants to be treated as a girl, I realized. Shall I say 'Sorry, babe' to bring a smile to her face? Just then, my phone buzzed. I looked at the screen. It was Bala, my Tamilian friend, and the message read, 'Bro, did you see babes in Goa?'

This idiot always has to come into my life at the wrong time.

My phone rang the next second. It was Bala. I picked up the call and pressed the speaker by mistake. Bala asked the same question, 'Bro, did you see babes in Goa?'

The lady heard that and looked at me disgusted. I tried to switch off the loudspeaker but it was not happening.

'Bala, one second, *macha*, one second, just let me . . .' I mumbled close to the mic but Bala was asking the same question again and again.

At that moment, I could see a 'GOA Central Jail' signboard right in front of my eyes. I was sweating in terror. I immediately ran out of the women's washroom and entered the gents' one. I looked in the mirror. My face had turned red as I took a deep breath and disconnected Bala's call. My hands were shivering. This Bala would have got me into big trouble today. I realized I had to get a new phone. I heard a few women laughing. It felt as if Avni was there. I quickly popped my head out of the washroom to check, but it wasn't her.

'What the hell is Avni doing in Goa?' I asked myself, looking back into the mirror.

'And who is that guy? Is she really married to him?'

'Why didn't she have this haircut in college? She looks so nice. Okay, enough. I'll text her and call her here.'

'Can we meet now?' I messaged and waited. No response came.

A message came after a few seconds—from Bala. I forgot to mention one thing about him. He's never had a girlfriend.

'Did you see girls on the beach or not, macha?'

Man, this guy should get married as soon as possible. Or get a girlfriend. He is dying to get married. I really feel bad seeing his mental condition as the days go by. This is what happens when you are twenty-six and you don't have a girl in your life.

'Did you see girls on the beach or not?' Bala messaged again.

'Yes. All the girls on the beach have said hi to you', I replied.

Avni still hadn't replied. Was she busy? With her . . . that guy?

'Macha, please send pics from the beach', said Bala's next message.

'Oh god, please get this guy married to the hottest and most beautiful Tamilian girl on the planet. Please,' I prayed.

I had taken a few pics of the beach. I scrolled through my phone gallery but there were no girls in my pics. There was only water and sun and palm trees. My phone buzzed again. It was Maa.

'Where are you?' she asked.

'I am coming, Maa,' I said.

After splashing some more water on my face, I left the washroom. The lady who had just screamed at me was at the reception. I smiled at her without saying a word and walked by. I heard her mumble 'Jerk', but I ignored it. There were things more important than that.

I came back to my annoying relatives. Anjali Mami was now sitting beside Maa so I switched places and ended up sitting next to Amit Mama.

'Who is she?' he asked, gesturing toward Avni.

'What the hell? You were stalking her?' I hissed.

'Do you like her?'

'N-n-no. No, no, I don't,' I mumbled.

'Okay, have your breakfast before it gets cold,' Amit Mama said and looked at Avni again.

'Mama, please,' I said, hoping that Avni wouldn't notice some middle-aged guy staring intently at her.

'Okay, okay. I won't look at her. But she is nice. If you want, I can talk to her parents,' he said.

All my family members have become psycho and fat. It is a deadly combination.

Avni got up and smiled at the guy beside her. He got up too and hugged her. It wasn't a tight hug. Her parents looked happy. Maybe their marriage was fixed or maybe they were already married. I don't know.

'Congrats Dhruv, you will die single,' the inner me said.

'Dhruv, look here. We're taking a selfie,' Alok Mama said, his right hand still clutching a dosa morsel. He never left food go uneaten. No wonder he has so many gastric issues.

'If Avni is still single, should I acquaint her with my family? Will that make them happy about my life too? At least, I should acquaint Avni with Maa.'

'But what will you tell them when they ask you who she is? Avni is not your girlfriend, Dhruv,' the inner me responded.

I tried to throw a smile at Alok Mama's phone camera but my mind was already thinking about Avni's wedding night. Damn it. *What was wrong with me?*

Avni and her family left. The guy who was with her got busy on his phone when mine buzzed.

'I will call you in some time', read Avni's message.

'Wait near the reception. I'm coming', I messaged.

'Not now Dhruv. My parents need to talk to me'.

'Cool', I replied, with a smile on my face. Actually, I was smiling a lot looking at Avni's messages. After all, it was our first conversation after so many years. I was smiling ear to ear.

Single guys should never have a girl as a friend especially when she is beautiful. We have no idea when our heart starts falling for her.

'Why are you smiling so much?' Shreya Didi asked.

'What? Smiling? Me? No way.'

I finished my breakfast and checked Nidhi's picture once again on Facebook. She looked beautiful but I didn't care any more.

'Maa, I'm going to my room for a bit. I just want to rest a little. Please don't disturb me,' I said as I got up.

'Dhruv, stay with us for some time,' Shreya Didi said.

'No Didi, please,' I replied.

'Okay, fine, go,' Maa looked disappointed but I just wanted to be alone for a bit.

I came back to my room and lay on my bed, which looked neat now. The housekeeping girl was also beautiful. It could mean that even she would have a boyfriend. Only Dhruv Mehta never got a girlfriend.

'Relax, all beautiful girls don't have a boyfriend,' the inner me said.

I didn't realize when I fell asleep. I woke up because someone was knocking on my door.

'Dhruv, come down for snacks!' It was Maa.

I got up, rubbing my eyes, and looked at my phone. There was a message.

'If you are free, we can meet', the message from Avni read.

It was evening already and I had not even realized that I had slept for so many hours.

I came down thinking about Avni and the guy she was with.

Is that guy her boyfriend? Is he here to convince her parents? Am I too late to tell Avni my feelings?

I came to the open area where my relatives were sitting with their smiling faces. My phone rang. It was Avni.

'Shit, I didn't even reply to her message,' I cursed myself and picked up the phone immediately. I moved away from my family towards the beach and sat on a rock facing the sunset.

'Where are you, Dhruv Mehta?' Avni asked.

In college, when Avni said Dhruv Mehta, it meant she was really upset.

'What happened? You sound angry, Avni.'

'When people don't reply to your messages, what else are we supposed to feel? Screw you.'

God, she was fuming. But it was so good to hear that again. 'Screw you.' She used to say this to me all the time in college. All those memories came back in a flash.

'I am sorry. I was sleeping,' I said, trying to pacify her.

'Dude, tell her you missed her,' my inner voice said.

'You shut up. I am not saying anything.'

'What are you doing here with your parents?' Avni asked.

Instead of replying, I asked her the same question.

'What are *you* doing here with your parents?'

'So, whom should I come here with? I don't have a boyfriend.'

I punched my hand in the air knowing Avni was single. It felt like I had won a lottery. Thank god.

'Oh okay,' I said calmly, as though it didn't matter to me.

'You still haven't told me what are you doing here,' she said again.

'You won't laugh, right?'

'What? Why would I laugh? Just tell me, Dhruv.'

'I was kinda tricked into this trip. I didn't know all my relatives would be here, and now my parents are showing me marriage proposals,' I said.

One second later, Avni started laughing. This girl had not changed even a little. She always did the same in college every time I was tense.

'Why did you tell her that, loser?' the inner me said.

'Dude, it's better to indirectly tell her that I am single.'

'Oh yes, you're right.'

'I am always right.'

'Okay, fine. Laugh. Now tell me, where are you?' I asked.

'I am near the spa centre.'

Amit Mama was near the spa centre, getting his evening massage done. He was already stalking her in the morning.

'Move from there right now,' I said.

'Why? What happened?'

'Why do you ask so many questions? Just move, *na*. You'll see me,' I said, as I waved to her.

'Oh hey! I see you!'

She waved and started walking toward me. Avni looked almost radiant in a white salwar kameez and an orange dupatta. As she came closer, I saw a tiny red bindi on her forehead. And that mole below her lower lip. It still looked so beautiful on her face. And she still didn't know that the mole was my heartbeat.

'Why were you not responding to my messages? You were not sleeping. I know that,' she said playfully.

'Sorry, but you are wrong just as you were in college. I was actually sleeping.'

She looked at me and then at my legs. She smiled looking at my waxed legs. I had paid three thousand rupees to get that done.

'Can we sit down?' she said, smiling.

'Yes,' I said. Avni looked at my waxed legs again, hiding her thirty-two teeth with her hand.

'What are you doing, Avni?'

'Nothing,' she said and giggled. Girls have to giggle at everything.

'What have you done to your legs?' she asked, still giggling.

'Same thing that girls do when they come to Goa,' I replied.

Avni burst out laughing this time. A few people roaming around the rocks turned towards us. It took her a minute to calm down. She had tears in her eyes. She wiped them. She adjusted her dupatta and sat beside me.

'Okay, tell me one thing,' she said.

'Yes.'

'Why did you punch your hand in the air when I said I don't have a boyfriend?' Avni looked at me, a big question mark forming on her face.

'Oh no. Did she see me doing that? What do I tell her?'

'Tell her that it was your phone. Your phone suddenly hung,' the inner me said.

'Oh actually, my hand hung,' I said.

'Huh? What?'

'No, I mean my phone hung,' I said immediately, my heart beating fast.

'Oh, okay.'

'You know why I came here, Dhruv? I came here to meet a guy,' she asked and answered herself.

I looked at her earrings. They were long and matched her outfit.

'And you did not like him?' I said.

'How do you know?' Avni asked.

'I know you. Dhruv knows everything about Avni,' I chuckled.

Avni gave a mini smile.

'Dude, you are getting better at romance,' the inner me said.

'Am I right?' I asked.

'Kind of, but what is your whole family doing here? Look at them. It feels like the entire Patna is here.'

'I mean, everyone isn't close family. Most of them are extended relatives. Tortuous relatives.'

'Oh wow. A joint family trip,' Avni said.

'I am on a suicide trip, Avni,' I sighed.

'I am so happy we met,' she suddenly said.

I looked at Avni closely. Her hair looked silkier now than I saw it in the morning. And then I looked at her face closely. How could someone's face be so soft? Why can't we men have such faces? Damn it. What was I thinking? I looked at her again. She had also put on a light kajal, which made her look so pretty that any guy would die to be with her.

'This is called love, you fool,' the inner me said.

'Shut up.'

'Dhruv, I think I said something,' Avni said, waving her hands at my face.

'Yes, I like you too,' I said.

'What?' she asked, her eyes widening.

My heart started beating faster than a bullet train. That is why most guys don't express their feelings. Girls ask 'What?' and then we forget everything. My mind was really not in my control.

'No, I mean what did you say?' I asked, calming down my heartbeat.

'Where are you lost?' Avni asked.

How do I tell her I am lost in her eyes, in her thoughts, in her dreams; that I am seeing Avni everywhere right now? Oh god, why did you make her so beautiful? And then you gave her that mole. How do I focus on anything else?

'Nowhere,' I said.

'So, you are here to discuss marriage with your parents?'

'What else can a single guy do in Goa, with his Indian parents?'

'Party?'

'Does it look like I am partying, Avni?'

Avni looked at me.

'You look happy,' she said.

How do I tell her that I am happy because she is here with me now and not because of anything else?

'No Avni, I am not happy. Guys like me only get ready-made wives and not girlfriends. You know how painful it is,' I said, making a sad face.

'Don't worry. Even girls like me get ready-made husbands and not boyfriends.'

We both looked into each other's eyes and paused there. After a few seconds, I don't know what happened but we both started laughing loudly.

'Has someone ever told you that you look cuter when you are angry?' she asked.

Has someone told you that girls like you are meant for love?

'No. Never. And about that marriage thing, I told my parents clearly that I don't want to marry someone I don't know.'

It is so difficult to make a girl say what she feels for you. I was trying my best.

'Actually, even I don't want to marry a guy whom I don't know,' she said.

'Our parents think once we get a job, we should have someone to take care of. I agree, we should have someone, but then please don't force us.'

'My parents didn't force me. In my community, girls of my age have two kids.'

'Shit. That's fast. But I am clear. No arranged marriage.'

'Any specific reason?' she asked.

'Many. First, they show you a girl's photo and ask you if you like her. If you say yes, then they check if your *nakshatra* matches. If that matches, then they check if your *kundli* matches. If it doesn't, they show you another girl. And after infinite attempts at last, you finally find a girl with whom your kundli, nakshatra, in fact, everything matches, but the girl refuses to marry you. So, no more arranged marriage drama,' I said, frustration in my voice.

Avni laughed.

'So where is the guy who came to meet you?' I asked.

'He wants to meet me at dinner too.'

'Will you go?' I asked.

'I need to go or else my parents will kill me,' she sighed.

'You look different now. I mean, different from how you looked back in college,' I said.

'Amma says I am too old-fashioned. She's been pushing me to try western outfits,' she smiled.

'Hahahaha,' I laughed, seeing her irritation.

'Look, even you are laughing,' she pouted.

'No, not like that. I mean, you look really beautiful in Indian wear.'

Am I really flirting with her right now?

'Really?' Avni asked, her eyes twinkling. There is a thing about Indian girls or, in fact, all girls in the world. They just love it when you tell them they look beautiful.

'Yes,' I said.

Yes, dude. Come on. Praise her more. Be romantic, my boy,' the inner me practically screamed.

'Can I say something, Avni?'

'Hmmm, go ahead.'

'You won't beat me, right?'

'That depends on what you want to say,' Avni replied, a mischievous twinkle in her eye.

'It is personal but that's okay. Let me ask you. How come your mom married your dad?'

'What did you say? How dare you?'

'I am sorry, I didn't mean to offend you. But, I mean, your mom is too beautiful for your dad. Don't you think so?'

Avni paused for a moment

'You are right in some way, but they fell in love,' she said.

I almost fell from the rock when I heard that.

'Are you serious?'

'Dead serious. They are the most boring couple I have ever seen.'

'I still can't believe it,' I said.

'Shut up and don't say a word about my dad,' Avni said, mock-threateningly.

'I am just praising your mom. Look at you. No doubt you are her photocopy.'

Avni smiled and tucked a strand of hair behind her ear. That mole had arrested my attention and it was hard to look away from it, but I had to.

'But their marriage was a big drama,' Avni said.

'I can understand. North India and its cultures are complex.'

'My mom is from South India,' Avni corrected me.

'I think, in college, you said that you're a North Indian. Didn't you?'

'My dad is a North Indian. My mom is South Indian. My dad fell in love with my mom and then I was born. Do you want to know anything more?' Avni said playfully.

'Yes, just one more thing.'

'Ask,' she said, making a cute face. I felt like pinching her cheeks. Oh my god, I was so happy today.

'Was the guy, whom you met in the morning, a South Indian?'

'Yes.'

'So, you are ready to marry a South Indian guy now?'

'No. Yes. I mean, I don't know . . . it was just because my parents insisted, Dhruv,' she said.

Just then, I saw Didi and Jiju coming towards us.

If Jiju comes here, he will directly ask Avni whether she loves me or not. Seeing Jiju's mental state, right now he can ask any girl if she wants to marry me or not. No one in my family is as desperate as Jiju to get me married. And my love story will end before it starts. What do I do now?

'Look there,' Avni said, pointing at Jiju.

'Why are you pointing at strangers, Avni? It's bad manners,' I said teasingly.

'Shut up. I know your Didi, I'd met her once in college. Is that her husband?'

'Didi? She is not my Didi. I am an only child. She is some stranger. Don't point at them like that,' I said.

'Hahaha. You are very funny,' Avni smiled.

Avni had no idea that if I stayed here with her for a few more seconds, Jiju would make my life a little unfunny. He would make sure that I died single.

'What do I do now?'

'Dhruv, run.'

'What?'

'Run, bro. Run as fast as you can. Nothing can save me from dying single if Jiju reaches here.'

I looked at Jiju and Didi. They were getting closer. I looked at my legs. Thank god I was wearing shoes.

'Avni, are you coming with me or not?' I asked firmly. She didn't care as usual.

'Let's go, please,' I pleaded.

'No, I want to meet them. They look so cute, holding hands.' Avni was practically squealing.

'Avni, are you coming or not? I am asking for the last time,' I said, my voice firmer this time.

'No.'

I knew what I had to do now. Just run. Without wasting a second, I ran from there as fast as I could without turning around. I had never run so fast in my entire life. Usain Bolt would have lost today if he had run a race with me. I stopped where no one could see me. I was panting and totally exhausted. I needed water.

'Dhruv, wait! Stop!'

Avni had chased me down. Thank god. I was totally safe now. I looked at her. She looked even more beautiful, all sweaty and exhausted. *Uff*, her white salwar kameez. Avni still looked so beautiful in it. I wish I had seen her like this in college. She only wore jeans and a top in college. Girls in salwar kameez steal our hearts.

'Why did you run away like that?' Avni asked.

'You ask a lot of questions. I mean, a *lot* of questions. And you don't listen to me. I had no other option.'

'But why did you run?'

'Avni, you are asking questions again? Do you want me to go mad?' I said, folding my hands.

'Okay, fine. Don't cry. But can I ask something? Just one thing?'

'You girls are in a habit of asking questions, right?'

'Yes,' she said.

'Okay, then ask.'

'Can you talk to my mom?' she asked.

My eyes twinkled, my lungs had air all of a sudden, my legs had the energy to run a marathon right now.

'Is she proposing?'

'Yes, dude.'

'Talk to your mom? About what?' I asked, trying to be calm. All great things should be done calmly.

'Marriage,' she said.

Oh my god, I have been waiting for this day for so many years.

'What shall I tell your mom?' I asked, even more calmly. My heart was beating really fast.

'That I don't want to have an arranged marriage,' she said. I slapped my forehead. My dreams were shattered in a second. I thought she would say, *'That I want to marry you, Dhruv.'*

'What happened? Why did you hit your forehead?'

'Who me? Oh no. There was a mosquito on my forehead,' I said, cursing my fate. 'I will talk to your mom later. Right now, I can't. My mom is behind me for an arranged marriage. Let me sort that out first,' I added.

'Thanks,' Avni said, pinching my cheeks. I liked that, and I tried not to blush.

'Don't you think she's pinching your cheeks for a reason?' the inner me said.

'It's okay. I like it when she does that.'

'Just a second,' Avni said as her phone rang.

'Hi Amma. I am close to the rocks,' she said. Her phone was on speaker. Avni has hated keeping her phone to her ears since college, whether she is alone or with me. She hadn't changed a bit. Her mom spoke for another minute while Avni replied in a South Indian language. I wasn't sure if it was Kannada or Tamil.

Her tone got louder and she finally said, 'I am not meeting him now. That's it.'

Cutting the call, she looked away at the water. She was obviously fuming.

'What happened?' I asked.

'I don't want to go with him for dinner,' she almost spat out her words.

'Okay, so your mom is a Tamilian?' I asked. I just couldn't control myself. I had to know a few things about Avni's family. Avni looked at me from head to toe.

'She is half Tamilian, half Kannadiga,' Avni said.

'What? What does that mean?' I was totally confused now. She laughed.

'I mean, she was born in Tamil Nadu but brought up in Bangalore,' she said, smiling.

My phone buzzed. Now it was my mother.

'Okay Avni. I have to go now, otherwise my mother will eat my head. I'll call you later?'

I had to leave now or else my entire family would have come to meet Avni. I didn't want my love story to end before it started.

'Yeah, okay,' Avni said, as I stood to leave. 'I'll wait for your call, Dhruv Mehta.'

My name had never sounded sweeter.

2

It was 9 p.m. and starting to get cold outside. Avni had messaged me to meet her. I wore the same clothes I'd worn in the morning. I saw Avni coming from a distance, wearing a green salwar suit. I wondered how girls managed to change so many outfits in a single day. Don't they get tired? She wore something in the morning, something else in the evening and now she was wearing a third outfit.

She came and shook my hand; her hand was like cotton. If I wasn't too careful, I felt I'd crush it. She sat down beside me and my eyes fell on her mole once again. My heart started beating fast.

'You called me here at this time? If my relatives see me with you, there will be level-three drama. Do you have any idea?' I said, secretly glad that she called me.

'If my parents see me with you right now, there will be a tsunami in Goa,' Avni rolled her eyes.

I chuckled. Girls have a better sense of humour than boys. I realized.

'Pratap wants to talk to you, actually,' she said, interrupting my chuckling.

'Pratap?'

'My cousin, Dhruv. You forgot?' Her eyes widened in surprise, making them even more beautiful. Just then, Avni's phone buzzed. She picked up and spoke for some time. Then, she handed her phone to me.

'Who is it?' I asked.

'Pratap.'

'Wait, hang on. Oh wait, I remember him now! Pratap is your cousin who was with us in college, right?'

'Yes. Talk to him. Put the call on speaker.'

'Hey Pratap. How have you been?' I barely remembered his face properly, except for his huge body.

'Hi Dhruv. I am good, yaar, and I have called now to invite you to my wedding.'

'Oh wow. When is it and where?'

'Chennai, day after tomorrow. You have to come,' he said.

'Sure bro. I will try my best.'

'No trying. Come with Avni. I'll see you there. It was nice catching up. Bye!'

'Same here,' I said and disconnected the call.

'He couldn't talk for long because he was driving. Okay, listen,' she said.

'Go ahead. I'm listening.'

'Will you come to Chennai?'

'But when did Pratap move to Chennai? He was in Bangalore, right?'

'After college, my dad and his dad got posted there.'

'What about Bangalore?'

Oh no. I live in Bangalore. If Avni lives in Chennai, how will we meet?

'I still live in Bangalore, Dhruv. I just visit my parents in Chennai on alternate weekends,' she said, adjusting her dupatta, causing her bangles to make a tinkling sound— exactly how my heart was beating right now.

'You will come, right?' she asked, almost pleading.

'I am thinking about what I should say to Maa.'

'When are you going back to Patna?' she asked.

'After four days.'

'Then you can come for a day to Chennai and return the next day,' she said.

'Okay, let me talk to Maa. I will let you know,' I said.

She looked at me with disgust. A girl thinks that when she asks a guy to do something, he should just do it. They should understand that we have another woman in our life called Maa.

Girls don't understand anything.

'Just let me convince Maa. I'll try my best, I promise.'

'Okay, fine.'

'You want me to come or not, Avni?'

'I just want you to come to Chennai to attend the function but you are showing attitude.'

'When did I show attitude?' I asked.

'Yes. I know you. That is why no girl in college ever spoke to you.'

'Ha! But you spoke to me.'

'Because . . .' Avni hesitated.

'Because what?'

'You felt safe, Dhruv Mehta.'

'Safe. What do you mean? Are you saying the other guys were unsafe?'

'I just knew that you would run away from girls if they even came close to you.'

'Hahaha. True that. Not all girls are nice like you,' I said.

I just have one rule in my life. Be friends with a girl you want to marry and who wants to marry you. No complications.

'Other guys just want to talk to every beautiful girl or flirt with them, but you were different,' she said.

'Still, you haven't answered, Avni. Why did you speak only to me in college?'

'Because you are . . .' she said and stopped.

Damn it. Girls will keep everything in suspense until the last minute.

'Because I am your friend?' I asked.

I needed to be clear. Either a banana falls on the knife or a knife falls on the banana, it's the same thing.

'No, you are not just my friend,' Avni said and got up.

'Then who am I?'

Avni just stood there for a while and looked at me. I felt my heart beating faster and faster, and it was almost in my mouth.

'No one,' she said. And added, 'Will you come or not?'

'Give me some time. Let me talk to Maa. I will confirm tonight.'

Avni's phone started buzzing. She got up and started walking away from me.

'Get lost. Bye,' Avni said and left.

I kept looking at her, the way she walked, the way her bangles tinkled, the way her hair had smelt when she'd sat beside me.

Damn. Why did I never do all this in college? Damn. I was so boring back then.

3

I came back to my room, thinking of an excuse to leave for Chennai the next day. My brain was not working. Why does everything have to happen today itself? Damn it. My life is so messed up. I had no option but to call Didi.

I explained to her everything that had happened and said I needed her help to go to Chennai. After listening to my story, Didi reached my room within a minute. Girls love drama but there was an issue. She came to my room along with Jiju, who is the only person I am really scared of. He wants me to get married as soon as possible and right now, he can go to any extent to get that done.

'When is Avni leaving?' Jiju asked, jumping on my bed. My mattress shook for almost thirty seconds and we both kept looking at each other in that time.

'She is going back to Chennai tomorrow for her cousin's wedding,' I said.

'Wow. Everyone is getting married but you won't,' Jiju said.

'Marriages are boring, Jiju. Avni has asked me to come to Chennai but I can't. Maa will not allow me, I'm sure.'

'What? So, you literally said no to a girl who was asking you to go to a wedding with her?' Jiju asked.

'I said I would let her know if I could come. I need to talk to Maa.'

Jiju looked at Didi and in turn, Didi looked at me in slow motion just like in those Star Plus serials. I knew what she was thinking.

'Avni really wants you to be with her, Dhruv. She didn't just ask you to come to Chennai,' Jiju said politely.

'How can you be so sure?'

'*Accha*, tell me, what did she say when you refused to go to Chennai?' Didi asked.

'She said "*Get lost*".'

'It means she definitely wants you there. Is your brother all right, Shreya?' Jiju said.

'I am ashamed I have a brother like you,' Didi said and threw a pillow at me.

'What do you both want me to do? I am here to spend time with you all. How can I go to Chennai all of a sudden?'

'Dhruv, Avni really wants you to go to Chennai. Goddammit!' Jiju said.

'But Aadi, what will he tell everyone? He can't leave like this. Rather, Dhruv should tell Avni that he'll come to Chennai in a few days,' Didi said.

'Will you let me talk to him, Shreya? Please, yaar,' Jiju said.

'Okay, fine,' I said. 'Tell me what to do, Jiju. I am confused. Maa won't allow it.'

'Yes, Dhruv. Don't go. Leave it, Aadi,' said Didi.

'Shreya, don't overreact, yaar. Let me speak to him,' Jiju said.

'No, Dhruv. You stay with us,' Didi said.

'If you listen to your sister, you will be single for your whole life,' Jiju said.

Didi threw a pillow at Jiju, which he easily caught and put on his lap.

'But what about Maa? And what about everyone else?' I asked.

'Dhruv, we are not going anywhere. Avni has met you after so many years. Don't pass up this opportunity to let her know how much she means to you,' Jiju said.

I like the way Jiju explains everything. It goes from my brain cells to my heart cells directly.

'But what would she think if I told her now that I am coming? She should not feel I am a despo,' I said.

'But you are a despo, my boy,' Jiju said. My ears went into shock on hearing that.

'Just kidding,' he said. I felt relieved.

'She won't feel like that. I am telling you,' Jiju added.

'But what if she feels so?' I asked.

'Aadi, leave it,' Didi protested.

'You trust me, right, Dhruv?' Jiju asked.

'No.'

'I don't care, just message Avni that you are coming to Chennai,' he interrupted.

I did not know what to do. I looked at my phone. I recalled Avni's last words before she left: '*Get lost*'. Maybe she really wanted me to come. Maybe she did not. Do any men understand girls? They are really confusing.

I looked at Didi and then at Jiju. I picked up my phone and messaged Avni that I was coming. The double tick mark confirmed that it got delivered.

'Did you send the message?' Jiju asked. I nodded. Didi patted her forehead.

'I'm so happy you are coming, Dhruv', Avni messaged.

I showed the message to Jiju. He jumped to his feet as if he had just proposed to his girlfriend and she had said yes.

'Avni is happy,' Jiju shouted and threw his hands in the air and started dancing. Seeing him so happy, I joined him too. And then we both did a little bhangra and a little dandiya with our hands. Didi clapped at our mini performance and finally, a smile came to her face.

'My two heartbeats,' she said, blowing a flying kiss at us. Jiju caught it. And then, I made them both pack my bags, which they happily did, to leave for Chennai the next day.

But after dancing the bhangra and dandiya, I asked Jiju, 'How will we convince Maa?'

Jiju said that he would plan something and left for his room. I went off to sleep hugging the pillow as though it was Avni.

4

I woke up and the first message I saw was Avni's.

'Good morning', it read.

'Why don't you tell her that you like her before going to Chennai?' the inner me said.

'Are you mad? She will kill me!'

'She won't. She missed you all these years. Didn't she say that?'

'Dude, we need to wait. I just met her after so long. Sometimes girls say something and mean something else. Millions of guys have gotten friend-zoned because of this misunderstanding. I need to wait.'

'Until when, Dhruv? Until she gets married?'

'Shut up.'

There was a new message from Jiju, which read:

'Only Avni can convince your mom for your Chennai visit. If Avni asks your mom personally, your mom will not be able to refuse her. Shreya told me that Aunty knows Avni. Why didn't you tell me this?

Also, it would be better if Avni invites your entire family to Chennai so that Aunty doesn't feel bad. Women can feel bad any time, I am telling you from personal experience.'

Sometimes Jiju made sense. Without wasting a second, I called Avni.

'Where are you? Come fast, Dhruv. Need to plan for your Chennai visit. There is a flight tomorrow morning. You will have to reach before 11 a.m. I will send a driver to pick you up at the airport,' she said.

'Wait, Avni. You have to do something,' I said.

'What?'

'Do you have a nice dress?'

'What are you saying?'

'Listen. Dress up nicely, like a proper Indian girl, and come to my room.'

'Proper Indian girl! Do I look like an improper Indian girl?'

'Oh no. Why do you have to misunderstand me all the time? Avni, you have to meet my Maa if you want me to come to Chennai.'

'Meet your Maa? For what, Dhruv?'

'You have to ask her if you want me to visit Chennai for your cousin's wedding. She knows you from college. Also, it would be better if you invited my whole family, just for formality's sake, so that Maa doesn't feel bad. Women can feel bad at any time. I am telling you from personal experience.'

'What did you just say? How dare you?' she asked.

'I didn't mean it that way,' I said, my heart skipping a beat.

'You guys are all the same,' she said.

'So, you're coming to meet my Maa, right?' I asked, keeping one hand on my heart. Girls can really feel bad at any time. Jiju was right.

'Of course, I'm coming. Your Maa will get convinced, right?'

'Depends on your convincing skills, Avni. Can you be here in thirty minutes?' I asked.

Avni muttered something inaudible, probably scolding me as she used to do in college.

'Come in half an hour. Maa will be here any moment,' I said.

'Okay, I am coming. Bye,' she said and cut the call.

I called Jiju's number but Shreya Didi picked up.

'Where is Jiju?' I asked.

'My husband is not even speaking to me. What is going on between you two?'

'Avni is coming to my room, Didi,' I said excitedly.

'What? Why would she come to your room?'

'She is coming to talk to Maa and invite all of us to Chennai.'

'All of us? Was this Aadi's idea?'

'Well, your husband is smart.'

'Aadi is too much. So, now I have to come to Chennai with you?'

'No, what? No, no, no. Who said that?'

'You just told me that Avni will invite all of us to Chennai.'

'That's just for formality's sake. Only I have to go with her,' I said.

'What a master plan! Aadi has gone mad again,' Didi said.

'Be happy, Didi. For the first time, I'm doing something like this.'

'I am happy for you, Dhruv, but sad for that girl,' Didi said.

'What did you say?'

'Look at yourself and look at her. No match.'

'We both are the best match,' I said firmly.

'Didn't I tell you that he likes her?' Jiju said in the background.

'You are always right, Aadi,' Didi said. I heard both of them clapping. I was shocked.

'So, you were listening to everything? And Didi, you were acting all this time?'

'Who do you think gave the idea to Aadi?'

'Your sister has never given one single good idea in life. This is my idea. Marrying her was also my idea,' Jiju said.

'Okay, now please don't fight and tell me the plan,' I asked.

'I told your sister to book your Chennai ticket,' Jiju said.

'Didi, have you booked the ticket?' I asked.

'Flights are very costly, Dhruv,' Didi said.

'Shreya, money doesn't matter this time. Book it,' Jiju said.

There was utter silence for a few seconds.

'Done. The ticket is booked,' Didi said.

'Oh *balle balle*,' Jiju started singing. I started dancing on the bed, with my left hand on my waist and my right on my head, when Maa suddenly entered my room. I jumped down and fell on the floor.

'Why were you dancing, Dhruv?'

'Dancing? Why would I dance?'

Maa looked at my phone.

'Aadi is on the phone?' Maa asked.

'Yes Maa. No Maa,' Jiju said.

'Haan Maa,' Shreya Didi said.

These two are the craziest couple I have ever seen.

'What is going on, Shreya? I told you and Aadi to get ready and come to my room. And you are talking to Dhruv?'

'Maa, I am going to take a bath,' I said and entered the bathroom. I was done listening to *Yes Maa, No Maa*. When I came out, my room was all tidied up. Maa was checking my phone.

'Maa!' I screamed.

Maa dropped the phone with a shock and clasped both hands to her chest.

'What happened, you idiot? Why did you shout? I got scared,' Maa said.

'I've told you so many times, please never check my phone,' I said and picked up my phone from the floor. Thank god it was not damaged.

'I left my phone in my room, Dhruv. I was just checking about cabs,' Maa said.

'The resort has its own cab. And besides, I have something important to tell you. A girl is coming to meet you. Please be good to her.'

'What girl?'

'College friend. Avni. Remember?'

'Is she married?'

'No,' I said. Maa looked so happy, as if I had given her the best news of her life.

'But what is she doing here?'

All women have to ask questions. Without questions, their lives would be so boring.

'Maa, please don't ask questions until she comes here. And please wear a nice saree.'

'This is my nineteenth anniversary saree,' Maa said.

'Okay, Maa. Anyways, you are beautiful,' I said.

'Thanks, beta,' Maa said and smiled.

There was a knock at the door. I had kept it slightly open already as Maa was in my room. Avni wore a pink top and grey jeans. Simple. Beautiful.

'Hi Aunty,' she said as she came in and sat down on the sofa across my bed.

Maa was sitting on the bed. I was sitting close to Maa on another sofa-cum-chair. No one spoke.

Then Maa mumbled, 'She is so pretty.'

'Talk to her, Maa. She said hi to you,' I mumbled back.

'Hi Avni,' Maa said.

Avni was twisting her fingers as though she did not know what to say to Maa.

'It is really nice to finally meet you in person, Aunty. I have heard a lot about you from Dhruv. He used to talk about you in college all the time,' Avni said.

'I hope he said good things about me,' Maa chuckled.

'Of course, Aunty,' Avni said and smiled.

Come on, Avni, ask what you have come to ask. I want to go to Chennai with you.

'Aunty, I have to attend a wedding in Chennai,' Avni said.

'What? Whose wedding? Yours?' Maa asked.

'No Maa, her cousin's wedding,' I intervened.

'It would be really nice if all of you could come to Chennai, if it is okay with you. I know you are here with your family to spend time with each other,' Avni said.

It did not sound convincing at all. Avni should not have said the last sentence.

'Her cousin Pratap studied with me in college, Maa. He has invited me,' I said, trying to save face.

'Thanks for inviting us, Avni. We won't be able to come right now, but we will soon come to Chennai and visit all the temples over there with you,' Maa said.

Come on, Avni, ask Maa if it would be okay if at least I can come with you.

'Wouldn't it sound bad if she wants only you to come without the rest of the family?' the inner me asked.

'But I want to go to Chennai at any cost.'

'You call Shreya Didi here. She will handle it'.

I called Didi and disconnected immediately. Jiju might be with her and if he got to know I needed Didi's help, then even he would come along. And I am scared of Jiju. He is an unpredictable man who could make my future unpredictable if he came here.

Avni and Maa were now talking about the resort and the food. Maa also told Avni that she saw some girls wearing short clothes on the beach. How do I explain to Maa that in Goa they won't wear lehengas and sarees on the beach? Avni was giggling listening to Maa.

'These days girls are very modern,' Maa said.

'Yes Aunty, I agree,' Avni said.

'You Chennai girls are so nice and traditional,' Maa said.

Suddenly, there was a knock on the door. I got up and opened it to find Didi and Jiju standing there.

'What do you both want from me? Please go from here. I beg both of you,' I said to them, folding my hands.

'Move aside. Let me handle it,' Jiju said.

'I am handling it, Jiju,' I pleaded, not moving from the door.

'Who's there, Dhruv?' Maa asked.

Jiju and Didi pushed me aside and entered.

'Oh Avni, you're here,' Jiju said as though he and Avni were college friends.

'Hi Aditya, Jiju!' Avni said.

'You can call me Aadi,' Jiju said, shaking hands with her.

'Hi Avni. It is so nice to see you after we met last at your college,' Didi said.

I had no idea about the drama this husband and wife were going to unfold. So, I got ready to run away from the room at any moment.

'Dhruv messaged me that you wanted all of us to come to Chennai,' Jiju said, looking at Avni.

'When did I message this man?' I asked the inner me.

'Check your phone.'

I checked my phone. There was no sent item to Jiju. This man is very dangerous. I need to be careful.

'Yes, it would be nice if all of you could come to Chennai,' Avni repeated.

'Maa, Avni will feel bad if none of us go to Chennai. She has invited us to her home town. It is just for a day. In fact, I suggest that Dhruv can go with her and come back the next day. After that, he can spend time with us for the rest of the week,' Jiju said calmly.

I wanted to scream with joy. This man was good at heart, I realized. Maa glared at me as though I was the one who had given her the million-dollar suggestion.

'But it would be great if you all came with me to Chennai,' I said, just to be on the safe side.

Maa turned towards me and smiled.

'Come on, Dhruv. Don't ruin my plan now,' Jiju mumbled.

Maa thought for a few seconds and then relented.

'Okay. You kids have fun. Dhruv can go with you, Avni,' Maa said, looking at her. Both of them smiled. Jiju and I winked at each other. If Maa was not there, we both would have done the bhangra. I love bhangra. It relieves you of all your anxiety.

'Okay great, thanks Aunty! I have to go now, my mom is calling. We have to leave for the airport soon,' Avni said, touching Maa's feet. Jiju looked at Didi and smiled.

'Okay, Avni. Please do come to Patna to meet us,' Maa said. Avni nodded, bidding goodbye to me, Jiju and Didi.

Jiju hugged Avni and said, 'Nice meeting you, Avni.'

Maa looked at Didi and Didi looked at Maa. When two women look at each other, especially when a man is hugging another girl, it means they do not like it at all. Jiju was perhaps in deep trouble. But he did not care. I wanted to hug Avni too but I couldn't. At least not in front of Maa.

'Such a nice girl,' Maa said as Avni left the room.

'Yes. Very nice,' Jiju said. Didi and Maa looked at each other again. I left the room after that.

5

The Next Day

I landed at Chennai airport at sharp 8.45 a.m. Avni had sent a driver to receive me, who would take me to a hotel where I could freshen up.

The driver gave me a written note smilingly as he picked up my luggage.

'What is this?' I asked.

'Didi asked me to hand it over to you. Her phone battery died and she did not have time to charge it. So, she wrote this and gave it to me,' he said.

I took the letter from him. He was smiling as though he had read the letter already.

'Didi? Who is Didi?' I asked.

'Avni Didi,' he said.

I wanted to tell him *she is your Didi, not mine*, but I kept quiet and opened the letter. It smelt of some kind of perfume. I don't know why girls use so much perfume. Did she spray it on purpose? I don't know. I entered the cab, placed my laptop bag on the seat and started reading her letter. I was seeing her handwriting after years.

'Hi Dhruv. Too much drama early morning. My phone had no battery; so, I have left it in your hotel room for charging. I thought I would be there in the hotel to receive you but Pratap's mom called me to the hall. I will come to the hotel in some time to take you to the pre-wedding celebrations. One more thing, I have kept a dhoti and kurta on your bed which you have to wear. Hope you like it. Sorry again for the mess.'

Dhoti and kurta. No way. I can't wear that. I have never worn a dhoti in my whole life. There are two reasons for this. One, it is risky, and two, it is very risky.

I folded the letter and put it in my shirt pocket. I took out my phone to call Avni when I remembered that her phone was charging in my hotel room.

'You like Didi, sir?' the driver started talking as soon as we hit the road.

'What?'

'I mean, Avni Didi. She is very sweet.'

'How do you know her by the way?'

'I am her family driver,' he said. 'For thirty years, I have been driving for them.'

'How are her mom and dad? Are they strict?'

'Sir is very strict. But don't worry. Amma is cool.'

'You mean, her mom?'

'Yes sir. Very nice lady.'

All men are the same, I realized. Maybe he agreed with me that Aunty deserved a better husband. Just kidding.

'Great. Can you play some Hindi songs?' I asked.

'Here, only Tamil. No Hindi,' he said.

'Then play any Tamil song, please,' I said.

'You understand Tamil, sir?' he asked.

'Uh, I know a little Tamil. Avni and I were in college. She taught me.'

'I know. Avni Didi told me about you,' the driver said as he put on a Tamil song. It was a famous one whose lyrics were good even though I did not understand all of them. I just remembered, it was from a movie in which Dhanush had acted. Listening to the music, I fell asleep as I was tired.

We reached the hotel when I saw a few girls looking at me as I got out of the car. They spoke to the driver from a distance and giggled.

'What did they say?' I asked.

'They were asking about you. They haven't seen such a handsome guy here before.'

'Very funny,' I said.

'Sir, you are a nice guy, right?' the driver asked.

'Why do you ask that?'

'Avni Didi is like my daughter, sir. She has a good heart but people are not good these days. I mean, boys.'

'Don't worry. She is my best friend. I understand what you are saying.'

'Thank you, sir,' the driver said, as we reached the door to my room.

'And please don't tell her that I told you she is my best friend,' I said. The driver smiled.

I just didn't want to be friend-zoned at this stage of my life. Life is not easy for boys today.

I smiled and gave the driver a small tip, which he refused. I entered the room and saw another letter on the table to the left of the door.

'Hi Dhruv. Pick me up' it said on the envelope.

I smiled, picked it up and opened it. Girls are really sweet. They know how to make you feel special.

The letter read: 'Thanks for coming. You don't know how much it means to me. I never knew we would meet like this after so many years and then you would come to Chennai for Pratap's marriage. I still can't believe you are here; I can't believe we met, I missed you so much. Thanks again for coming. Now please call Amma's number from my phone. I will pick up.'

I checked the clothes kept on the bed. I had no idea how to even wear a dhoti. I looked around. There was a phone charging near the lamp. It was switched off. I switched it on, searched for Mom in her contacts and called the number.

'You reached?' Avni asked excitedly.

'Yes, ma'am.'

'Oh my god, I'm so excited. Did you wear the clothes?'

'Avni, I am already wearing clothes,' I said.

She laughed and then said, 'I mean, I am talking about the clothes I have asked you to wear. Did you like them?'

'Yes, I like them. But would it be okay if I wear my own clothes?'

'Why? Wear the dhoti and the kurta, no? Please? You'd match with all the guests here.'

I couldn't refuse her when she said it like that. How could I resist that tone?

'Okay, fine. I'll get ready now.'

'Dhruv?'

'Yeah?'

'Welcome to Chennai.'

'Hahaha. Thanks a lot,' I said.

'It means a lot to me,' she said and cut the call.

I smiled. Now I had to learn to wear a dhoti. Bala was the only person I could think of. I called him. It was a video call. Bala was wearing a white dhoti and a white shirt.

'Aren't you in the office?' I asked.

'I am in office, bro. There is some celebration and our manager asked us to come in regional dress.'

'And you wore a dhoti?'

'Yes, dhoti is my pride,' Bala said puffing his chest out.

'Actually, I came to the office in casuals and then changed to dhoti in the washroom,' he added, still puffing out his chest. Bala always has to explain things in detail.

'Okay, relax the chest, and tell me how to wear a dhoti,' I said and showed him the dhoti in my hand.

I still hadn't told him that I was with Avni in Chennai. I had told Bala once that Avni was the girl I used to like in college. If I had told him that she was with me, he would have left everything and come to Goa. My life was important to Bala. If I talk to a girl, he has to know it or else he won't have any reason to live.

'But why you are wearing a dhoti in Goa, macha?'

'Mom and dad's anniversary. We are going to the temple. Do you want to join us?' I asked, irritated.

'No, macha. You did not send me girls' pics.'

'Bala, will you teach me how to wear a dhoti?'

'Oh yes. It is very simple,' Bala said and started opening the knot on his dhoti.

'No, Bala, no. Please stop. I can't see this,' I shouted.

'Shut up, you fool,' he said, cursing me and completely undid his dhoti. My eyes popped out after what I saw. I shouldn't say this because it is top secret. Bala was wearing Mickey Mouse bumchums underneath his dhoti. After seeing that, I laughed for half a minute.

'Okay, if you are done laughing, can I teach you? I have a meeting soon,' Bala said.

He taught me how to wear a dhoti in the washroom. Friends like him are called best friends for a reason. Who gets half-naked in the washroom to teach his friend how to wear a dhoti?

'Okay, I have a meeting now. I will call you later,' he said and cut the call.

That is how I learnt to wear a dhoti in five minutes. I took a quick bath. Chennai weather had already started showing its effects; I was sweating continuously. I lay on the bed for some time when my phone rang. It was Avni.

'Hi Avni, where are you?'

'I am reaching in another fifteen minutes. Are you ready?'

'Yeah, I am waiting for you.'

'Coming soon. Bye!'

I got ready immediately. I was looking good, if not really good. Dhoti-kurta was not that bad a combination after all. Someone knocked at the door and I opened it. Avni looked really beautiful in a maroon saree with a gold border. She wore a matching blouse with a similar border. I closed my mouth, blinked and smiled. She entered the room and then turned around to look at me.

'Perfect.' Her fair hands had mehndi designs up to her elbow.

'You like it?' I asked.

'Love it.'

'Me too. Your . . . uh . . . saree I mean.'

'I know,' she said.

Girls know everything. She looked at the mirror and fixed her hair and lipstick right in front of me. I was standing like a mannequin looking at her, wondering how a girl could look so beautiful. Isn't it a crime? I realized that I hadn't seen a girl in a saree for a long time.

Girls have stopped wearing sarees these days and that is why boys have stopped falling in love.

'Let's go,' she said as she picked up her phone.

We reached the ground floor where she gave me a set of keys.

'What is this for?'

'The car,' she said.

'What? There is no driver?'

'Our driver who dropped you is at the wedding hall. He left the car here. I came by cab. Now will you drive, please?'

'Avni, I am in a dhoti. How can I drive?'

'Like others do.'

'Are you serious?'

'We are getting late, Dhruv. There is so much fun going on there. Let's go!'

I tried to sit with the dhoti stretching up to my toes when my waxed legs got exposed. Avni looked at them for a few seconds without blinking. I don't know what she was thinking when I covered my legs and she burst into laughter.

'Boys also wax. I didn't know this,' she said and laughed again, clapping her mehndi-painted hands.

'Now don't do that. Come here and drive then,' I said.

'Okay, I'm sorry. I won't say a word now,' she said and smiled.

'Look Avni, I can't drive like this. It is uncomfortable.'

'Come out,' she said.

'First of all, you don't know how to wear a dhoti. Let us go to your room.'

'What are you saying?'

'Is this the way you wear a dhoti? It is so tight. Loosen it,' she said, as we got to the room.

'Go to hell,' I said.

'I mean, loosen it from the top close to your waist. You have tied it really tight. It's not supposed to be worn like that,' she said.

'Turn around.'

I loosened it. I hoped it wouldn't come off in the marriage hall or else I would never forgive her.

'Look now,' I said.

'Better but a little more would be even better,' she said.

'Avni, it's a joke for you, haa?'

'No, I am not kidding. Show me.'

'What?'

'I mean, let me help you, if you don't mind?'

I smiled. Avni held me from both sides and pulled me a little closer. My breath was rapid and my eyes were closed. For a moment, I felt my dhoti would fall but it didn't. I would have never forgiven her if she had done something like that.

'It's done,' she said.

'You are my sweetest friend,' I said, pinching her cheeks.

'I am not your friend. Will you come now?' she said as she reached the door.

I nodded. I was about to pull up my dhoti when I thought Avni would look at my waxed legs again and laugh.

'Okay, I will close my eyes. You can pull your dhoti up and drive,' she said.

'Why can't you drive?' I said.

'I'm sorry, but I can't drive in a saree.'

'Okay, I'll drive but you have to sit in the back,' I said.

She looked at me in frustration and sat in the back seat, banging the door while closing it. I pulled my dhoti up as Avni had advised and started the car.

'Dhruv?'

'Yes?'

'Can I say something?'

'Yes. Go ahead.'

'Your legs are sexy,' she said and laughed, clapping in glee.

I chuckled when I heard that. Then, Avni kept telling me about Pratap's fiancée and Pratap's wax story too, which was funnier than mine. I couldn't stop laughing after listening to what Pratap had done. I didn't even realize how time passed.

6

We reached the venue and Avni had asked me to wait near the wedding hall as while she went inside the guest house. She was wearing a lehenga when she came back.

'You changed your dress again? Why?'

'I have to dance. I can't do it in a saree.'

'But you didn't get a lehenga from the hotel, if I recall.'

'One of my cousins had got my lehenga already, Dhruv. I took it,' she said.

'And what about me?'

'I did check but there's no lungi available here. You North Indians wear lungi, right?' she smiled.

'I hate you,' I said.

'Same here,' she said, laughing now.

I looked at the guy and girl dancing on the stage. The guy was good—just like I used to be when I was younger. I had hardly danced in the last ten years. Every nook and corner of the hall was decorated. There was a huge rush of waiters all over the place. The entrance had a red carpet which took us straight to the Ganesha idol on the right, where a pandit was seated along with a few family elders. My eyes went to a few guys who were pointing at Avni as they passed by us. They sat down pretending to watch the dance, but they were looking at Avni.

'Where are you lost, Dhruv?' Avni asked.

'Let us go and meet Pratap. Where is he by the way?'

'I will go and get him. Sit in the first row, okay?'

'Yes, ma'am.'

Those guys were still pointing at her as she walked away. Avni walked briskly, holding her lehenga with both her hands. She hadn't changed a bit since her college days—the same soft-spoken, innocent girl I had met in college. Oh god, I had missed her so much.

I ignored the guys and took a seat in the front row when someone patted my shoulder. I turned around. It was Pratap.

'Oh my god. Look at you,' Pratap said, as he hugged me.

'Congratulations, man,' I said.

'It is so nice to see you. You've become more handsome,' he said.

'Not more than you,' I said. We both laughed.

'You look so nice in a dhoti,' he said.

'Your cousin insisted. You know how stubborn she is.'

'Hahaha,' Pratap laughed.

'So, where did you find Bhabhi?' I asked.

I had seen her pics on Avni's mobile. She is so beautiful.

'It is an arranged marriage, man. In today's time, we don't get girls like your Bhabhi easily,' he said.

'Lucky you,' I said. We both hugged again tightly.

'We are meeting after so many years, Dhruv. I can't tell you how happy I am to see you here. None of my friends could come for my wedding, but you came with just one phone call.'

'I am glad to be here, man.'

We sat down for a few more minutes and relived our college days, remembering how our 'mechies' group used to wait outside the mechanical corridor just to stare at girls from the computer science and information science branch.

Pratap had once saved me from senior girls while they were ragging me. He told them that I was the younger brother of their super senior, Bhagel sir. The girls ran away after hearing that and we had a good laugh after that.

Every girl in our college was terrified of Bhagel sir. But that same day, Bhagel sir ragged me after he found out that I was his long-lost brother. He wanted to show me his brotherhood in his own style.

We also spoke about one night when Pratap stayed back in the college hostel on my birthday and he realized that staying in the hostel was no less than madness. That night, he saw late-night singers, card players and, most importantly, frustrated guys talking about who was the most beautiful girl in our college and if she was single or not. We shared all the fading memories of our college days and kept laughing throughout our conversation.

Avni came back holding a soft drink. I looked at her kajal-lined eyes, which made her look even more beautiful, but I was worried about the guys who were staring and pointing at her a few minutes back. I turned around. They were still looking at her.

'People are looking for you, Pratap,' Avni said.

'Pratap!' an old uncle called out.

'I'll catch up with you guys. Have fun, and Avni, make him dance too,' Pratap said.

'Dance?' I repeated, as Pratap left.

'Yes, dance. I don't think you can even do one step properly, Mr Writer,' she said.

In the car, while coming here, I had told Avni I was working on a book.

Dhruv, you are wearing a dhoti. Don't dance.

'Don't dance,' the inner me said.

'Yes, you are right Avni. I can't dance,' I said.

Avni and I moved towards the DJ area, manned by two guys with huge headphones on. They looked cool. I wished I could be cool like them.

'My dance is next. Wait and watch,' Avni said.

I looked at the stage where another couple was dancing.

'Wow,' I said, looking at them.

'That girl is from Bhabhi's side.'

'They are awesome. Probably the best.'

'Oh please. Stop it. You haven't seen me dance.'

'I'm waiting,' I said, when Avni nudged me.

'After the dance, I'll introduce you to Appa,' she said.

'And Aunty? I would like to meet her too. I am not good with uncles. I don't know what to say to them. With Aunty, I will be more comfortable.'

'Okay, I'll make you meet Amma first. She is the coolest.'

'Don't you have a partner like that girl to dance with you on stage?' I asked.

'Will you dance with me?'

'Me? No, Avni. Sorry,' I said.

I would have loved to dance with her. It would be odd to see her dancing alone. I danced in my school days like Hrithik Roshan but I was not confident enough now.

'It's my turn to dance now,' Avni said, holding her lehenga as she climbed the stairs to the stage.

Thank god, there was no guy to dance with her. I might have felt a little jealous. The DJ changed the song as Avni climbed on to the stage.

'Ma'am, you don't have a partner?' the DJ asked. Avni shook her head.

'Anyone who'd like to join the beautiful lady here?' the DJ asked.

Those guys staring at Avni stood up and started walking towards the stage.

Come on, Dhruv, do something.

I looked at the pandal ceiling and prayed to god. I climbed on to the stage to join Avni before any of those guys could join her.

'Your name, sir?' the DJ asked, looking at me.

'Dhruv.'

I was holding my dhoti and checking if it was tight enough.

'Dhruv, do you really know how to dance?' Avni asked.

'I know, but a little,' I said.

The DJ was busy adjusting the song track for us.

'I don't want a *nagin* dance on the stage. You North Indians only know nagin dance, isn't it?' she said and giggled.

'What did you say? You are also half-North Indian. Don't forget that,' I said.

'That's not the point. I have seen on TV how you guys do the nagin dance,' Avni said and laughed. I felt hurt. It felt as though the self-respect of all North Indians was at stake. I remembered my Hrithik Roshan stage performance from my childhood years. The DJ was about to play the song. The light focused on Avni.

'Are you sure, Dhruv?' she asked, as she moved ahead.

'I am going to dance better than you.'

'Are you serious?' Avni said.

'Of course I am.'

Avni and I stepped to the front. As soon as the light focused on me, I held my dhoti tightly.

There was just a piece of white cloth between my self-respect and tomorrow's news headlines. What if it falls? What if Newton's law of gravity comes out to be true in front of hundreds of people? Everyone in the crowd will laugh and all my 'maan-maryada' *will be lost forever.*

'Are you ready?' Avni asked.

Ready? I was ready to run away but the DJ had already started the song.

Avni started dancing—it was the '*Nimbooda Nimbooda*' song. She was damn good right from her first step and, to my surprise, I was actually dancing . . . well. I held my dhoti and followed her steps carefully, but Avni was quick. The quicker she got, the more I was scared that my dhoti would fall off on stage in front of hundreds of kids, men and women.

People were clapping as though they had never seen such a dance in their life. Maybe I did dance well. The song ended in a few minutes. Avni was really good. We gave each other a high five before we got down from the stage.

'Sir, one request,' the DJ said. Avni and I turned around.

'Can you dance once more? Only you, sir. People loved your performance,' he said and Avni clapped like a kid in sheer excitement. I looked at her.

'Go, Dhruv, please. People would love to see you dance,' Avni pleaded.

I was once again at the centre of the stage. I asked the DJ to play '*Ek Pal Ka Jeena*'. The dance from my childhood was going to redeem me. As the song started, I just went nuts and kept dancing until I heard people clapping and hooting. They had too much entertainment after all. I got down from the stage bowing to people as though I was Michael Jackson.

'Wow, Dhruv Mehta. What a performance!' Avni said.

'Thanks, Avni Mathur. Hope you are impressed.'

'I don't get impressed so easily,' she said. I chuckled. I felt like pinching her cheeks, but then I had to restrain myself as I saw an intimidating-looking man walk up behind her. *Her dad?*

'My dad,' Avni said, as she turned around.

Uncle stood at a distance and scanned me. Maybe the outfit hadn't impressed him. I don't know what impresses a girl's father.

Come on, Uncle. Let another North Indian win another South Indian girl's heart. If North Indians won't help North Indians, who will? I will wash your daughter's clothes, cook for her, keep your baby like my babe, I mean baby.

Uncle looked at me as though he had heard what I was saying to myself. He faked a smile and shook hands with me. It felt as though he wanted to crush my fingers.

Why can't a girl's dad keep his identity as a father aside for some time and think on humanitarian grounds? It is inhuman to break a guy's heart. People should know that.

'Who is this man, Avni?' Uncle asked grumpily.

'Man? Do I look like a man? I am a guy, not a man, for your information,' I wanted to say but I didn't.

'He is Dhruv, Appa. I told you, right?' Avni said.

Uncle looked at me from top to bottom once again as though he would also ask me to dance just like his daughter did.

'Hello, Uncle.'

'Hmmm. Hi. You were the one dancing on stage, right?'

'No, Uncle. I mean, yes, Uncle,' I said.

'Yes or no?' he asked.

'Yes. Avni insisted. So, I danced,' I said.

'So, if Avni asks you to jump from the top of a building, you will jump?' he asked.

I did not know what to say.

'Hahahaha,' Uncle laughed loudly. My heart skipped a beat.

'I was just joking,' he said and patted me on my shoulder.

'Papa is very funny,' Avni said.

If this is called being funny, everyone will die of a heart attack.

'Hmmm. What is Dhruv's native place, Avni?' Uncle asked.

'I am from North India, actually. I studied in a college in Bangalore,' I said.

'Oh, North India. Which city?' Uncle asked politely this time.

'Patna, Uncle,' I said.

'Oh, that is my native place too. Avni didn't tell me this before,' Uncle said.

'Are you serious? Are you also from Patna, Uncle?' I asked.

'Do you think I make jokes all the time?' Uncle asked grumpily.

'Appa, relax. He was just confirming it with you,' Avni said.

'Hmm. Anyway, the pandit has called me. I will join you in some time,' Uncle said, looking at Avni. Then, he looked at me and turned around, walking away briskly.

'My god. He is so scary.'

'What? Oh no, he's always like that. Chill.'

'How do you deal with him every day?' I asked.

'You shouldn't talk like that. He is my dad.'

'How is your mom?'

'She is stricter than him.'

'But the driver who dropped me off at the hotel said that your mom is cool. If she is not cool, then how are you surviving with these people around you, Avni?'

'That is why I live in Bangalore, Dhruv,' Avni said sarcastically.

I laughed.

The rest of the day was entertaining except for the wedding rituals part. But the atmosphere became lively when Pratap kissed his wife while tying the *mangalsutra*. No one does that in an arranged marriage usually. Maybe that is why people enjoyed that moment even more. I had even taken a perfect shot of that moment on my mobile.

Avni, on the other hand, burst into tears when she saw that. She had told me about Pratap and his ex-girlfriend. Pratap had almost ruined his life after that incident. But Avni helped him recover by telling him about Moksha Foundation, an NGO that helped people with depression. Their world-class team helped Pratap get back to a healthy life once again. Today, the same guy was happily married.

After that, Avni and I got some pictures clicked with the bride and the groom in multiple poses. After all, he was my college friend. I lifted Pratap in my arms and got a picture clicked. That turned out to be the best photo of the day.

My first visit to Chennai turned out to be a great experience. I could not meet Avni's mom as she was busy, but I knew I'd meet her someday. Avni got some sweets packed for my family, especially for Didi and Jiju. They had all been calling me and I had barely attended Maa and Didi's call that morning.

I was back in Goa. My entire body hurt because of the dance and the festivities, but it was worth it. Amit Mama told me to have a massage session. He had taken it thrice in a single day in the resort premises. He told me that it was awesome, emphasizing a lot on *'awe'*.

When I went for the massage session, a beautiful girl entered the room. I felt a little shy. It was my first massage by a girl. God was really kind, but I was not ready for this.

'Remove your clothes, sir,' she said.

'Excuse me?'

'Sir, you have to remove your clothes so we can proceed,' she said, without any hesitation.

Mama ji got me into big trouble. Oh no. How could I take off my clothes in front of a girl? She was arranging the cot on which she was going to give me the massage. I did not know what was going to happen. If Maa saw me with this girl, she would beat me with her slipper. Oh no, I don't want any drama.

'Uh, ma'am, if you don't mind, could I get the massage from a male masseuse?' I asked politely, with a smile on my face.

She looked at me as though I had committed a crime by saying that. Of course, she just lost a client.

'As you wish,' she said, quite impolitely, and left the room.

After she left, a giant man came inside the room. He was so serious that it felt as if he would slap me if I dared to talk to him. The entire massage session went off without any conversation.

It felt really good after I was done with the massage. I gave him a small tip but I was scared to even give him one. *What if he slapped me for giving him a small tip?*

Every joint in my body was relaxed after that session and I came back to my room. I picked up my phone to see some messages from Avni—she'd sent me the photos. As I was scrolling through them, Jiju entered the room.

'What are you doing here alone?'

'You guys can't leave me alone, right?'

'Wow, are you blushing?'

'What? No, nothing like that.'

'Tell me. Did Avni kiss you?' he asked.

'Shame on you, Jiju. What are you saying?'

'Hahahaha,' he laughed.

'She is a nice girl. She won't do all that, okay?' I said and threw my pillow at him.

'Good girls don't kiss? Is that what you mean?' he asked.

'Seriously, Jiju. Something is really wrong with you,' I said and threw another pillow at him.

'Look, you're still blushing. What happened in Chennai?'

'Everything.'

'Did Avni tell you that she likes you?'

'I have no story to tell.'

'Come on, Dhruv. Tell me,' Jiju insisted.

'Let your wife come or else she will ask me to repeat the whole story again,' I said.

Jiju dialled her number and the next second, Didi was in my room.

'Did Avni kiss you?' Didi asked, with her eyes wide open.

'Yes, on my left cheek. There is a mark. See,' I said out of frustration.

'Shameless,' Didi said.

'Don't you guys have any other work to do?' I said.

'Will you start the story, please?' Jiju said, holding the pillow under his chin and sitting like a schoolkid. Didi stood right in front of me.

'Do you want to dance on my head?' I asked Didi. She sat down on my bed.

I told them the whole story from the beginning.

I said that Avni had left a letter for me at the hotel room and that I became famous in Chennai overnight. If my dhoti would have fallen, I would have become famous all over India by now. Jiju laughed listening to that.

I also told them that Avni showed me a few clicked pictures of us together from our college days. I was always camera-shy. So, Avni had got my photos clicked along with her, without even telling me. She might have asked Pratap to click those. In most of the photos, I looked like an idiot whereas Avni was pretty in all the pictures.

Avni's mom and dad had insisted she drop me off at the airport. So Avni did just that. I also told Didi and Jiju about Pratap kissing his wife publicly during the ceremony. Didi and Jiju's mouths and eyes fell open on hearing that. Yes, they hadn't done this at their own wedding despite the fact that they had a love marriage. Pratap had done it in an arranged marriage.

'Shreya, let's get married again,' Jiju said, out of excitement.

'Again? And that too with you? No way,' Didi said. I laughed.

'There is no value of a guy after marriage. Did you see that, Dhruv? Before marriage, this girl used to cry for me,' Jiju said.

'I still cry being with you,' Didi said.

I laughed again, holding my stomach.

'Shame on you,' Jiju said.

'Same to you,' Didi said.

'I just love seeing you both fight. I just love it,' I remarked.

'Dhruv, you don't know my situation and how I cry every night under the pillow being with your sister,' Jiju continued.

'He uses a pillow because I don't want to be disturbed while sleeping,' Didi clarified, looking at me.

This time, I fell from the bed laughing.

We stayed in Goa for two more days, visiting all the temples and seeking blessings from god. When we all left Goa, only one person was truly sad—Amit Mama. I knew what he was missing. If I told his wife, it would be the most memorable trip of his life. But later, Mama ji revealed that he, too, had gotten a massage from a man. One other common thing about our massage experience was that there was pin-drop silence during our sessions.

7

I was back in Patna. The song 'Let Me Love You' was playing on my laptop and I was dancing in my room. I was missing dancing with Avni. Life would have been so beautiful if I could dance with her every single day.

I was swinging all over my room when our housemaid saw me and giggled as though she had never seen a guy dancing. I shut the door and continued dancing. It was just a few seconds, and then Maa came into my room at full speed and slapped my bum. I felt the pain and rubbed my bum immediately.

'You don't have time to talk to girls I am choosing for you but you have time to do all this nonsense in my house,' Maa said.

'No, Maa. I'm ready to talk to the girl. I was listening to the song to get in the mood.'

'Really?'

'Yes, Maa. Swear on that girl,' I said.

'Don't swear on her. If you are lying, she will get ill.'

'Why Maa? Why would I lie? I know you will choose the right girl for me.'

'My sweet son.'

'Maa, I can understand your frustration these days. I totally understand,' I said.

'What do you understand?'

'That I am the most eligible bachelor in my family but I am still not getting married. So, it's obvious that my mother will get frustrated.'

Maa looked at me puzzled.

'What do you mean by *most eligible bachelor*?' she asked.

'It means boys who are in demand, Maa,' I said politely, holding her hand.

'Who told you that you are in demand? Girls have started rejecting you,' Maa said, very impolitely I thought.

'Maa, please don't shout. The maid will hear you.'

'Then you have to listen to me.'

'Okay, fine. I'll talk to the girl.'

'Good then. She'll call you in another fifteen minutes,' Maa said and left for the kitchen.

Maa had invited a girl's family to our home today but they couldn't come. I was at peace when I got to know that they were not coming but Maa doesn't like peace. She likes war. So, she threatened me to get ready to talk to the same girl on a video call. I agreed peacefully.

Maa actually asked me to tell her everything about Avni the previous night. Maybe she liked Avni but I did not utter a word about her to Maa. It was a sensitive matter. I needed to be sure first if Avni liked me.

I got a message on my mobile. It was from Ritu, the girl everyone had told me about in Goa. I had told Maa last night that I didn't like Ritu's photo but still, Maa insisted on having a conversation at least. Maa politely said that there were other things apart from a girl's face that we should focus on, such as the way a girl talks, the way a girl listens and the way a girl smiles.

Maa kept telling me I should always have a smile on my face while talking to Ritu. I could not sleep the whole night practising that. My jaws had already started hurting. My laptop screen blinked. There was a call from Ritu. My fingers were shivering and suddenly my heartbeat quickened when I realized that I wasn't wearing my jeans. I was wearing only a T-shirt and shorts. Seriously, if Ritu saw me like this, she would reject me right away. Thank god I was sitting on a chair. On the bed, I would have got exposed. But, I didn't want to accept her video call. I did not like her in the photo. How could I talk to her?

'Bro, relax. Talk to her first,' the inner me said.

'Okay, fine.'

'What if she is actually beautiful and you fall for her?' the inner me said.

'What about Avni then?'

'Let us focus on one girl at a time. Okay?'

'Okay, fine. One girl at a time.'

The call was still on. This girl seemed so eager to talk to me. I looked at my legs. They were still waxed and smooth. I faked a smile and without further delay, I answered the call.

Arranged marriages suck.

I saw Ritu on the video call but Avni's face was flashing in front of me. Maybe that is why I did not find Ritu too attractive.

'Hi,' she said shyly.

'I can tell you clearly that she has already spoken to many guys before you. She is just faking it,' the inner me said.

'Shut up, dude.'

'Hi Ritu. How are you?'

'I am good and sorry for the early morning call. I had a meeting.'

'It's fine, I can understand,' I said smiling, just like my sweet Maa had told me to, or shall I say, threatened me. Looking at Ritu smiling for no reason, I too could not stop smiling. She was smiling constantly.

How can a human smile so much? Maybe she was threatened by her mom too.

'So, Dhruv. I am a very straightforward girl,' Ritu said.

'Is that so?'

'Dude, you are not supposed to talk like that.'

'What did you say?' she said.

'I love straightforward people,' I corrected myself immediately.

Ritu smiled again.

My life will be full of laughter if I marry her.

'So, did you have a girlfriend?' Ritu asked that one question I was running away from, all my life.

'I mean, I want to make things clear from the start,' she added.

'Dude, this is a trick question,' the inner me said.

'What do you mean?'

'If you say that you never had a girlfriend, she will think you are a loser and if you tell you had a girlfriend, then she will reject you.'

'Then what do I do?'

'Tell her that you have been too busy with your career. Anyways, you can't tell her the truth—you have a problem with Vitamin "SHE" around you.'

'Shut up.'

'No, I never had a girlfriend, Ritu. I have been too busy with *vitamin she* and I had no time for my career all these years,' I said, smiling.

'What?' she asked.

Oh no, what did I just say to her? Now Maa will beat me and kill me.

'I mean, I have been too busy with my career all these years, Ritu.'

'Oh my god. I was so scared!'

'I was just kidding.'

'You are so funny, really,' she said and threw out a bigger smile, as if she had been declared the queen of my heart.

'Did you have a boyfriend?' I asked. 'Just to be clear at the start,' I added.

'Yes, yes, you can ask me anything. Be frank,' she said.

'So, did you have a boyfriend?' I asked.

Ritu looked to her left and then to her right. She had a earring in her left ear but not in the right ear. That was one thing I noticed.

'I had a boyfriend a few years back,' Ritu said.

'Wow,' I said.

'What?'

'I mean how and why did he leave you?' I asked smiling.

'He didn't leave me. I left him,' she said without smiling. It seemed as if she felt bad about what I had said. No one wants someone to leave them. They all want to be the ones who leave.

'But don't tell my mom. Just telling you because I really liked your profile and you are a good match,' she added.

If I tell her right now that I don't like her, there is a two hundred per cent chance she is going to get hurt. Oh god, please help me.

The next second, there was a call on my phone. It was a video call from Avni.

Shit.

'What happened? You look tense,' Ritu asked.

'Nothing, but I've to go now, actually. My Maa's calling me.'

'Your Maa calls you being in the same house?' Ritu said, laughing. 'You're funny, Dhruv,' she added.

'Hahahaha, yeah, I try. But yeah, she's just like that.'

'Are you serious? I still have five minutes to talk.'

'But this is urgent. I'm sorry, Ritu. It was nice talking to you. Bye!'

'Is it from your girlfriend? Ex-girlfriend? Are you hiding it from me? You don't like me?' Ritu asked with a puppy face.

I didn't know which answer to give first. Yes or No. The phone was still ringing.

'I don't know and I'm sorry, Ritu. Bye,' I said, disconnecting her call and switching to Avni's.

'Video call?' I asked.

'Yes, I wanted to see you.'

'All girls want to see me. No problem,' I said, flattering myself.

'Hahaha. That is so true. All the girls at the Chennai wedding were talking about you.'

'But I only want to talk to Avni,' I mumbled.

'What did you say?'

'Nothing. By the way, you look nice in that pink top with a teddy bear. Even that pillow behind you has a teddy bear. You girls like teddy bears a lot.'

'We like SRK a lot too,' Avni said.

'SRK and his female fan following will never end. The whole world loves him.'

'Gauri and his love story is so unique.'

She was saying 'Gauri' as if she was her school friend.

'Gauri ma'am. Yes, she is a romantic girl. Very difficult to find girls like her.'

'Impossible,' Avni said.

'But guys like SRK exist,' I said, pointing at myself.

'Umm hmmm. Someone is trying to say that they can beat SRK in romance.'

'Yes. But guys like us don't get a chance to prove it.'

'Hahaha. Very funny. SRK is the god of romance.'

'Okay, I agree on this. No one can argue with girls about SRK. I bow down.'

'Good boy,' Avni said, smiling.

'Okay listen,' I said.

'Yes.'

'I am writing a love story.'

'Oh wow, that's crazy! Can I read it?'

'Not yet. Let me finish it at least.'

'Please?'

'Okay, fine.'

'Is it a true story, Dhruv?'

'Of course. A love story that will inspire the world.'

'Wow, Dhruv. You were doing theatre in college. I knew you would do something great in life.'

'Relax. I haven't done anything yet.'

'Let me know if you need any help and please send me a few chapters. I want to read it.'

'Hahaha, you girls are crazy about love stories.'

'Of course. Our generation is so unlovable.'

'True that. Okay, I'll send you a few chapters but you have to give me an honest review.'

'I take an oath on the Gita that I will give you an honest review,' Avni said, placing her palm on a newspaper.

'Hahaha. That much drama is not needed.'

'But when did you start writing and why?'

'India needs to read real love stories. We have to talk about our culture and inspire youngsters.'

'Wow. So romantic,' Avni said.

'It's called patriotism. You girls think everything is romantic.'

'Yes, we do. You have a problem?'

Just then, Maa entered my room like a whirlwind and looked directly into my phone camera. She has no etiquette.

'Hi Aunty,' Avni said.

'Oh, so pretty you look,' Maa said, rolling her hands around her ears, to ward off the evil eye.

'I missed you at the Chennai wedding, Aunty,' Avni said.

'Oh, I missed you too. We all missed you, in fact. Both my brothers were asking about you.'

'So, when are you coming to meet me?' Avni asked.

'Give me some time, beta. I just have to make sure Dhruv is settled down and then I'll be free,' Maa said, and I felt like banging my head against the wall.

'Tell him to talk to girls, Avni. He never listens to me. He says that he will have a love marriage.'

'I will try to talk to him, Aunty.'

'When are you getting married, beta?'

I really wanted god to disrupt the network right now. Maa was crossing all the borders and I was in the mood of *Gadar 3*.

'Just waiting for the right guy, Aunty. Mom and Dad are searching.'

'Beautiful girls should get married soon.'

'Hahaha. Yes, Aunty. I will marry soon.'

I had to do something or else Maa would spoil my love story before it even started.

'Maa, have you left the gas switched on in the kitchen?'

'Oh yes. Go and close it.'

My plan did not work. I got up and ran to the kitchen and came back to my room as fast as I could. I did not want to miss their conversation. My future was at risk after all.

Maa and Avni were talking as though they were school friends. Maa had no idea that she was talking to her prospective daughter-in-law but now nothing could be done. She was talking to Avni only about my arranged marriage and I had tears in my eyes thinking about my future in darkness once again. I had to do something.

'Maa!' I shouted.

'What happened, Dhruv?'

'Maa, I'm hungry,' I said.

'Then go and brush your teeth.'

'No, I want to eat without brushing my teeth. Will I get food or not?'

'Okay, Avni. Dhruv has gone mad. I will talk to you soon,' Maa said and gave me the phone.

I placed it on mute immediately and looked at Maa angrily.

'Why are you looking at me like that?' she asked.

'Thanks for ruining my life, Maa,' I said.

'I don't have time for your nonsense. I am going to make breakfast,' she said.

'I hate you, Maa,' I said.

'But I love you,' Maa said and left.

Avni giggled as I was back on the call.

'Avni, please delete everything that Maa just said. There is no truth in that and you know I won't lie to you.'

'So, you are not talking to girls?'

'I told you that I don't want to have an arranged marriage.'

How do I tell her that I like her?

'Same here.'

'Then why did you tell Maa that your parents are looking for a guy?'

'Aunty threw a bomb at me. What was I supposed to say?'

You could have said Aunty, I love Dhruv and will marry him only.

'Agree. So, you are not talking to guys?'

'Yesterday, Amma made me speak to another guy.'

Ouch.

'Did you like him?'

'Shut up.'

'Even I spoke to a girl this morning.'

'In the morning? Are you serious?'

'Yes, Maa forced me to. If I don't listen to this lady in my house, then the entire neighbourhood will get to know what is going on in my life,' I said. Avni laughed.

'The girl I spoke to also had an ex-boyfriend,' I said.

'All girls and boys have exes these days.'

'We don't have,' I said.

'Yes, we are clean and clear just like SRK and Gauri.'

'You and your SRK love will never end in this birth, right?'

'Never ever,' Avni said.

'Thank you, SRK sir, for keeping Avni like this,' I said.

Avni laughed. I stared at her. I wished every morning could be like this. Light. Fun. With Avni.

'Dhruv?'

'Hmmm?'

'Come to Bangalore, *na*.'

'Bangalore? What for?'

'I want to show you around.'

'Are you serious?'

'Yes. I have to go shopping.'

'You want me to come to Bangalore for your shopping?'

'You don't understand anything.'

'Yes, I am dumb,' I said

'I miss you.'

Butterflies.

'That sounds good,' I said.

'When are you coming then?'

'In a week or so.'

'Oh no, Appa is here. I will cut the call,' Avni said.

'Why are you scared of your dad?'

'Okay then, I will make you talk to him.'

'No Avni, please. I am scared of your dad. Please don't give Uncle the phone.'

'Whom are you talking to?' came a male voice on Avni's side.

'Dhruv, Appa,' Avni said and handed her phone to her dad. I cursed my fate. Uncle looked into the mobile screen.

'Hi young man. What's up?'

'Hi U-U-Uncle. I am good. I was just discussing our college days with Avni.'

Maa came into my room with a plate of my breakfast and gave it to me. She peeped into my phone once again and then looked at me.

'Who is he?' she asked.

'My sasur and your samdhi,' I wanted to say but I didn't.

'Avni's dad,' I said.

'Vanakkam ji,' Maa said. I was surprised to see her addressing Avni's dad like this.

'Vanakkam, madam, but even I am a North Indian.'

'Oh is it? How come? Which city?'

'Your city only, madam,' Uncle said, laughing. I don't know why Avni's dad laughs after each sentence.

'Wow. Dhruv never told me,' Maa said.

'He has no time to tell you the real facts. He is busy talking to my daughter every day.'

'Yes, yes. They both keep talking and talking and talking.'

After that, Maa and Uncle started discussing their school days in Patna. Just then, Dad came into my room.

'Who is your Maa talking to?' Dad asked.

'My sasur,' I wanted to say again.

'Avni's dad,' I said.

'Namaste,' Dad said.

'Namaste ji. We were talking about you only,' Uncle said.

After that, I knew I should leave the room. Avni's mom had also joined the call and they all were laughing for no reason. Dad took the phone from Maa. Maybe he was feeling insecure. Avni's dad can make anyone feel insecure.

Maa did not look happy with Dad's intervention. Maybe she liked talking to Avni's dad.

Will I also become like this after marriage? What am I thinking?

I came out of the room with my laptop. There was a message from Ritu on the matrimonial chat box.

'Let's connect soon. I hope you liked talking to me. See you', Ritu's message read.

I did not reply.

Maa and Dad were done with the call after fifteen minutes. They went into the kitchen shouting loudly at each other. I ran to the kitchen with my plate.

'Why were you talking to that man?' Dad asked Maa.

'What are you saying? He is Avni's dad,' Maa said.

'I know that, but why were you talking to him?'

'Even you were talking to his wife,' Maa said in her defence.

'I spoke to her in your presence.'

'I know how much you were smiling talking to that lady. So, don't ask me why I was talking to her husband.'

'What is going on here?' I asked.

'Ask your Maa,' Dad said.

'I didn't do anything, Dhruv,' Maa said.

Their drama continued and I came back to my room.

'My mom and dad are fighting after the call, Dhruv. I don't know what happened. I'm cooling them down. I'll call you later'—it was Avni's message. I laughed reading it. North or South, East or West, Indian husband and wife are all the same everywhere.

8

I reached Bangalore and it was raining. I took a deep breath and looked for a cab, which I got in less than a minute. The driver picked up my luggage and placed it in the boot as I sat inside comfortably.

'Dhruv, are you back?' came a message from Aditi.

Goddammit, Aditi. How does she know that I reached?

'Maybe she was stalking you on Instagram. Good-looking boys have no privacy, dude,' the inner me said.

'Sure, dude.'

I forgot to tell you about Aditi. She works in my office and she is a little crazy. No, she is totally crazy. You will get to know the reason, soon. She's a character.

'Yes, I'm back', I replied.

Aditi immediately called me. 'Can I come to meet you? It's urgent.'

'In your life, everything is urgent. Were you even born in urgency, Aditi? What happened?'

'Yes. I was born very urgently. Happy now?'

'Not at all. I have been suffering since I met you.'

'Good for me. Okay, I'm coming to your flat. I have boyfriend troubles. Please don't say that your flat owner will kill you.'

Again?

'I don't know about killing, but he will increase my rent if he sees you. Even I won't feel comfortable with you in my flat.'

'Oh my god, how come you are like this? You are so old school.'

'Because I'm a one-woman man?'

'Oh yes. How can I forget your dialogue of a one-woman man? Dhruv, these days nobody is a "one-woman" man. How can you be?' Aditi said.

I laughed. *What did she know about my Avni?*

'A few girls are there,' I said.

'Yes, like me, right?'

'You're joking, right?'

'Why do you say that?'

'Every weekend you are with someone new from the office.'

'What to do? I lost my . . . my boyfriend.'

'Just kidding. I didn't mean it. You are a nice girl, Aditi, and you didn't lose your boyfriend. He is still there.'

'Can you help me?' Aditi persisted.

'Me? No way.'

'Just because you are single, it doesn't mean that you can't see others mingling, Dhruv.'

'Aditi, there are two things I want to make clear. First, I am not single. And second, I am mingling too.'

'Are you serious? So, Mr Dhruv Mehta went to Goa to see a girl and he is getting married soon?'

'Shut up. I didn't go to see a girl. I will have a love marriage.'

'Am I talking to the same guy who left Bangalore a few weeks ago? You sound different.'

'Yes. I am in love.'

'Dhruv, are you serious? I never thought you could fall in love. You are so boring,' Aditi said.

'How dare you?'

'Hey, I'm sorry. I shouldn't have said that,' Aditi said.

'It's okay. When a boring girl calls another person boring, I don't mind.'

'How dare you?'

'Hahahaha,' I laughed.

'Won't you ask why I called?'

'So, you won't tell me if I don't ask?'

All girls in the world can't live without speaking their mind.

'Actually, I am in love once again, Dhruv.'

'You found a new guy? Again? How do you get new guys every week, Aditi?'

'No, wait. I am talking about my only love. He was my first. I don't feel for anyone else the way I feel for him.'

'And what about the guys you hang around with?'

'They are just for timepass,' Aditi said.

'Aditi, please stop doing this. What if one of those guys starts liking you? You are going to spoil his life.'

'Oh, yes. I'm sorry. I never thought about it. How can I be such an idiot?'

'Aditi, we should not spoil anyone's life just for timepass. They are also someone's kid. You do not know if the other person is serious about you.'

'Dhruv, you know me. I am not a girl who will fool around. I got your point. Will you help me talk to my boyfriend?'

'First, we'll talk about him. How do you know that you really love him?'

'I don't feel for anyone else like I feel for him even now.'

'I can't believe you're saying this. It feels so nice to see girls being loyal to guys. They are so rare.'

Another call was coming in—from Avni. Damn it. I picked it up.

'Hi Avni,' I said.

'Hi handsome,' Avni said.

'Handsome?' Aditi said.

'Who is this other girl, Dhruv?' Avni asked.

'Dhruv, is there a cross-connection? Someone is calling you handsome,' Aditi said, laughing.

'Avni, you are on call with Aditi, my colleague. Aditi, you are talking to Avni. We both studied in the same college. I merged the call by accident, my bad,' I said.

'Hi Avni,' Aditi said.

'Hey, hi Aditi,' Avni said.

'Sorry for creating this confusion, girls,' I said.

Aditi then asked Avni how we met. Avni described to her our Goa trip and the Chennai visit. She also told her about my dance performance. Aditi told Avni about my female fan following in the office.

I did not know that so many girls in the office liked me. Aditi never told me that before.

After that, Aditi requested a video call. We switched our cameras on. I saw Avni and felt I was in love again. Aditi and Avni were seeing each other for the first time. After seeing Avni, Aditi messaged: 'Any guy will fall for Avni. She is so beautiful.'

Every time I see Avni, I just cannot stop myself from falling in love with her.

'You both were just in the same college or anything more?' Aditi asked Avni, after I messaged begging her not to ask personal questions. She would get my love story into trouble.

'He was my bestie in college, Aditi,' Avni said.

'Wow, we hardly see besties from college these days. All break up,' Aditi said.

Avni laughed and said, 'No girl can break up with Dhruv.'

I was on cloud nine after hearing this. No girl has ever praised me like this.

'Avni, shall I tell you one thing?' Aditi said.

'Yes, please.'

'You are very lucky,' Aditi said.

I almost had a heart attack. Aditi would put me at risk today. She was going to end my love story before it started.

'Did you tell Avni you like her?' Aditi messaged me.

'Aditi, please shut up or I will kill you', I replied.

'Lucky? Why's that?' Avni asked.

'Ask Dhruv,' Aditi said.

Shit.

'Dhruv, are you there?' Avni asked.

These girls will surely give me a heart attack today.

'I can't hear you guys. Looks like a network issue,' I said.

'But I can hear you,' Avni said.

'Me too. We can hear you clearly, Dhruv,' Aditi said.

'Hello, hello,' I said and disconnected the call.

'Two girls. Wow, sir. You are really lucky,' the driver said, turning around.

'Will you look straight and drive?' I said.

'Sir, how do we get girls in our life?' the driver asked.

'It's all fate, dude. If your fate is bad, you will get girls. If your fate is good, you won't get them,' I said.

The driver laughed out loud.

The next day, I was back in the office. Getting back to work is the worst feeling. Same meetings, same status calls, and same faces. In the break, I spoke to Aditi about her boyfriend.

Aditi was from Patna. She even knew my Maa. So, it was my dharma to help her, or else she would tell Maa that I liked Avni. Yes, she threatened me and I don't want anyone to know that I like Avni, especially Maa. It has to be top secret. For the time being, Aditi said that she would not tell anyone about Avni. A few months ago, I had asked Aditi to keep a secret and told her not to tell anyone. She told my secret to everyone and asked them not to tell anyone else. So, I have trust issues with *this girl* at present.

Aditi's boyfriend is a Tamilian. I told Avni about Aditi's lover boy and Avni found all his details in less than an hour. She also learnt that he is still single. I wonder how all Tamilians know each other in some way or another. Avni told me that we both could help them meet. So, officially I was now a matchmaker, whose own love story had not even started properly.

Anyway, I was going to a movie with Avni the next day but I did not know which one.

'Hi', I messaged Avni.

'Someone messaged me?' Avni replied.

'No. The message came for a walk on your phone'.

'Very funny'.

'I forgot to ask, which movie is it?'

'Guess. How can you ask me this question?'

'Please tell me it's not an SRK movie. Please.'

'You know me so well. Of course, it's an SRK movie and you are coming tomorrow'.

'So, you are ordering me now?'

'Of course'.

'Well, beautiful girls have the right to order guys'.

'Yes, and handsome boys should listen to beautiful girls'.

'Avni, no one has ever called me handsome before. You don't know how happy I feel when you call me handsome'.

'Hahaha. Is it so? But you are not more handsome than SRK'.

Damn.

'Dhruv, be ready for the movie at 6.30 pm, INOX, Galleria Mall'.

'What movie is it?'

'It's a surprise'.

'Done'.

'Thanks'.

'Avni, no thanks between friends'.

'You are not my friend'.

'Then, who am I?'

'Looks like Dhruv Mehta has no work today'.

She always dodges this question.

'Dhruv Mehta has a lot of work but it looks like Avni is missing Dhruv'.

'How did you know that?'

'I know everything'.

'Okay then, tell me. What colour dress am I wearing?'

I looked at my shirt. It was maroon.

'Dhruv, if she loves you, she will be in maroon too.'

'Why do you always have to be romantic, bro?'

'Because love is in my blood, bro.'

'You're wearing a maroon dress?' I messaged.

Avni immediately sent me a selfie. She was actually wearing a maroon salwar suit with light make-up.

'But how did you guess?' she messaged.

'I told you I know everything. But, who is the guy behind you?'

In her selfie, I had seen a guy behind her, looking into her phone.

'Oh no. He's my manager. I'll chat with you later. Bye'.

'Hahaha. Be safe'.

I could talk to this girl all day.

9

Avni and I were going for a movie today. I left my office thirty minutes early and reached my flat to spend an hour finding the right shirt to wear. Finally, I chose a white T-shirt.

'Today, Avni will see you and fall for you,' the inner me said.

'And then she will hug me.'

'And then you will propose to her.'

'And then we both will hug each other.'

'How romantic.'

'But I don't believe in this proposal business.'

'Why? Scared?'

'I am not scared. Avni is not like other girls. She likes being simple.'

'You both are boring.'

'That is why we both are made for each other.'

I had asked my college friend, Raj to lend me his bike but he had given it for servicing.

A message flashed on my phone.

'Dhruv, what time you are leaving?' the message read.

'Just leaving, Avni'.

'Good. I will reach in some time. Don't be late'.

'When will you reach Hebbal?'

'I am near Majestic now'.

Avni and I were supposed to meet at Hebbal, have an ice cream and leave from there. Avni loves the ice cream there.

'Ok Dhruv, see you soon'.

I left my room and took a BMTC bus. No seat was available and it was really hot outside. I reached Hebbal bus stop ten minutes late and saw Avni waiting there. She was wearing a yellow salwar suit with green embroidery at the edges. She wore long earrings, adding elegance to her beautiful face. Two boys almost fell from another bus while staring at Avni.

These guys will never improve.

'Look right, madam'. I messaged Avni, as I approached her. She turned to me and smiled.

'Sorry for being late,' I said.

'You are sweating,' she said and handed me a kerchief.

'Next bus to Galleria is coming,' she said.

'But that is not AC,' I said.

'You really want us to be late for the movie, Dhruv?' she asked.

'No, but please wait for a minute,' I said and ran to the ice cream corner. But it did not have Avni's favourite ice cream.

'They don't have it,' I told Avni, as I came back.

'It's okay. I almost forgot about it,' Avni smiled at me.

The other bus was less crowded. Avni took the ladies seat in the corner and I stood beside her, like I used to during our college days. Avni held my shirt as she sat down. Often the bus conductors don't allow men to stand close to women's seats. So, Avni used to hold my shirt even during college days so that the conductor would know that I was with her. The conductor looked at me and then at Avni. She told him something in Kannada after which he left.

After three stops, the lady beside Avni got down. Avni asked me to sit beside her but I refused.

'No woman is standing. You can sit, Dhruv' Avni said.

'No. It's okay. You sit,' I said.

'Sit, Dhruv, or else I will stand with you,' she said sternly.

I knew she would stand if I didn't sit. I sat hesitatingly and all the women in the front seats turned around in slow motion just like in those Star Plus serials. One woman nudged another.

'I should rather stand,' I told Avni.

'No need. Stay seated,' Avni grunted. I followed her order. 'Keep the tickets,' Avni handed me the movie tickets as we neared our stop. We reached Galleria in a few minutes. The entrance was jam-packed. We somehow managed to enter on time. The theatre echoed with a loud noise on SRK's entry. I was excited to see him even though I was not a huge fan. Avni asked me to whistle at his entry but I told her that I didn't know how to whistle. Avni

looked at me as if she really wished I could whistle too.
The movie was good. I was loving it. During the interval, I
told Avni I knew what was going to happen at the end, but
she warned me not to reveal anything.

All the girls are emotional about SRK as though he is
their boyfriend. One day, I would like to meet SRK and
ask, 'Why are girls so crazy about you?'

*I guess I knew the answer already. The answer was DDLJ
and every girl wants her love story to have an ending like
DDLJ.*

After the film was over, as Avni and I were walking out,
I saw my college friends Sandeep, Sunil and Dilip. They
had asked me today if I was free and I had told them that I
was going to the office. Oh god, if I had known they were
coming for this movie, I wouldn't have dared to come here
with Avni. Now, they would kill me if they saw me with her.

I was really scared. This is the issue when you have
male friends as well as a girl in your life. You have to choose
between them. I pulled Avni down back to the seats.

'What happened? Let's go out,' Avni said as she fell on
the seat beside me.

'No, Avni. It's an emergency. Please wait here for some
time,' I said.

'You look scared, Dhruv,' she said.

'Yes, I am scared because my friends are here.'

'Friends. Then let's meet them. It's nice to meet friends,
Dhruv.'

'Avni, these are not like normal friends. They will beat
me if they see me with you.'

'Beat you? But why?' she asked.

'Because I told them that I am in the office today. And if they see me here, they'd just . . .'

'So what?'

'I came to watch a movie with you. You don't know, Avni, how guys think. They get jealous when they see their friend with a girl,' I said. Avni giggled.

'Then for how long we are going to sit like this?'

'Avni, please stop asking questions. I am tense.'

'Okay, then we will eat ice cream after they leave.'

I looked at Avni. There was no hope with her.

'Okay, madam. Let them just go out.'

'But they seem to be nice guys.'

'Avni, I have spent four years with them in college, four years after college. I know them more than you,' I said.

'Are they so bad?' Avni asked, shocked.

'Avni, they are not simply bad. They are the worst when it comes to lies. They will first beat me and then if they feel they are done, they will leave me alive. They love me a lot, Avni.'

'Is this how friends love? What sort of friends do you have?'

'Yes, boys display love like this.'

'I think they are gone,' Avni said.

I got up slowly and checked everywhere. Avni and I spent some more time in the theatre before we left. I was really scared to go out. I dropped Avni and then I took another bus. I reached my room late at night when I saw Sandeep, Dilip and Sunil standing at the entrance of my apartment building. My heart started beating really fast after seeing them. My legs were automatically shivering seeing them but I faked a smile.

'Oh my god, what a beautiful surprise,' I said, keeping one hand on my heart as I approached them.

'Where were you the whole day?' Sandeep asked, flexing his huge biceps.

'Me. Office. I told you guys, right? Too much work,' I said.

'We all saw what work you were doing,' Sandeep said.

'Hahaha. You still joke like you used to during college days.'

'We also beat like we did in college days,' Dilip said and my heart skipped a beat.

'Gandhiji said, "no violence", guys. Remember?'

'Newton said, that for every action there is an equal and opposite reaction. Do you remember?' Sunil said.

'I'm scared, guys,' I said.

'Don't worry. We will not do too much damage. Let's go up.'

'I'm sorry. Please forgive me. I won't repeat this,' I said folding my hands and begging them.

'Dhruv, let's not create a scene. Let's handle things like grown-ups and peacefully.'

'Peacefully? Then why do you want to come up?'

'Dhruv, you want us to start here?' Sandeep asked.

'I don't mind,' Dilip said.

'But. If. I mean. I think,' I was blabbering senselessly.

'Dhruv. Relax. Keep your hand on your heart and take a deep breath,' Sandeep said.

'Today will be like Diwali for you,' Sunil said as we reached my flat entrance.

'What is your favourite cracker?' Sunil asked.

'I stopped burning crackers since last year,' I said nicely.

My hands were shivering while using the door key.

'Give it to me,' Dilip said.

'You look really scared, bro,' Sandeep said, placing his hand on my shoulder.

'Scared? No. Why would I be scared? You guys love me, right?' I said when the door finally opened. Swear on my mom's mom, I had never been so scared to enter my own flat before.

After entering, I can't explain how peaceful my night was. In the morning, the owner knocked at my door.

'Yes, Uncle,' I said as I opened the door.

'There was a lot of noise coming from your flat last night. All good, right?' he asked.

'Yes, Uncle. We were watching an action movie last night,' I said, smiling.

'Oh. Your friends told me that you went on a date with a girl and you told them that you were in the office. They were inquiring a lot about you yesterday.'

'Hehehe. They were joking, Uncle.'

'It must be paining a lot, right?' Uncle said, chuckling.

'What?'

'Your action film,' Uncle looked at me and laughed.

I faked a smile.

'Dhruv, I can understand. Let me know if you need Iodex balm,' Uncle said.

The culprits, Sandeep, Dilip and Sunil came out from the bedroom and looked at Uncle. Uncle gave them a thumbs up.

'Well done, boys,' he said.

'Thanks a lot, Uncle. You rock,' they all said.

I stood at the door, shocked. My owner uncle was against his own tenant. It is really not easy to trust anyone these days.

After Uncle left, Sandeep, Dilip and Sunil belted me again to get me to reveal Avni's name but I did not open my mouth. Also, I changed Avni's name in my contact details to 'Mummy Aircel'. Thank god these idiots had seen her when it was dark, or else they would have recognized her.

10

Bala had come to meet me when he found out that I was not well. I had a 101-degree fever. Bala was eating Lay's chips. I hate it when people eat Lay's in front of me and I can't—they are my favourite. Bala had found three packets in the kitchen and had finished one already. He was eating the second Lay's with chilli flavour and he had tears in his eyes. No, his tears were not due to the chilli but because of his ex-girlfriend.

'I wish I had never broken up with my girlfriend,' Bala said.

He was recalling his college days as he had got a marriage proposal yesterday. Old people often say that before you die, your entire life runs through your mind. Marriage is like death and Bala was recalling his golden days when girls used to fall for him. Thank god he was not in my college.

'Bala, how did you get a girlfriend, bro?' I asked.

'What do you mean by *how*? Can't I have a girlfriend?' Bala looked at me angrily.

'No, I mean, tell me about her.'

'She was beautiful. And a Tamilian, just like me.'

'Why did you leave her then?'

'Do you think I can afford to leave a girl? She was the only girl I ever had a chance to get married to in this lifetime.'

'She would have been the mother of your kids, *da*. Just imagine,' I said, adding some fuel to the fire.

'I feel like crying now,' Bala said.

'Focus on the chips, Bala, or else I will eat them.'

'Today, she would have been your bhabhi. Oh, my bad fate. When will you stop chasing me? Why can't I forget her?' Bala said, looking at the ceiling, probably complaining to god, and then he ate another chip.

'Was she beautiful, Bala?' I asked.

'Yes, da. Very beautiful.'

'Wow, Bala. You are awesome.'

'No, da. You are awesome. At least, you have someone who cares for you and is coming here.'

'Bala, what are you saying? Whom did you inform about my fever?'

'Avni's coming.'

'What?'

'Dude, what is the problem if she comes here?'

'Bala, this is a boy's apartment. Girls are not supposed to come here.'

'You are saying it as if it's a crime if she comes here.'

'There is no point arguing with you now.'

Just then, there was a knock at the door. Bala still had tears in his eyes.

'Bala, open the door,' I said.

He wiped his tears, ate two more Lay's chips and got up with a lot of effort from my sofa.

'Hi Avni,' Bala said.

I looked towards the door. Avni had glasses on and was wearing a saree. I really find her cute in glasses. For a moment, I forgot I was looking like shit. Damn. My clothes were all crumpled.

'How are you feeling?' Avni asked as she sat beside me.

'Avni, there is a problem,' I said.

'What happened?'

'My flat owner does not like girls coming over. So, tell me one thing. Did any old man with well-combed grey hair see you coming?'

'Dhruv, Avni will feel bad. Don't say it like that,' Bala said.

'No, Dhruv. No one saw me,' Avni said.

Then we heard another knock at the door.

'Dhruv, are you at home?' It was my owner.

Oh my god. If he found out there was a girl in my flat, he would ask me to leave immediately.

'Avni, please hide somewhere.'

'Dhruv, you are sick. You can tell him that I came to see you,' Avni said.

'Dhruv, open the door. Is anyone inside?' Owner Uncle shouted.

'Avni, hide,' I said.

'Go to the bedroom,' Bala said.

'Avni, hide behind the fridge,' I said. Avni looked confused and I was scared. I showed Avni where and how to hide.

'One second, Dhruv. There are no lizards, right? I am scared of lizards,' Avni said firmly.

'Will you hide or not?'

'Not until you tell me if there are lizards here.'

'There are no lizards, Avni. Trust me, and please don't shout once the owner is inside.'

'Even if you find any lizards, don't shout,' Bala said.

'Bala, don't scare her,' I said.

'Dhruv, why are we doing this?' Avni asked.

'No time for questions. Hide.'

Avni hid herself behind the fridge. Bala opened the door.

'Why did you take so much time to open the door?' Owner Uncle said.

'I went to pee, Uncle,' Bala said.

'You take so much time to pee? Are you a human or dinosaur?' he asked.

'Sorry, Uncle. I drank a lot of water this morning.'

Owner Uncle came to look at me. I was pretending to be sicker than I was.

'Hi Uncle. Anything urgent?' I asked.

'Are you sick?' he asked.

No, I am acting.

'Yes, Uncle. I am very sick,' I said, making a puppy face.

'Be a man. You will be fine,' Owner Uncle said and turned towards the kitchen. My heartbeat started speeding up. He looked at the cooker which had khichdi in it.

'Who made this?' Uncle asked.

'I made it, Uncle,' I said.

He was walking towards the fridge when my mind stopped working. I coughed loudly but Uncle didn't stop. Suddenly, Bala dropped his phone on the floor.

'Oh no, oh no. What have I done? Mom will kill me. Mom will kill me,' he screamed like a kid.

Owner Uncle came running to him. Bala had actually broken his phone to save me.

'Your phone is gone,' Uncle said.

'Now, what to do, Uncle? Where can I repair this? Mom gifted it to me on my birthday,' Bala said.

'Get it repaired as soon as possible,' Uncle said, turning towards the bedroom. Bala gave me a thumbs-up, and I returned the gesture. I realized he was a true friend. Uncle checked the bedroom but didn't find anyone.

'Did you see any girl coming up?' Uncle asked Bala.

'No, Uncle. How was she?' Bala asked.

'What do you mean, how was she? Do I look like a stalker to you?'

'Sorry, Uncle. I mean, was she beautiful? What was she wearing?'

'She was a beautiful girl with a fair complexion,' Uncle said.

'What colour saree was she wearing, Uncle?' Bala asked.

'How do you know she was wearing a saree?' Uncle asked. I cursed my fate. I realized we didn't need friends like Bala.

'Uncle, you only told me she was wearing a saree,' Bala said firmly.

'Did I?' Uncle asked. I hid my face in the blanket.

'Yes. Beautiful girls are not good, Uncle. Mom told me,' Bala said, overacting, which I hate.

'Where did she go then?' Uncle asked.

'Maybe she went upstairs,' Bala said.

'You mean on the terrace?' Uncle asked.

'Uncle, thanks for coming to check if I am doing well. I will be fine in a few days,' I said, to distract Uncle's attention.

'Okay Dhruv, if you need anything, don't call me,' Owner Uncle said and turned around to leave.

Bala and I smiled. Uncle was about to leave when we all heard a loud scream. Of course, it was Avni. Uncle turned towards the kitchen. I hid my face in the blanket. Bala stood at attention. Avni came running into the living room and climbed on my sofa.

'Sorry Dhruv, there was a big cockroach,' she said.

I looked at Uncle, Uncle looked at Bala and Bala looked at his broken phone which he had dropped to save me.

'Who is she?' Uncle asked.

'She is the new maid,' Bala said.

'Who is this idiot guy, Dhruv?' Uncle asked, looking at Bala.

'He is my office friend, Uncle,' I said.

'Such friends are dangerous to have,' Uncle said.

'I agree,' I said.

'Madam, will you please come down from the sofa? I have placed a sofa here, for people to sit on,' Uncle said.

Avni came down, adjusting her glasses.

'Who asked you to hide?' Uncle asked Avni. She pointed with both hands at me and Bala.

'You look like a nice girl from a nice family. It is not good to come to a guy's apartment alone. Do I make sense?' Uncle asked. Avni nodded. Uncle looked at me. I nodded too.

'I totally agree, Uncle,' Bala said.

'You keep quiet. *I went to pee,*' Uncle mocked Bala.

'I am sorry, Uncle. I won't lie again,' Bala said, looking at his broken phone.

'I am sorry, Uncle. Dhruv is not well,' Avni said.

'It's not a big issue. Don't do all this nonsense next time. Okay?'

'And keep the door open until she leaves. People will talk nonsense about her. You don't know how people think,' Uncle said.

'Sure, Uncle,' Bala said.

'*I went to pee*, it seems,' Uncle said and left.

Maybe my owner wasn't as bad as he'd seemed.

'He is so sweet,' Avni said.

Bala looked at his broken phone.

'Sorry, da,' I said.

'Don't worry. I will ask Avni to pay for it,' Bala said.

'I won't pay for it. If that cockroach was not there, I wouldn't have come out,' she said. I laughed. Bala didn't.

'I take an oath on my ex-girlfriend that I will never trust this girl ever again,' Bala said, looking at Avni.

I laughed.

'Avni, can you make some tea?'

Bala and Avni looked at me.

'Why do you drink tea all the time?' Avni asked.

'What shall I do then? Drink cold drinks?'

'Eat ice cream. Ice cream is life.'

'You girls eat ice cream, but you don't get fat at all. We boys have to maintain our figure by going to the gym. Do you know how difficult it is for us to sacrifice ice cream?'

They both stared at me.

'Figure?' Avni said and laughed, clapping her hands. Bala looked at his belly and became even sadder.

'See, she distracted the main topic. Avni, will you make tea or not?'

'Macha, as per Avni's track record, I am two hundred per cent sure she does not even know how to make tea.'

'Very funny,' Avni said.

'Who said I was being funny?' Bala said.

I laughed.

Avni cooked fresh khichdi and fed me. She too ate some of it. Avni stayed until the evening in the flat and I started feeling better. We all went out for a walk where we gave Bala's phone for repair. That's when Bala informed us that the phone was a gift from his ex-girlfriend which he had kept safely all these years. We looked at him. My idiot, sweet friend. Both Avni and I teared up.

11

Sandeep and I met after a week again. He asked me if the back pain had gone. I told him it was still there. He was so happy to hear that. Friends find happiness when they see us in pain that they gave us.

Today, Maa and Dad are coming to Bangalore. So, I asked Sandeep to lend me his car for a few days. We both ran towards the Arrivals as we saw Maa and Dad. Maa was not looking well but I did not say anything. I placed their luggage in Sandeep's car.

'Why did you trouble Sandeep to come here?' Dad said as he opened the door of the back seat.

'He wanted to meet both of you,' I said.

'It's really nice to see that you have such nice friends. Nowadays, most guys are not that great. They do not want to meet old people,' Dad said.

'Who said you are old, Uncle? You look more fit than both of us,' Sandeep said.

Dad laughed at that and settled into the back seat along with Maa. Sandeep sat beside me. I played some soothing music. My phone was with Sandeep as he was helping me with the shortest route to my flat. There was traffic everywhere. Suddenly, my phone rang. Sandeep looked at the screen. It flashed 'Avinash'. I had changed Avni's name to Avinash so that Maa and Dad would not question me if they saw Avni's message or call.

'Who is Avinash?' Sandeep asked.

'I am driving, yaar. Please disconnect,' I said, getting a bit worried.

Sandeep picked up the phone and I turned the music volume really loud.

'Lower the volume, Dhruv!' Maa and Dad screamed.

'Hello, hello,' Sandeep said.

Avni might have heard Maa and Dad's musical voices. Thank god she did not say a word. Sandeep would have screwed me if she had.

'Your Avinash is not talking,' Sandeep said.

'She might be facing a network issue,' I said.

'She?' Sandeep asked.

'Who said she?' I asked.

'You.'

'No, I didn't and please don't pick up my calls,' I said.

'I would like to meet this Avinash someday,' Sandeep said suspiciously.

'What is going on between you two?' Maa asked.

'Nothing, Maa,' I said.

'Aunty, what did you get for me from Patna?' Sandeep asked.

Maa took out a pack of kachoris and gave it to him. Not fair. They were mine. Sandeep winked at me while he took them from Maa. I felt bad.

'You should have got something for Dhruv also, Aunty,' Sandeep said.

'I have one packet for him also. I knew his friends would meet us,' Maa said.

I felt nice after knowing my kachoris were safe. I saw Maa take a pill when we stopped at a signal.

'What happened, Maa?' I asked.

'Is everything all right, Aunty?' Sandeep said.

'BP issue,' Maa said.

'Get married, Dhruv. Aunty got BP because of you.'

'That is true. Are you married, Sandeep?' Dad said.

'I will get married soon, Uncle. My parents will find a nice girl for me.'

'See how nice he is. He listens to his parents,' Dad said.

I glared at Sandeep. He asked me to drop him near the lane to my flat; he said he'd take a cab to his office. After he left, Dad gave me a lecture for borrowing his car. I kept quiet. As we reached my flat, I did not open my mouth or else Dad and Maa would start giving me more lectures. Maa kept fixing my entire flat for half of the day. After she was done, I realized my room was actually dirty before.

In the evening, Sandeep came to my flat along with Dilip and Sunil. I had no idea they were going to come but later on, it turned out to be the best evening for Maa and

Dad. They had brought sweets for us. Dad loves sweets and Maa loves to stop him from eating sweets. So, it was a mini-war situation for a few minutes between them. After that, we all played Ludo. Sandeep and I were in one team. Dilip and Sunil were busy discussing girls in their office. Maa won the game finally. She actually cheated twice. After that, she made an amazing dinner for us. We gathered in the kitchen and chopped onions, potatoes, fried paneer—you name it, so that Maa would not feel overburdened.

Dad got the vegetables from the market while we were preparing the menu for dinner. For the first time, we realized we were amazing cooks too. Just kidding. Maa guided us throughout the process. After dinner, we went downstairs to the society lawn and sat on the green grass under the sky. We played *antakshari*, singing old Hindi songs. Many people in the society were staring at us. Maa, Dad and I enjoyed it thoroughly. Sandeep, Dilip and Sunil stayed back at night as it was really late. We spent the whole night in the living room discussing our college days.

Another surprise came the next morning. Aditi, my office colleague, had come to meet Maa. I had told her not to come to my flat because my flat owner does not like it, but she insisted that she wanted to meet Maa. Aditi hailed from Patna too. Maa has known Aditi since I started sending pictures to her of my office trips with Aditi. Sandeep, Sunil and Dilip were supposed to leave at 10 a.m., but they did not once they saw Aditi. They were behaving like good kids since Aditi had arrived. My flat owner too came to check after seeing Aditi. He was okay after seeing my parents. I don't know why he hates girls in his building. Aditi and Maa made a nice cup of tea for all of us. Maa asked me if Aditi was married and I clearly told her that she had a boyfriend.

'Where is Avni?' Maa asked.

'She is busy, Maa,' I said.

'I want to meet her.'

'Why, Maa?'

'Dhruv, every girl has a boyfriend. Even Sandeep is getting married. Only my son is not getting anywhere.'

'Maa, relax. Give me this year.'

'Dial Avni's number now,' Maa said in a threatening tone.

'Okay, fine,' I said and edited Avinash's name back to Avni and dialled.

'Maa is here,' I said when Avni picked up the phone.

'What? Aunty is in Bangalore? Give the phone to her,' Avni said excitedly.

I don't know why women and girls are always excited. We men never get excited like they do about these things.

I gave the phone to Maa. She switched on the speaker.

'Hi Aunty!' Avni said.

'I have been waiting to talk to you since yesterday. I just met Dhruv's friends, Sandeep, Dilip, Sunil and Aditi.'

'Yes, and now you have to come to meet me. I am inviting you for lunch. Take some rest in the morning and come in the afternoon.'

'Okay. I will come to meet you, but don't cook anything. I will come and cook,' Maa said.

'No, Aunty. It's my treat,' Avni insisted.

'Hahahaha. You kids are so stubborn.'

'See you, Aunty. And did you get anything for me?'

'Do South Indians eat kachoris?'

'I am half North Indian also, Aunty, and I love kachoris.'

'Then I will bring fresh kachoris for you,' Maa said.

'You are so sweet, Aunty. I'm waiting to meet you,' Avni said.

Maa handed the phone back to me; I rolled my eyes and went to my bedroom to continue the conversation in private.

'Hello, ma'am. Any other order for me?' I asked.

'Bring Aunty safely. The next orders shall be given after that.'

'Miss Avni. First and foremost, you don't know how to cook, and you have invited my Maa for lunch?' I said.

'Mr Dhruv Mehta, I will order from a restaurant. Don't worry,' Avni replied.

'Seriously? Who does that?'

'I do. Now, I have already invited Aunty. I didn't think about this. I will manage,' Avni said.

'No, manage. Just tell Maa that you have made the food even if it is ordered from a restaurant. Shall I place the order before reaching your flat?'

'No. I will order the food myself,' Avni insisted.

'Okay, but please don't tell her that you ordered it. Maa will kill me. She hates outside food,' I emphasized.

'Okay, fine,' Avni said.

Aditi left with Sunil, Sandeep and Dilip. I had already warned the three of them that Aditi was in love with someone else. So, there was no chance for any of them. Maa and Dad were really happy to get such a warm welcome in Bangalore from all my friends.

Dad's friend was coming to meet him. So, he couldn't join us to visit Avni. Maa and I reached Avni's flat at 2 p.m. Avni was wearing a red churidar salwar suit with a golden border. Maa and Avni hugged each other like mother and daughter. Maa handed kachoris to Avni along with some rasgullas which we had bought from a Kanti Sweet Corner nearby.

'I will eat all of this in a single day. Hope you don't mind, Aunty,' Avni said, as she took the kachoris and sweets.

Maa laughed.

'Where is your roommate, Anju?' I asked.

'She has gone back home,' Avni said.

Avni's room was way cleaner than I had expected. Avni gave Maa a tour of her house except for her bedroom. I don't know why. Guys never show their rooms to anyone because they are always dirty. I stood on Avni's balcony enjoying the cloudy weather.

'Please come inside and tell me you are hungry, Dhruv. The food is getting cold', I got a message from Avni.

'You have kept it in the cooker, right? It should look authentic', I replied.

'Yes, come fast'.

I immediately ran inside.

'Maa, I'm hungry,' I said.

'Relax, Dhruv,' Maa said.

'Oh sorry. I forgot that I had invited both of you for lunch. Please sit down in the living room. And sorry, Aunty. I have a very small dining table,' Avni said.

'It's okay. Let me come with you to the kitchen first,' Maa said.

'Oh god. Please save Avni,' I mumbled as I sat at the dining table. Maa and Avni came to the living room with three plates of biryani.

'I have made raita also, Aunty. I'll just get it,' Avni said.

This girl will get herself caught with her overacting. Why did she say she made raita? Damn,' I thought to myself.

'You know how to make raita also?' Maa asked as Avni came back and sat right next to me.

'It's very simple, Aunty, and good for the stomach too,' Avni said. I closed my ears. Avni was flattering Maa a lot. We set the table and Maa helped Avni serve the food.

'It is really tasty,' I said.

'Very tasty, Avni. How did you learn to cook?' Maa said.

'I am used to it, Aunty. I hope the biryani is not too spicy?' Avni asked.

Avni will for sure get herself into trouble today.

'She has been cooking since childhood, Maa,' I put in.

'He is kidding, Aunty,' Avni said and pinched me real hard.

'I'm still shocked. How did you cook such tasty food, Avni?' Maa said.

'We are singles, Aunty. We have no option but to cook food ourselves rather than eating it from outside,' Avni said.

Now, I was damn sure that today Avni was going to get caught by Maa. This girl was saying too much. I was scared that if Maa asked her for the recipe, what would Ms Avni say?

'I can taste pudina, turmeric, red chilli and garlic. What other masalas have you put?' Maa asked.

My heart skipped a beat and then stopped beating completely. Now what would Avni say? She was in trouble now. She looked at me.

'Maa, take some more,' I said, trying to change the topic.

'You didn't say anything, Avni,' Maa said, looking at her.

Avni looked to her left, then to her right, then she looked up and then she looked at the biryani. She had sweat all over her face as though she had eaten a hundred chillies. Of course, when you flatter people so much, you are bound to get into trouble. I gave Avni my kerchief to wipe the sweat on her face.

'Stop flattering her, please,' I mumbled in Avni's ears.

After that, Avni started naming all the masalas in the world. She didn't even leave one masala out.

'We cook biryani with only two to three masalas. No wonder, ours is not so tasty,' Maa said. I think she was suspicious already. Avni faked a smile and looked at me.

After lunch, Avni took us to a gurudwara where her friend Inder was waiting. We had to cover our heads while getting inside. There was a huge rush of men, women and children of all age groups. It was really peaceful inside, with the humming of people praying. Inside the premises, there was a huge square-shaped pond. We sat down near the pond for some more time, enjoying the peace.

'Aunty, can I say something?' Avni said.

'Yes, beta. Tell me.'

'Aunty, I ordered the food from outside. I did not make it, actually,' Avni said. Maa looked at Avni and then at me. I smiled, holding my ears.

'Hahaha, I already knew that,' Maa said and laughed.

'You're not angry with me, right?' Avni asked in Hindi. Her Hindi sounded really cute as it had a slight South Indian accent.

'*I have cooked raita also, Aunty,*' I imitated Avni, making fun of her words.

Maa pulled my ears. Avni giggled. We explained the whole story to Inder, after which she started laughing. Maa thanked Avni and Inder for a wonderful evening. She kissed Avni's forehead as we left for our flat. Even I wanted to kiss Avni's forehead. At least I should have pinched her cheeks. She was looking even cuter with that dupatta over her head.

12

We all were at the dining table that night.

'Are you free tomorrow?' Dad asked.

'Yes, Dad. I am on leave.'

Dad looked at me in shock when I realized that the next day was the weekend. I felt like an idiot.

'Come with us to—' Dad said and Maa held his hand.

'Where?' I asked.

'Nothing,' Maa said.

'Tell me, Maa,' I said.

'We are going to the hospital,' Dad said.

'For what?' I asked.

'Ask your Maa.'

I just looked at her and put my hand on hers.

'Maa, are you fine?'

'Yes. Just a little BP issue. I am all right,' she said.

'How come you got BP issues? I thought it was just a minor issue when you came last time,' I said.

'She is not sleeping the whole night. She walks all over the house at night. Ask her,' Dad said.

'What happened, Maa?'

'Nothing. Once you are married, I will be fine,' she said.

'Maa, what is this? Why do you have to worry about my marriage? I will get married soon.'

'No, Dhruv. Just do it as soon as possible. I can't take it any more. I want you to be settled now. I am old. Both your brother and sister are married. See, they are so happy. They have someone to take care of them. Seeing you alone, working day and night, I feel tense all the time,' Maa said, tearing up a little.

'Maa, I am totally fine.'

'No. You kids don't understand our problems. Everyone keeps asking about your marriage and I don't know what to say.'

'It will be fine, Maa. Now, don't worry and eat. We will talk about it tomorrow.'

'Come with us tomorrow,' Dad said. I nodded.

'No need,' Maa said.

'I am coming with you both tomorrow, Maa,' I said holding her hand.

We reached the hospital, the next day. The doctor was a lady and she was very good-looking. Maa told me twice that the doctor was really beautiful and she looked prettier than Hema Malini.

Looking at the doctor, I could definitely say that she had a boyfriend. Girls with boyfriends look different. Dad was waiting outside. The doctor checked Maa's reports and looked at me.

'Are you guys not taking care of her? She is not well at all. She needs a lot of attention and care,' the doctor said. She continued, 'Do you sleep enough, ma'am?'

'Yes, yes,' Maa said.

Dad entered the room immediately and sat down with the doctor's permission beside Maa.

'No. She has been sleeping for only three hours for the last few weeks,' Dad said. I looked at him.

The doctor looked at Maa, probably ready to send her to jail for the small lie she had just said. A patient should never lie to their doctor. Doctors hate it.

'Your wife is not well, sir,' the doctor said.

'What do you mean?' Dad asked.

'She is taking a lot of stress lately. Any reasons for stress, ma'am?' the doctor asked.

Now, which doctor asks such personal questions?

'Not really, doctor,' I said.

'Ma'am, can you tell me whether you feel stressed right now?'

'Yes. She is. We are looking for a girl for our son's marriage. His mom is worried a lot about that,' Dad said, looking at me.

Dad sounded as though he was inviting the doctor to marry me. I felt like hiding my face. I felt so insulted. No one has ever insulted me publicly in front of a beautiful doctor like this before.

Oh my god. Kill me.

'I understand,' the doctor said. 'But Aunty, your stress will not get things done fast. Some things take time. You shouldn't worry about it. Your son will get married when he has to. Please don't worry.' She sounded like my mom's daughter. Which means she would have been my sister.

Oh no, what am I thinking?

'No more overthinking and no more stress. Everything will be all right,' the doctor said.

'Anything else you want to tell me, Uncle?' the doctor asked.

Come on, Dad. Now, don't tell her that I never had a girlfriend all my life.

I didn't want a beautiful woman to judge me.

Most girls think that if a guy does not have a girlfriend, he is a waste. We guys, on the contrary, think that if a girl does not have a boyfriend, she is a very nice girl.

'Nothing more, doctor. Please ask my son to listen to his mother.'

'Okay. I am writing a few medicines. You both can go outside and get them. You wait here,' the doctor said, looking at me.

After my parents left, the doctor looked at me. I felt nice but my body started shivering all of a sudden. I was nervous. There were two reasons. One, she was beautiful and two, I had been distracted right from the time I sat in front of her. I was somehow stopping myself from asking if she had a boyfriend. If not, could she please marry Bala, my best friend? He is under too much stress these days because of his marriage.

'Your mom is really not well. It is serious. You need to take good care of her. Make sure she's not stressed.'

After that, the doctor gave me a few more tests to run and I rushed out. We all drove back home without saying anything. Now, I was really worried about Maa.

Maa and Dad left for Patna after a week of check-ups. The doctor had called me personally and told me not to give Maa any stress. She asked me to inform her if anything serious happened. She would change the medicines if needed.

13

It was two weeks and three days since I lost my job. I did not even know why I was asked to leave the company. I still remember the day I got the mail from HR. That day, I wanted to give a letter to Avni. It was 14 February. I thought I would finally tell Avni everything, that I have loved her since the first day I met her, but I couldn't give her the letter that day. After seeing that mail from HR, I forgot everything. My mind stopped working.

It said:

Hi Dhruv,

Due to the organizational changes and business decisions taken, this is to state that tomorrow is your last working day. Kindly complete all the final formalities by tomorrow morning. Our concerned team will reach out to you to collect your laptop and perform the remaining formalities.

No reason was stated as to why I was fired. I had not even finished my work on an ongoing project.

How could they do this?

When I reached out to the HR manager, she said that they had been instructed not to discuss anything with employees as it was a business decision. I insisted repeatedly on knowing the reason but the HR lady did not answer. She kept repeating the same sentence:

'Is there anything else I can help you with?'

I felt helpless. I wanted to tell her so many things, scold her, sue the company, but I did not do anything.

The day before I got fired, Dad needed some money. I was so happy that Dad had asked me for something for the first time and I immediately transferred him the money. And now I'd gotten fired.

He had said, 'It does not feel right to ask your sister or brother for money as they are married now. They have their own responsibilities.'

I told Dad to let me know if he needed more money. But the very next day, I got the HR mail about my last day in the company. I did not tell anyone in the family that I was laid off. I only told Bala and requested him to let me know if he knew of any job openings in his circle.

I thought I would find another job soon but I couldn't. It was getting difficult to manage so many responsibilities. I had a home loan to pay for my house. I felt lost. I stopped talking to the friends I often spoke to. They would talk about their promotions and salary hikes but I would feel disturbed when they asked about my life.

How do I tell them what was going on with me?

I was busy preparing for interviews but nothing was working out. I had given a couple of interviews, but they had all put me on hold. After a few days, they stopped answering my calls and emails. Avni would call me at night but either I did not want to talk to her or maybe I did not want her to know that I had lost my job.

She was in Chennai as her youngest cousin was getting married and her dad was not well. So, I did not tell her anything. But I really wanted to talk to her and tell her how low I was feeling, how much I needed her in this situation, how much I needed a hug from someone who would tell me that everything was going to be all right. I was not even able to focus on the novel I was working on. Avni had told me she would help me in publishing it. She really liked the story. I really missed her.

I kept waiting for a few more days but there were no calls for any interviews. The only option left was to cut down my expenses to save some money for the upcoming months. I had stopped talking too much to my parents too. It's not that I did not want to talk but I was not able to speak to them happily. Moreover, I wanted to tell Maa what I was going through but I just couldn't. If she told Dad that I don't have a job any more, he would hesitate to ask me for any help. It felt good to help Dad after such a long time. I felt really nice.

Two more weeks passed. I still hadn't got a job. I spoke to a manager from my previous company. He said that he would let me know if he found something. A few times, even Shreya Didi asked me on the call why I was upset. I did not tell her the reason. I just told her about too much workload in the office. She would relax me and make me feel good, crack jokes to change my mood and talk about our childhood memories. She would tell me how jovial I used to be in my school days and how girls from the colony used to complain that I troubled them.

I was depressed most of the time. I had met a doctor for the constant headache I had been facing for the last few days. He gave me some medicines and told me that I might get migraine issues if I did not stop getting stressed. But I did not know how to stop that. Life is not easy after losing a job, especially when you are all alone. Bala was busy with his marriage plans. Sandeep too was meeting a girl's family for his marriage. Their life was so normal. My life was totally messed up. I needed to talk to someone but I did not know whom to talk to.

'Dhruv?' There was a knock at the door. It was my landlord. I got up from my bed and opened the door.

'What happened? I don't see you coming out these days,' he said, looking at my face.

'Nothing, Uncle. Just busy with few things,' I said.

'Hey, are you all right?' he asked.

'Yes, Uncle, I am totally fine,' I said.

'You don't look fine, son,' he said and checked my forehead.

'You have a high fever.'

'No, Uncle, I am good.'

'Shut up. Have you taken any medicines?'

'Medicines? No, Uncle.'

'Did you eat anything?'

'Not yet. I will cook something now,' I said and almost fainted in front of him.

'Dhruv!' Uncle reached out to hold me.

I could barely hear him. I did not know for how long I was unconscious. When I woke up, Uncle was sitting beside me. I actually felt nice to see someone caring for me. I really needed someone. I was feeling broken from inside.

'Are you feeling better, beta?' he asked.

'Yes, Uncle. Sorry for troubling you.'

'You kids stay alone and don't tell your parents your issues. What have you done to yourself? Look at you,' he said.

I don't know what happened then, but tears started flowing from my eyes as I looked at him. I felt totally lost.

'Dhruv, what happened, beta? What is happening to you?'

'I lost my job, Uncle. I lost my job,' I said, sobbing.

'Dhruv, Dhruv, stop crying, beta. It is all right,' Uncle said.

'I don't know what to do, Uncle. I am really feeling alone here,' I cried.

Uncle wiped my tears. He stayed with me for some more time until I calmed down.

'No need to pay rent until you find a job. Don't take tension. And I will arrange for your food too. You are like my son. I will come back with something for you to eat,' Uncle said and left.

'Are you all right?' a message flashed on my phone after a few minutes. It was from Maa.

'Yes, Maa. What happened?' I replied.

'Had a bad dream, beta'.

The next second, I received her video call. I faked a smile and answered. Maa saw my smiling face.

'Why haven't you shaved? You look sick, beta,' she said.

'I am fine, Maa. See?' I said, trying to smile, but wasn't able to. I wanted to cry.

'I always want to see you smiling,' she said.

'And I also want to see you happy, Maa.'

'All good, right, beta? Why do I feel something is wrong?'

'Nothing, Maa. All good. Look at me,' I showed her my happy face again.

'My sweet kid. You are not hiding anything, right?'

'No, Maa. I'm not. Why do you say that?'

'Had a very bad dream, beta.'

'What was the bad dream?'

'We should never reveal a bad dream. Leave it. You are fine. That is everything for me.'

'Maa?' I said.

'Yes, beta, tell me.'

'I miss you, Maa. I miss you a lot. I feel lonely here, Maa,' I said and broke into tears. I don't know why I couldn't control myself.

'Dhruv. Come on. Stop crying. Why do you miss me? See, I am right here, in front of you na, beta?'

'I miss you, Maa,' I said sobbing. I was really feeling lonely. Maa had tears in her eyes too.

'Maa, am I not a good guy?'

'Who told you this, beta?'

'Then why am I facing so many issues? Why doesn't god want me to be happy?'

'Dhruv, will you please stop crying now? See, now you made me also cry,' Maa said.

I didn't say a word and kept crying. Maa consoled me.

'Okay, drink water. Get up now,' she said. I drank a glass of water.

'Are you okay now?' Maa asked.

'Yes. I am fine. Sorry Maa, I made you cry.'

'Now, tell me what happened?'

I explained everything to Maa. She spoke to me about random things; my childhood memories just like Didi often does and she also reminded me how I used to top my class when I was a kid. Maa kept talking to me until I calmed down. I felt better after talking to her as though a huge burden was taken off my head. She also told me to read Hanuman Chalisa regularly as it gives us strength.

The next day, I felt better. I woke up early, spoke to Maa and performed my puja. Bhaiya, Bhabhi, Didi and Jiju had reached Bangalore. They were all in Patna when they found out about Maa's health. Didi and Jiju did not return to the US as they were stuck with their new flat in Delhi. They were going to be in India for a few more months. I felt so happy to see all of them. They invited even my landlord over for lunch.

Bhabhi spoke to me for a long time while Bhaiya was busy with his office work. Since Bhabhi had got married to Bhaiya, we hardly spoke much. She showed me photos of her beautiful female cousins and asked me if I liked any of them. Bhabhi also told me about her 'Miss Fresher' title which she won in college.

Bhaiya joined in our conversation while Didi and Jiju were busy preparing lunch. We had already chopped the vegetables for them. Now, it was their turn to show their talent. While speaking to Bhaiya and Bhabhi, I got emotional for a moment and thanked them for coming to Bangalore. I really needed them. With them, my flat had suddenly turned into a lively place. I heard a knock at the door. I got up and opened the door. It was Avni.

'When did you come to Bangalore?' I asked Avni.

'Can I come in, Mr Dhruv?'

'Avni,' Didi said as she came running to the door. I was still in awe.

'Hi Didi,' Avni said. Bhabhi came running too when she heard Avni's voice.

'Avni, this is Bhabhi and he is Prithvi Bhaiya.'

After that, the most important man came up, Jiju.

'Oh, I was waiting for you,' Jiju said and hugged Avni.

'So, it was your plan,' I told him.

'It was Shreya's plan,' Jiju said.

'Actually, girls are not allowed in his flat, Jiju. So, he never allows me to come here,' Avni said.

'But beautiful girls are allowed here,' Jiju said. We all laughed.

'Only Avni is allowed,' I clarified.

'Ahem, ahem, we can understand,' Didi and Bhabhi said.

'Come in,' I said to Avni and we sat in the living room. I remembered the time when she came running from the kitchen and jumped on my sofa.

'Don't worry, there is no cockroach,' I said. Avni pinched me as she sat down.

Didi called Bhabhi to the kitchen and she gave me and Avni extra potatoes to peel. She also gave me a few onions. I had tears while peeling the onions while Avni happily peeled the potatoes.

'Can we exchange vegetables, Avni?' I asked authoritatively.

'No way. Get lost,' Avni said.

I wiped my tears and continued peeling onions.

'Dhruv, can I tell you something?' Avni asked.

'Yes, please,' I said and wiped my tears again.

'Dhruv, don't peel onions with your dirty hands. You are wiping tears and using the same hand to peel them. Yuck,' Avni said in an irritated voice.

'Is this what you really want to talk about? Onions? You're a mean girl.'

'No. Not just that.'

'Then?'

'Shall I?' Avni said.

'Will you tell me or not, Avni?'

'I like you, Dhruv,' she said and continued peeling potatoes.

I stopped chopping the onions. *Did I hear it right? Avni liked me? Avni? Liked? Me?*

At least, she should have made eye contact with me. I was already on cloud nine. I wanted to pinch Avni's cheeks but I didn't. Bhabhi was moving around the living room.

'Dhruv, I said something,' Avni said.

'So?' I said.

'What about you?' Avni said.

'You like me or love me?' I asked.

'Okay, fine, I meant the second one.'

'What second one, Avni?'

'The second option you gave.'

'Is *KBC* going on here?'

'I feel shy.'

'Wow. This is the first time I've seen you this shy.'

'Now, please tell me what you feel about me,' she said, pointing the knife at me.

'Is this how a girl asks a guy if he loves her?'

Avni put the knife aside and held her ears. She looked cute.

'Okay, fine. Same here,' I said.

'Do you feel ashamed to say "I love you"? What sort of a guy are you?' she said.

'My whole family is here. Try to understand, and even you did not say "I love you". So, it's balanced.'

'Can I ask you one more thing?' she said.

'Why do you have to ask so many questions?'

'Because you guys are so confusing.'

'Okay, ask.'

'Why do you love me?'

'Because you have a mole on your chin,' I said.

'Wow. What sort of answer is this? How can a guy be so unromantic?'

'I tell you, Avni, we guys are like this only. We fall in love with simple things. We don't fall in love with a girl for her figure and body measurements.'

'Wow. That is so nice. So, my outer beauty doesn't matter?'

'It is your body. I will love you even if you become a hippopotamus.'

Avni smiled and put her hand on my cheek. I got a warm feeling in my belly. Thank god no one saw us. We both were done cutting our vegetables. Actually, Avni had exchanged the vegetables after I told her that I loved her. Girls are good at heart, I realized.

'Why are you crying?' Didi asked Avni, as we entered the kitchen.

'Didi, Avni was peeling onions. So, they are not real tears. They are crocodile tears,' I said.

Didi punched me. Bhabhi also punched me.

'Very nice. It is balanced now. I cried. You got beaten,' Avni said. Everyone laughed.

Didi had spoken to one of her friends regarding a job opening. After lunch, Didi got a call from her friend who was a manager. She gave us the good news that she had found a job for me but it was in Hyderabad. I would have to join in a couple of weeks. We all felt happy to hear that. I felt so relieved. Within a day, because of my family, my problem was solved. I immediately called Maa and informed her. She cried as she heard that.

'Dhruv?' Avni asked.

'Yeah?'

'Dad is not keeping well. So, I am leaving Bangalore and moving to Chennai for a few months.'

'Okay. You do what you need to.'

'But, how will we meet then?'

'Dhruv will travel to Chennai to meet his Avni. Simple.'

'Will you?'

'You doubt me?'

'Never. Congratulations on the new job, Dhruv,' Avni said and hugged me.

This is how it feels to be on cloud nine.

14

I was about to reach Hyderabad. Avni's roommate in Bangalore, Anju, had been transferred to Hyderabad a few weeks ago. So, Avni had shifted her Bangalore luggage to Anju's flat in Hyderabad as she would try to get a posting in Hyderabad once her dad was fine.

Avni had said that she would come to pick me up but she informed me last night that she was not coming. She got some work at the last moment. She had given me the address and flat owner's number to contact once I reached the apartment. But I wanted to see her. I wanted to meet her.

I reached Hyderabad in another half hour and it took me a few more minutes to come out to the Arrivals. I looked for a cab to take me to the flat as soon as possible. There was an important mail which I had to drop to my US manager. I kept looking for a cab when my eyes fell on a girl. She was simple, in fact, very simple, standing in the crowd, wearing bangles and waving at me. Yes, she was Avni, my Avni. I immediately ran towards her.

'How do I look?' she asked.

'The most beautiful girl I have ever seen.'

She continued, 'I look like shit right now. No make-up, nothing. I am not even wearing a good dress. I just ran from the railway station to receive you.'

'Railway station?' I asked, puzzled.

'Long story. I will tell you in the cab,' she said.

'But you still look hot,' I said.

'Very funny,' she said and walked holding my hand.

Avni got me a trolley.

'Dhruv, I told Amma about you,' Avni said.

'Are you serious? What did Aunty say?'

'She said that she has no issue,' Avni said, suddenly shy.

'Did you tell your dad?'

'Of course I told him. That is why I missed the flight and had to catch a train to Hyderabad.'

'What did Uncle say about me?' I asked, biting my nails.

'He said you seem like a nice guy but he would like to meet you.'

'It means, we will get married soon.'

'What about your parents, Dhruv?'

'Maa loves you already. And we do not have any caste issue at all. So, our marriage will be easy-peasy. Moreover, after you invited her for lunch that day in Bangalore, she was really impressed by you.'

'Very funny,' Avni said.

We reached the rented flat in another fifty minutes. Avni called a security guard to help us with the luggage. He happily helped. Of course, when a beautiful girl asks, no security guard will refuse. The guard looked really happy lifting my bags. He didn't even ask for money. Avni paid him a hundred bucks anyway.

'It's really nice,' I said as I entered the room, and immediately ran to the balcony. It had a swimming pool view.

'No girl comes to swim here,' Avni said.

'Do I look like a stalker to you?'

'No, but what is wrong with looking? You won't close your eyes if a girl swims there, right?'

'Okay, so now you got this pool view to tell me all this.'

'No, I am just telling you that I don't want any drama here. This was the best society. So, I asked Anju to take this flat on rent.'

'I will have two affairs here,' I said.

'No girl will give any footage to you except me,' she said and laughed.

'You are so bad,' I said and remembered that I had to drop the mail to my US manager. I ran and opened my laptop.

'You came here to work or be with me?'

'Just a few minutes,' I said.

Avni took a broom and started cleaning the room. Thank god. For a second, I thought she was going to beat me up.

'Isn't the room already clean, Avni?'

'No, can't you see this?' she said, showing me the dust which had gathered on the floor.

'Sorry. Continue then,' I said.

'Only today. From tomorrow, you have to do this yourself.'

'I can't do all this.'

'Dhruv, learn to keep the room clean. Tomorrow, you will get married. What will your wife think? What if she leaves you?'

'Is it a threat?'

'Kind of,' she said.

'Okay. Then I will clean the room. I know you mean it,' I said.

There was a knock at the door. Avni and I looked at each other.

'Who could this be?' I asked.

'How would I know?'

'Open the door then,' I said holding my laptop. Avni went and opened the door. I heard two women laughing and talking. Avni came inside with a lady. She was beautiful. She was wearing a yellow saree with a golden border.

'He is Dhruv,' Avni said pointing towards me.

'Hi Dhruv. I am Puja. Please let me know if you need anything. I live in the opposite flat,' she said.

Avni glared at me.

'Sure, Puja ji,' I said.

Please, god, I don't want any affair at this stage of my life. Please, god.

The lady and Avni kept talking for some more time when I saw another girl entering our flat.

'Now, who is she?' I mumbled to myself. She was also beautiful.

How many girls will I have to meet today?

'Dhruv, you are not safe in this apartment, dude,' the inner me said.

'I feel the same.'

'You should immediately vacate, bro.'

'My daughter, Divya,' Puja said.

Avni looked at her and smiled but I knew what was going on in her head.

'Hi Divya ji,' I said.

Yes, at twenty-six, I never thought I'd have to address a seventeen-year-old girl with 'ji'.

'I heard you write books,' Divya said.

'Yes, one is in progress.'

'I am waiting for it to be published, Dhruv Bhaiya.'

'Sure, the first copy will be yours,' I said when Avni gave me the eye. I did not feel safe among the three women.

'Oh god, which apartment have you got me into? All my life, I never got the chance to have an affair and now, when I have a girl in my life, I am scared that I will end up having an affair. Why god? Why me?'

'You are lucky, bro. Most men die without even thinking of an affair,' the inner me said.

'Shut up, you fool.'

'No affair, god, please.'

'What happened? Why are you looking up? They left,' Avni said.

'Nothing. I was just thinking if we could change the apartment or the building.'

'It's okay. I know what you're thinking. Puja Didi is married and Divya called you Bhaiya. I am safe now,' Avni said.

'Oh wow. What an explanation.'

Both of us laughed.

'Mr Dhruv Mehta.'

'Yes, Ms Avni Mathur?'

'I have rented a flat in Chennai as well. You can stay there when you visit.'

'You rented a flat for me? Are you nuts? I am not paying rent for two flats.'

'No, silly. I'll pay rent for the second one. Yeah. I want you to be close enough to me. We can meet easily.'

God. I love this girl.

'That makes sense. My girl is getting more romantic by the day,' I said and pinched her cheeks.

15

I was in Chennai and Avni had not even come to pick me up at the airport. Bala had come with me but had left early morning. He had to meet his cousins. His parents were in the US, inviting their relatives to his marriage. Yes, Bala's marriage was fixed and he had not slept for the last three days.

'I am coming to meet you', I messaged Avni. She had told me not to call.

'No, please don't come now. Amma Appa are here', Avni replied.

'You told me you want me to meet your Amma Appa. Now, you are saying no. Is your brain all right?'

'Shut up. You guys don't understand anything'.

'What?'

'Relax Dhruv. We will take this slowly'.

'Avni, I hope I won't be in a problem if people see me with you here'.

'Dhruv Mehta, you are in Chennai. Not even a mosquito knows you here. Rather, I should be scared of being seen with you'.

Avni made sense.

'I am coming to meet you soon. Bye'.

I changed into my home clothes and played Hanuman Chalisa. I feel nice and peaceful when I hear it. After thirty minutes, I heard a knock at the door. I ran to the door with a smile. Avni stood there holding three boxes.

'Sorry, ma'am. Not interested. Try another door,' I said.

'Very funny,' she said and entered.

'What's in these boxes?'

'These are sweets,' she said.

'Oh my god, I love sweets, let's eat—'

Avni slapped my hand away.

'No. Don't even touch it. You have to bring these to my home.'

'Huh? Who does this?'

'You are coming to my home for the first time. Amma's friends are coming tomorrow.'

'So, I should not come to meet your parents?'

'You have to come tomorrow to my house. Amma wanted you to meet them.'

'Are you serious?'

'Everything I had never thought of is finally happening. So, be happy.'

'Do your mom's friends speak Hindi? I can't learn Tamil overnight.'

'They speak a little. And you should learn Tamil, now that we'll be married.'

'I will learn and speak better than you. After all, Tamil is the world's most ancient language.'

'Wow, you know that?'

'That is our history. We must know that.'

'Tomorrow, you have to be at my house at 11 a.m.'

'Just wait,' I said and got up. I pulled out all the clothes from my suitcase that Bala had chosen personally for me. He said that I would look cool in these. Avni fumed looking at them.

'You don't like them?' I asked.

'You don't have a dhoti kurta?'

'Avni, why would I have that?'

'Because you are coming in a dhoti kurta.'

'Not again. You know that I feel uncomfortable.'

'And please don't wax your legs this time.'

'Even if I do, how will you know? I am not going to fold the dhoti like South Indians do.'

'Then how will you sit on my Scooty?'

'Go to hell. I am coming in a cab.'

'They will loot you, Dhruv. I have some work here. I will pick you up while returning.'

'Are you mad? If I come in a dhoti on a Scooty, people will laugh at me.'

'I will be in a saree. So, shut up.'

'What? You will ride a Scooty in a saree? Are you out of your mind?'

'Dhruv, stop arguing with me and be ready tomorrow.'

'How will I get a dhoti kurta now?'

'That's not my problem,' Avni said and got up. 'Be ready on time,' she added and left.

Bala arranged a dhoti kurta for me in the evening. He was very happy after meeting his fiancée. He had lied to me that he had come to meet his cousins.

Avni reached my flat the next day, looking stunning in a saree.

'You are still getting ready?' she asked.

'Since 5 a.m., he has been trying on different kurtas,' Bala said.

'This is perfect, Dhruv. No need to change. Let's go now,' Avni said.

'Let us go then. But Avni . . .' I said.

'What happened?'

'Can I sit sideways on your Scooty if you don't mind?' I said.

Avni looked at me with eyes wide open.

'Are you in your senses? You want to sit sideways like a woman on my Scooty? People will laugh at both of us,' Avni said and Bala chuckled.

'You can't say no to everything, Avni. You have to listen to me,' I said.

'You are not sitting sideways. You fold your dhoti and sit like all guys sit.'

'Then I will ride the Scooty. You sit behind me.'

'Dhruv, let's go, please. Everyone must have reached.'

We reached downstairs. I sat on the Scooty in my full-length dhoti but I was not feeling comfortable.

'Dhruv, you waxed your legs? Again?' Avni asked.

'Yes, and let us not talk about my sexy legs today. I am already tense.'

We reached Avni's home in fifteen minutes. I felt relaxed when I saw only ladies there. Thank god there were no males. I feel nervous in front of them.

Avni's mom introduced me to all her friends. I handed the sweets to her.

'What was the need of this, Dhruv?' Aunty said.

'Avni insisted, actually,' I said, looking at Avni.

'Avni, you told Dhruv to get sweets?' Aunty asked.

'No, Amma. I told him if he wanted to, he could get some,' Avni said.

'She is right, Aunty,' I smirked.

Avni glared at me. I smiled.

'I will kill you', I got a message from Avni instantly.

'Your Mom is really beautiful', I messaged back.

'Shut up'.

'I don't see Uncle,' I told Aunty.

'He is out of town. He had some urgent work.'

'Thank god,' I said and realized that I shouldn't have been so loud.

'Why thank god?' Aunty asked.

'No, I mean thank you for inviting me.'

Aunty looked at Avni and they headed towards the kitchen.

Dude, what are you doing? Do something to impress your future mother-in-law. Cook something for them,' the inner me said.

'Bro, please shut up. I am not in my home. I have been invited here.'

'Soon, this will be your home. Get up and impress her. This is your best chance. Avni's father is also not at home,' my inner voice pleaded.

'Leave it, bro. Why do you want me to get into trouble? What if my food is not tasty?'

'That is why your Jiju is more romantic than you.'

'No, I am more romantic than him.'

'Then prove me wrong.'

'Aunty,' I said.

Aunty turned around just like Kajol did in *DDLJ* when SRK said, '*Palat.*'

Damn it, what am I thinking?

'Yes, Dhruv beta?' Aunty said.

'Can I join you in the kitchen, if you don't mind?'

'Sure. Feel at home.'

I followed Aunty towards the kitchen.

'Dhruv, what are you trying to do?' Avni asked, holding my hand.

'Will you please not interrupt?'

'Dhruv, this is my home.'

'Aunty told me to feel at home. So, keep quiet,' I said and entered the kitchen. Avni followed me inside.

'What are you cooking, Aunty?' I asked.

'Avni told me that you are a vegetarian. So, I am cooking Mysore masala dosa. It's Avni's favourite.'

'Come on Dhruv, tell her you want to cook something for them. Be a man,' my inner voice prodded me.

'Okay, fine, I will.'

'Aunty?' I said.

'Yes, Dhruv?'

'I am a man,' I said and realized that I am an idiot.

'What?' Aunty said. Avni giggled.

'Aunty, I want to cook something for all of you.'

'You know cooking?'

'Better than Avni,' I said.

'Amma, he is a very big liar. Don't trust him,' Avni said.

'No, Dhruv. You are our guest today!'

'Relax, Aunty. Give me one chance to impress you.'

'We are already impressed by you,' Aunty said and laughed.

'Not me,' Avni said.

'Today, you will be impressed too, Ms Avni,' I said.

'Let's see. Huh,' Avni said. She was looking really cute today but I couldn't pinch her cheeks in front of her mom or else Aunty would turn me into lunch.

I started cooking. Aunty helped me with all the masalas and ingredients that I needed. I told Avni not to disturb me when I was cooking. She went into a corner and stood there alone. When I asked her what she was doing in the kitchen, she said, 'It is my kitchen and I am shopping on Myntra.'

Girls and their shopping never end. Thank god, at least she was not distracting me. I was done with my dish in half an hour.

'Aunty, can you please taste this?' I asked.

'I will taste it first,' Avni said.

'How is it?' I asked.

'Veg pulao is awesome but dum aloo is salty,' Avni said.

Damn, my first impression was not good.

'Let me check,' Aunty said.

'Pulao is really good. I will correct your dum aloo in one minute,' Aunty said, adding a little water to the dish and heating it for a few minutes.

'Now taste it,' Aunty told Avni.

'Wow Amma, you are awesome,' Avni said.

'No, Dhruv is awesome,' Aunty said.

'Thanks, Aunty. Your daughter never praises me,' I said.

'Hahaha. She never praises me also,' Aunty laughed.

'Okay, now all her aunts are hungry. Let me feed you all together. You must be hungry,' Aunty said.

'I am starving,' Avni said.

'You are always eating but always hungry and still, you don't gain weight.'

'I gained 1.2 kgs, Amma.'

'In two months. Okay, Avni, now move aside and arrange the dining table.'

After Avni left, Aunty took me aside.

'Dhruv, can I ask you something?'

'Yes, Aunty.'

'Who taught you to cook all this?'

'My Maa.'

'She must cook really tasty food.'

'My dad cooks tastier food than her.'

'Amma don't worry. I am safe with him. Your daughter won't die of hunger after marriage,' Avni said. She was listening, hiding behind the door. We both laughed.

We had an amazing lunch. Avni's mom and her friends were all so sweet. They did not let me feel even for a second that I was not at home. After that, Avni dropped me back to the apartment on her Scooty.

'Thanks for the amazing day, Avni.'

'Thanks for the amazing food, Dhruv Mehta.'

'Avni, can I ask something?'

'No.'

'But I will ask.'

'Okay, ask.'

'Are you impressed by my cooking skills?'

Avni paused for a few seconds. She was thinking about something.

'Actually, I don't get impressed so easily,' she said, smiling.

'How insulting!'

'You deserve it. First, learn to put salt properly in dum aloo.'

'I hate you, you should know that.'

'But I love you.' A smile covered my face.

This girl is mad and I am madly in love with her.

Avni was getting a call from her mom. She left but she gave me a tiffin box for Bala. He had asked her to send Aunty's handmade food. It was a great day even though I spent only a couple of hours there. A girl's mother is so sweet. Why can't their fathers be as sweet?

16

I have danced before but I have never played dandiya in my life. Avni has got this checklist fever lately, where she prepares a list of things to do and dandiya is at the top of that list right now. Today, I was going to play dandiya with Avni and we were participating in a contest. She informed me just a few hours before she landed in Hyderabad that we had to win the contest at any cost.

We reached the venue late. The gatekeeper was a nearly sixty-year-old man who looked at us as though we were aliens. He showed us his watch and then he showed us the exit. There are two things I don't like about any function: one, they keep gatekeepers who look scary, and two, these gatekeepers don't give a damn about couples. Avni looked at me.

'Give him some money,' Avni said. The gatekeeper wasn't letting us in. I looked at her. I couldn't believe she could go to this extent for dandiya. In my head, I had already booked a minicab to go back, as it seemed things had gone south.

'He is not a traffic policeman, Avni. Can't you see that he has a huge bamboo stick in his hand? I don't feel safe offering him money right now.'

'Okay, then I will give him. Give me a 500 rupee note,' she said.

'Are we really doing this?' I asked.

'What else do we do? I wanted to play dandiya for so long and our dance will start soon. They are calling names, Dhruv,' she said.

I could hear the announcements. I did not want to go because I knew we would lose the competition and then Avni would blame me for it.

'Wait, let me think, but I am not bribing the gatekeeper,' I said.

My mind was not working. I looked at Avni. Every time I am with her these days, I forget that I am in my late twenties. I feel as if I am in my early twenties and I want to do anything to keep this girl happy.

'I have an idea,' I said.

'What?'

'I saw a back gate while we were coming and it's dark. There is no security over there. We're jumping over the fence.'

'I am not doing this in a ghagra.'

'Fine, then stand here.'

'Why can't we pay him something?'

'Because one, I don't know if he would take the money and two, I am scared of his bamboo stick.'

'You are so scared all the time,' she said.

'Yes, I am. You have a problem?'

'Yes.'

'Then you can go and give him the money,' I said.

'No, why should I?'

'Just a few seconds back you were asking me for money to bribe him.'

'It won't look good if a girl gives a bribe, Dhruv. Try to understand. There are things which only guys should do.'

'Oh wow, Avni. Thanks for opening my eyes,' I said.

'Huh,' she said. I wish the Women's Rights team was here right now, the ones who always spoke about equality. They should meet the love of my life who always uses the girl card, every time I ask her to do anything daring. Avni kept looking at me.

'Ugh, fine. We will jump the gate,' she said.

We reached the back gate in a few moments. We saw lots of cars parked there. This was good news. I climbed on one of those cars and got over the fence. After that, Avni climbed on to a car and I pulled her over the fence.

'Happy?' I asked, as Avni came down.

'Very,' she said, smiling.

Most of the participants in the dandiya contest were ready. We cross-checked with the organizer. He explained the rules and then asked us to take our places along with the others.

'Dhruv, we have to win this,' Avni said.

'Look, I did not get time to practice.'

'Dhruv, just follow my eyes, legs and hands. It's simple. I will guide you.'

'Avni, you are making me nervous.'

'That is why I told you to watch the 'Nimbooda' song from *HDDCS*.'

'What is *HDDCS*? I told you not to talk to me in abbreviations, didn't I?'

'Leave it, you won't get it. Just follow my steps.'

The contest started. One wrong move from any of the partners meant one point deducted. We had around fifteen contestants. The famous dandiya song from *Kai Po Che*—'Shubhaarambh'—was playing in the background. I was following Avni's eyes, hands and legs as she had instructed. I had just requested her to be slow with her steps. Thankfully, we made it through the first round and we had seven contestants left. Avni seemed happy.

She told me to be faster in the next round. My hands and legs already hurt. I always thought dandiya was such a cute event every time I saw it on TV but today, I realized that it was really tough. After the second round, only two couples were left. We were one of them. Yes, we made it to the finals.

The final round started. People were whistling and that made me nervous. We lost one point due to my mistake. The other contestants got ahead of us. And then, I made another mistake. The other contestants got two points ahead of us. Avni was very tense. Twenty more seconds were left. I knew we were going to lose. But suddenly, the other contestants made a mistake back to back three times, and we were finally declared the winners at the last minute.

Avni was so happy. I could look at her forever. We gorged on the buffet food that had been arranged for everyone. After that, Avni asked me to take her to a peaceful place. I took her to a lakeside, where we sat down, far from the noise of the city, experiencing the soothing sounds of the water. My body was aching because I had not danced so much in a long time. I lay down on the ground and Avni lay down too with her head on my belly because she didn't want to mess up her hair. We both did not speak a word. I don't know why it felt so good there. Maybe because I was there with Avni this time.

After a few minutes, Maa called. I had almost fallen asleep. Maa asked me if I had reached home. I informed her that Avni was in Hyderabad and she was staying with her friend Anju. I checked my watch. It was already 8 p.m. I told Maa that I was still with Avni. Maa asked me to drop her safely to Anju's home personally and strictly ordered me not to send her alone in a cab. I looked at Avni. She was sleeping as if my belly was her pillow. I booked a cab and lifted Avni up once it arrived. The driver looked at me suspiciously as I entered the cab holding Avni in my arms.

'She is sleeping, driver sahib,' I said.

'Show me your ID, sir.'

I showed him my ID.

'What is the girl's name? Where are you taking her?'

'I am taking her to her friend's flat,' I said but the driver did not seem convinced. I had to wake Avni up. She told the driver her name and my name. She also told him that she loved me and went off to sleep again. The cab driver now relaxed.

'I rarely see guys who take care of girls these days,' he said.

'I understand, driver sahib, and I salute you for the care you showed for her. If all drivers become like you, girls will be so safe.'

'I have a daughter, sir. I know what it is to care for a girl. Their parents will die if any bad happens to them,' the driver said.

We kept talking for the entire route until we reached Anju's flat.

'Sir, if you don't mind, can I please come with you? Just to make sure that she is dropped safely,' the driver said.

'Sure, driver sahib,' I said.

Anju's flat was on the third floor. Somehow, I managed to wake Avni up once again. I didn't know why she was sleeping so much. Maybe she got really tired due to the dance. My body was aching even more now. Avni was still half asleep.

Anju opened the door and greeted us. I put Avni on the bed and asked Anju to call Avni's mom to inform her that she had reached safe.

'I have never seen a driver like you, sir ji,' I said, as I sat in the cab.

'Where should I drop you, sir?'

I gave him my address.

'You know why some guys destroy a girl's life, sir ji?'

'Why, driver sahib?'

'They do not realize that a girl is her parents' princess. And, if we have to make a better society, we have to care for these girls, or else their parents might die if anything wrong happens to them.'

'Wah, driver sahib. Very true. If we all start thinking like that, we will never spoil any girl's life.'

'Very true. But a few girls are also spoiling guys' lives. Girls also need to understand this about their boyfriends.'

'Really true. Both guys and girls have to understand.'

After the gyan session, we chatted and he played old Hindi songs till we reached my apartment.

'Will you come up and check my flat too?' I asked the driver.

'Hahaha,' he laughed.

'It was great meeting you, driver sahib.'

'Same, sir ji,' he said and left.

The next day, Avni and her college friends had planned to go shopping. Avni had told me not to come as she would directly leave for the airport. I wanted to meet her once before she left. I actually wanted to see her in a saree, because women look so beautiful in sarees. But I couldn't.

Don't worry, Dhruv. She misses you too.

17

Avni and I were in Bangalore for Bala's wedding. Bala had also invited Shreya Didi and Jiju who reached the hall after us. They were missing their wedding days seeing the celebration. During the ceremony, Bala was bare-bodied waist-up as per South Indian rituals. It started in the afternoon and finished in a few hours. South Indian weddings are so cool. You are free for the rest of the day. In North India, weddings happen late at night when both the bride and the groom are sleeping during the mantras as is the pandit.

Didi and Jiju left after the wedding as they had to be back in Delhi urgently. Jiju's friends were coming to meet him after many years.

'Hold my hand,' I said and held Avni's hand tightly. She insisted that she would not hold my hand on the road and I insisted that if she didn't hold my hand, I wouldn't walk with her. I would prefer to take an auto. But she had to try sweets and pani puri on the famous Commercial Street of

Bangalore. So, she had to walk. Avni held my hand. Now, I realize why most couples hold hands while walking. We had just walked a few metres when Avni pulled me back.

'Dhruv, wait,' Avni said.

'What?' I asked.

'My cousin is on the other side of the road.'

'So what? Your family knows, right?'

'Yeah, but my extended family doesn't. I want to keep this low-key for a while, before things are official. He will tell his parents that I am here with a guy.'

'So what? I am a guy.'

'No. You don't know how big a drama it will be and then they will ask me lots of questions about you. Right now, Amma has told me to keep things secret until everything is official.'

'So, now what should we do? There's nowhere to hide. It's a straight road Avni and your cousin is on the other side,' I said.

'Well, there is one place.'

'What, where?'

'I can stand behind you,' she said and giggled.

'Are you serious, Avni? Behind me?'

'You're an idiot. Okay, come here fast.'

'Okay,' I said and followed her instructions. Avni stood right behind me and held on to my shirt.

'Hehehe,' I laughed.

'Why are you laughing now?'

'You are tickling me, you idiot,' I said.

'Oh sorry,' she said and held my shirt loosely.

Now, we both were not walking, instead standing still on the road like robots. And I was looking at only one person—Avni's cousin. God knows why he looked at me. Yes, he looked right at me and called me.

'Oh no. Why is he calling me? Avni, shall we run? Looks like he saw us,' I said.

'No, he hasn't. Just stay still,' Avni said when I saw her cousin crossing the road and coming towards us.

'Hey hey, he is coming to this side of the road. Shall we run?'

'No way, Dhruv. We can't do that. Then double drama at home.'

'And what about the drama which is going to happen right now on the road? Damn it. I don't want to be seen in tomorrow's newspaper.'

'Stop joking. Where is he?'

'He is coming closer and waving at us. Avni, let's run, please. Let's run. Even I am scared now.'

'Oh no. Dhruv, save me, please.'

'Save you. Damn it. You save me now. I'm telling you, I'm running if he comes a step closer,' I said.

'Dhruv, you are scaring me,' Avni said.

'And what about the fact that I am scared?'

'Okay, just take a deep breath, In and out.'

'Deep breath my foot, Avni. I am not even able to breathe. Oh no, he is coming closer. He is calling me now. Avni, run,' I said.

Avni held me tightly.

'Will you please not run, Dhruv? I am wearing heels, for god's sake.'

'Who told you to wear heels, you fool?'

'Didn't you tell me that I look better in heels?'

'Oh yes. Damn it. Why did I say that?'

'Dhruv, stop shaking, please.'

'Listen, if I stand here for one more minute, I'll get a heart attack.'

'Relax,' she said.

'He looks scary, Avni.'

'From childhood he's been like that, heavy and monstrously tall.'

'Avni, please save me. I don't want to get beaten up in public for a girl. I am a future author, Avni.'

'And I am your future wife.'

'So what?'

'Be a strong man, Dhruv.'

'I'm not even feeling like a man right now and you are asking me to be a strong man,' I said.

He was just twenty metres away and coming up fast. Now, my heartbeat totally stopped.

'Maa, please save me, Maa,' I said, when the magic happened and the guy stopped suddenly. I was shocked and happy and shocked again. I saw an auto slowing down by his side. He hopped into it and left. Both my hands were clutching my heart.

'Oh my god. He was waving at the auto driver,' I said.

'He left?' Avni asked.

'Yes.'

After Avni's cousin left, I took a deep breath. I knew I would have been dead if he had seen me with his cousin. He would have thrashed me in public. He looked like a real rowdy. Some men are really scary. They are all tall and well-built and it appears as though they eat rice in the morning, afternoon and evening.

Who eats rice like this?

'I am sorry, Dhruv,' Avni said.

'Sorry? You put my life at stake to save yours and you just say sorry? You are a selfish girl.'

'Don't do drama. He wouldn't have done anything.'

'Oh, really? Then why were you hiding?'

'I was scared.'

'Then think, how I was feeling, Avni. If you were scared, I was dead scared.'

'You're stronger than me. You're a guy.'

'I am but that doesn't mean I'll go toe-to-toe with a monster.'

Avni laughed heartily.

'Funny for you, huh?'

She nodded and laughed again.

'I realized something today,' I said.

'What?' she asked, smiling.

'That you don't love me. You can leave me to save your life.'

'Shut up. It's not true. He is my cousin and he will tell all my relatives. I'll have to explain it to all of them.'

'Wow. So, let's put Dhruv in front and save myself. That's what you thought?'

My phone rang. It was Maa.

'Dhruv, are you ok? I had a bad dream,' Maa said.

'I am safe, Maa, and I love you more than anyone,' I said.

Avni punched one hand into her palm in frustration.

'That is love. Did you see?' I told Avni when Maa cut the call.

'I will give you chocolate. Will that be okay?'

'No. One tight hug is fine.'

'Wait till we get married.'

'Will your great dad allow me to do that?'

'Come to my home, talk to him respectfully, ask him for my hand. Then we will decide what to do with you.'

'Wow. What a bumper offer.'

'Hahaha,' Avni laughed and tied up her hair.

'Avni,' I said.

'Mmm?'

'I like it when you leave your hair open.'

Avni smiled and pulled the rubber band out of her hair, letting it cascade over her shoulders.

'Happy?'

'Very.'

We reached Bala's hotel and spent the rest of the time watching the girl cry during her *vidaai* ceremony.

'I am not going to cry like this,' Avni declared.

'There is only one person who will cry.'

'Who? My dad?'

'No. Me.'

18

A Week Later

I reached Chennai. Avni's mom had asked me to meet
her urgently. I was really nervous. Avni had not told me
anything. She just said that something had happened at
Bala's wedding because of which her mom and dad were
really upset. I'm already scared of Avni's dad. I reached
Avni's home and Uncle opened the door. He looked at me
angrily and went inside to his room. Aunty immediately
came to the door and welcomed me in.

'Dhruv, I think you are aware of what happened at
Bala's wedding,' Avni's mom said.

'I don't understand, Aunty. What happened?'

'Look, we know Avni likes you and even you like her.
But it will be good if you stopped meeting her from today
onwards.'

'Amma, please don't talk to him like that,' Avni
interrupted.

'Avni, let me talk, please.'

'Aunty, did I make any mistake? I am sorry if I have hurt anyone,' I said.

'It's not about you, Dhruv. It's about your family.'

'What happened, Aunty? Did anyone call and say something to you or Uncle?'

'What was the point of getting Avni's kundli matched with yours at Bala's wedding, when I haven't given any approval of your marriage with her?'

'Huh? When did this happen?'

'Ask your sister. She did all this,' Aunty said. I looked at Avni. She nodded.

'Your sister shamed my daughter in front of all the guests there.'

'But what happened? Avni, at least you tell me,' I asked.

'Avni is *manglik*. And, till date, only we knew that. But now, due to your sister, everybody knows. In fact, your sister and Bala's wife even laughed at Avni.'

'Shreya Didi didn't laugh, Amma,' Avni interrupted.

'Do you see my daughter? She's still defending your sister. But what did your sister do? She made a joke about my daughter in front of so many people. Do you know that the pandit said, in front of everyone, that my daughter is not a good match for you? How do you expect me to feel, Dhruv?' said Aunty.

'Aunty, I had no idea about all this. I am so sorry, I'll speak to—'

'Now, all my relatives know about this. This is a gross invasion of our privacy, Dhruv. I didn't expect this of your family. Does your mom know about this? Do you know how much we are being mocked right now? In our family, everyone has got to know that Avni is a manglik. Now, who will marry her?' said Aunty.

I wanted to say that I would marry her but it was not the right thing to say right now. I was really scared. Why would Didi do something so stupid? Damn.

'Does your mom know about this kundli match?' Aunty asked me.

'Aunty, I myself got to know about this today. How would Maa know?'

'Check with your sister. She must have already informed your mom as she did to the rest of the world.'

'I am really sorry, Aunty. Didi would not do anything to hurt Avni. This was all a mistake.'

'I am not saying anything to you, Dhruv. Just don't meet Avni from now on.'

Avni held her mom's hand tightly.

'We can't get our daughter married to you. Not today, not ever,' Aunty said.

'Aunty, I apologize again on behalf of Didi. Everything will be all right. My mom doesn't care about all this. She already loves Avni so much.'

'That is why your sister made a joke of my daughter. Is it?'

'Aunty, to be frank, everyone in our friends circle knows that Avni and I want to marry each other. Maybe that is why Didi might have asked the pandit to match our kundli.'

'And what about the mockery we are getting from everyone? Do you know what people are saying about my daughter now? We can't even go to their houses now.'

I did not know what to say. I shouldn't have come alone. I shouldn't have even come here. Why did you do this, Didi?

'I am sorry, Aunty,' I said, folding my hands.

'He is still here?' Uncle entered and spoke to Aunty while looking at me.

'Appa, please,' Avni said.

'Hi Uncle,' I said, as I stood up. Uncle did not say a word.

'Tell him not to meet my daughter from now onwards,' Uncle said.

'Uncle, I am really sorry for everything,' I said, folding both my hands again. I had no idea what to do to fix things now.

'I am extremely sorry. In fact, I'll ask Maa and Dad to meet you for our marriage as soon as possible. Will that be fine, Uncle?'

'Do you or anyone in your family have any shame? Is that how you treat our daughter publicly?' Uncle said.

'Dhruv, you don't understand. We don't want to marry our daughter into your family. There will be too many complications going forward,' Aunty said.

'But why, Aunty? I did not do anything. I want to marry her. My Maa and Dad like her too. Then, what is the problem?'

Avni didn't feel great about her parents' behaviour, but I could understand how they might be feeling when others were talking nonsense about their daughter. I was really screwed.

'You are a nice guy, Dhruv. But I want a family that respects my daughter and does not make a mockery of her publicly. Some things are very sensitive and we should do it only in the presence of the family. Your sister should have thought about it,' said Aunty.

'My family loves Avni a lot, Aunty. Didi loves her the most, in fact.'

'Talk to your mom and let us know,' Aunty said.

'No need,' Uncle angrily interjected.

'Let us know, Dhruv. We are waiting,' Aunty said, putting her hand on her husband's hand.

Avni looked at me. She was really upset.

'Sorry, Aunty. Sorry, Uncle. I will leave now,' I said, folding my hands. I left without looking at Avni.

I stood outside their door wondering what to do. Whatever happened at Bala's wedding was not intentional, but I was mad at Didi. I could hear Avni and her parents shouting inside. I quickly left. Avni called a few minutes after I entered the apartment.

'Tell me,' I said.

'Will you open your door?'

'You are here?'

'Of course,' Avni said.

I opened the door.

'Are you shocked to see me?' Avni asked.

'Of course. Your dad just told me not to meet you.'

'He is not your dad. Relax. I will deal with him,' Avni said and handed me a tiffin.

'What's this?'

'I cooked food for you but you didn't get the chance to eat it.'

'Someone is getting romantic these days.'

'Dhruv, I want to marry only you and no one else,' Avni said.

'I am not refusing, Avni. But I am really sorry about everything.'

'I know, I am sorry too. I did not know Appa would talk like that to you.'

'Avni, whatever he did was right. He is your father and he can't hear nonsense about you. Now, I have to talk to my Maa.'

'I am scared.'

'About what?'

'I mean, what would Aunty tell you if she found out about me?'

'Even I am not sure,' I said and opened the tiffin. Avni had made pulao and dum aloo, just like I had cooked at her home the last time.

'Why are you so sweet?' I said.

'Because I love you. Now can we eat?'

'Why would you eat? This is for me, right?'

'Dhruv Mehta, I haven't eaten anything since morning. I thought I'd eat with you.'

'Is that so? Then, let me feed you,' I said and gave her a handful of pulao mixed with curry.

'It is tasty,' Avni said.

'How will it not be? After all, I taught you,' I said.

'Shameless creature. You can never praise me, right?'

I ate the food peacefully but Avni kept talking.

'I had also cooked carrot halwa for you but I forgot to bring it,' Avni said.

'Give it to your dad. He needs sweets more than me.'

'Ah, I am sorry about him. He loves me too much.'

'It's fine. All dads are like him. What he did was totally justified.'

'Okay, I'm going to leave now. Get some rest. By the way, when are you going back?'

'Tomorrow, early morning.'

'I will come and meet you in Hyderabad.'

'But your dad told us not to meet. What if he gets mad again—'

'Sssh. Dhruv, I will come. That's it.'

19

Maa learnt all that Avni's mom had told me at their home from Didi and berated me over the phone. I immediately dialled Didi.

'What did you do, Didi?' I asked.

'What happened now?'

'Do you really want to see me getting married or not?'

'Of course, I want you to.'

'Then, why did you tell Maa everything I told you?'

'Dhruv, if you don't tell her, then Avni's parents will tell Mom when she talks to them about your marriage. So, I thought—'

'No, Didi, you are just messing up everything in my life. First, you did that kundli nonsense at Bala's wedding and now this.'

'Dhruv, is this how you talk to your sister?' It was Jiju.

'Jiju, you have no idea what Didi did just now. Earlier, Avni's parents were angry. Now, even Maa and Dad are angry.'

'Relax, Dhruv. Calm down. Your sister didn't do anything intentionally. In fact, she wanted you to get married as soon as possible. That is why she got Avni's kundli checked.'

'Leave it, Jiju. I will handle everything myself now,' I said and cut the call.

Someone has rightly said that when you love someone truly, then everyone wants to destroy that love story. Maa refused to meet Avni's parents after Didi told her everything. She told me that it was not safe for me to marry Avni. I mean, how could she? She liked Avni so much but now, Maa did not even want to talk about her. She was being extremely old-fashioned. Dad was also in Maa's favour. He told me not to stress out Maa as she was not well. I did not know what to do. Avni, on the other hand, kept asking me if Maa had replied. I keep giving her hope that someday I would convince Maa. Avni said that she would not marry anyone if I didn't marry her.

A week later, Maa informed me that she was coming to Hyderabad along with Alok Mama's family. They were going to meet a girl for Alok Mama's son, Hemant. I had asked Avni to come to Hyderabad as this was a nice way to make Maa realize that I was not going to leave Avni at any cost. I dialled Avni's number.

'Have you left?' I asked her.

'Dhruv, I am not feeling comfortable. Your mom is coming to meet another family. What if she is not expecting me?'

'Avni, you have to listen to me. We have to try.'

'Dhruv, what if Aunty feels bad if she sees me there?'

'I am here. Just come here. I will handle everything.'

'Dhruv, I will try to meet her some other day. You enjoy the time. Your entire family is coming. I don't want to spoil her mood,' Avni said and cut the call.

Maa and Dad arrived the next morning with Alok Mama and his family. They looked really happy. Why wouldn't they? Finally, Hemant Bhaiya was getting married.

'You are looking so handsome,' Maa said.

'Just like Hemant,' Alok Mama said. I touched everyone's feet at the railway station. We took a cab to the hotel. It was a fifteen-minute journey from the station.

'What happened? You look tense,' Hemant Bhaiya said.

'Me? No, nothing like that.'

'How is Avni?'

'She is good, Bhaiya.'

'I want her as my bhabhi. Remember that.'

I smiled. There was someone who cared about my Avni, other than me.

'Dilwale dulhaniya le jayenge, Dhruv. Remember.'

I laughed.

Everyone in the car turned around. I fell silent. We reached the hotel. Everyone freshened up and was ready in a couple of hours. We were supposed to meet Hemant Bhaiya's to-be-bride, Anjana, at 2 p.m. Her dad had sent two cars for us. We reached their house on time.

Alok Mama and Anjana's dad shook hands as we entered. Anjana stood in the corner of the living room, greeting us with a formal namaste. Hemant Bhaiya was overexcited to meet her. Anjana was actually very beautiful. Everyone in our family was really happy after seeing her. I missed Avni. If she was here, I would have tried something today.

The parents from both sides had started their talks. Their laughter filled the entire room. Hemant Bhaiya was constantly looking towards the kitchen because Anjana was inside and cooking something. This is what happens when a guy meets such a beautiful girl for the first time.

'Hemant Bhaiya, control,' I said, holding his hand.

'Hehehe. I was just looking at the house,' he said.

'This is not looking. This is called staring, and I know what you are staring at.'

'Dhruv, can I ask you something?' Hemant Bhaiya said.

'What?'

'Do you like Anjana?'

'I really like her. She is so pretty. Shall I go and tell her?' I asked.

'Are you kidding me?'

'I can tell her if you want me to.'

'No, Dhruv. Please do not break up my marriage before it is fixed. She will not like it.'

'Relax. You sit here,' I said and got up. Everyone was busy talking.

'Aunty, where is the kitchen? I need to have some water,' I asked Anjana's mom.

'That way,' Aunty pointed.

'Hi Anjana,' I said as I entered the kitchen.

'Hi Dhruv ji,' Anjana said. When Indian girls say the word 'ji', our heart beats in a different way.

'Actually, I wanted to have some water,' I said.

'Let me help you,' she said.

'And I also wanted to tell you something,' I added.

'Please tell me,' she said. Her voice was really sweet and she was looking as good as Yami Gautam in that beautiful saree. Girls in a saree can make us fall for them any time. Hemant Bhaiya was really lucky.

'There is a secret message from Hemant Bhaiya.'

'Oh, please tell me,' she said with a smile.

'Hemant Bhaiya has asked me to inform you that you are looking really beautiful,' I said.

Anjana paused for a moment.

'I don't know what to say, Dhruv ji,' she said, smiling.

'It's okay. You can just tell me what I should reply to Hemant Bhaiya,' I said.

Anjana paused again.

'Please tell him that he is also looking really great in blue,' she said.

'Thank you so much. I will convey it to him,' I said.

'Thanks, Dhruv ji. Do you want something else?' she asked.

'Yes. Could you take a class for all Indian girls to look as traditional and beautiful as you?'

Anjana Bhabhi laughed.

'I have one more request, Anjana, but you have to keep it top secret,' I said.

'Please tell me.'

'Actually, Hemant Bhaiya wanted to meet you. Is it possible?' I asked.

Anjana paused once more.

'We can meet in the garden. He can come there from the front door. I will come from this side.'

'Done. You are so sweet.'

'And you are so nice,' she said.

'What are you doing here, Dhruv? Anjana, I hope he is not disturbing you?' Maa said.

'No Aunty ji. I am good,' Anjana said.

Maa and I left the kitchen. Anjana's mom entered as we were coming out. I gave Hemant Bhaiya a thumbs-up.

'You are daring, Dhruv,' Hemant Bhaiya said as I sat down.

'Girls like daring guys. Be a man, Hemant Bhaiya.'

'What did she say?' Hemant Bhaiya asked eagerly.

'Oh ho. So, now you want to hear what she said?'

'Yes. Please tell me.'

'She said that you look nice in blue.'

'That's all?'

'Yes,' I said. Hemant Bhaiya looked sad.

'Okay listen, there is good news,' I mumbled.

'What?'

'Anjana Bhabhi said that she wants to meet you.'

'Dhruv, I feel really shy meeting her like this.'

'Oh, come on, Bhaiya. It'll be fun!'

'Okay, fine. How will we meet her? Shall I go to the kitchen?'

'If you go to the kitchen, my mom will throw me out of this house. So, relax. Don't get overexcited.'

'Sorry, man. I've not interacted with women that much.'

'That's okay. We'll figure it out.'

We got up together.

'Uncle, can we see the garden?' I asked Anjana Bhabhi's dad.

'It is your house. Please do,' Uncle said.

We reached the garden and Anjana was already standing there.

'Hi Anjana ji,' Hemant Bhaiya said.

'Hi Hemant ji. Please tell me what you wanted to say.'

'You called me here, Anjana ji. You should tell me,' Hemant Bhaiya said.

'But Dhruv said that you wanted to talk to me,' Bhabhi said.

'Shall I call Uncle ji here to ask who called whom?' I said. They both laughed.

'Will you please give us some space, Dhruv?' Hemant Bhaiya said.

'Can't I hear what you are talking about?' I said. 'Okay, I'm kidding. I'll keep a lookout.'

For the next few minutes, I stood looking around to see if anyone was coming.

We came back to the living room after five minutes. Anjana Bhabhi returned to the kitchen.

'Thanks, Dhruv,' Hemant Bhaiya whispered.

'Remember, Bhaiya. Dilwale dulhaniya le jayenge.'

Bhaiya smiled and hugged me.

Anjana Bhabhi came out of the kitchen with a variety of sweets and pakoras on a tray. She served us all tea and said thanks to Hemant Bhaiya in a low voice before she left.

'Totally my pleasure,' Hemant Bhaiya replied the same way.

After some time, Alok Mama and Anjana's father got up and hugged each other. As we were about to leave, I saw a girl in a saree entering from the main gate. My heart skipped a beat as she looked just like Avni for a moment. She touched everyone's feet as she entered including my Maa's.

'If you like her, I will talk to Anjana,' Maa said, looking at the girl.

'Maa, please. Why would you—'

'He's Dhruv,' Anjana Bhabhi said, introducing me to the girl. 'My friend, Akanksha.'

I missed Avni. I don't know why. It took us one hour to reach the hotel due to heavy traffic. I went to collect the keys at the reception when the lady there told me that a girl was waiting for me. I turned around and saw it was Avni. I had given her the address of this hotel a day before. She waved at me. I waved at Maa and asked her to come towards the meeting hall. I told the receptionist to give the room keys to Alok Mama.

'Thanks for coming,' I told Avni.

'How was the meet? I am sorry I came without informing you. I was not sure until the last moment whether I should come here or not, Dhruv,' Avni said.

'When did you arrive, by the way?'

'This morning. My luggage is at Anju's flat.'

'This is the best thing you could have done. I was missing you so much.'

Maa came to the meeting hall but when she saw Avni, her smiling face changed.

'Hi Aunty,' Avni said. Maa ignored her and pulled me aside.

'Dhruv, why did you call her here?'

'Maa, she came to meet you.'

'For what? Didn't I tell you that I don't want to meet her?'

'Maa, please. Don't create a scene. At least talk to her once, nicely.'

'No, Dhruv. I don't want her here. It is such a nice occasion. You shouldn't have called her.'

'Seriously, Maa. Why are you doing this? She is listening,' I said.

Maa looked at Avni and called her.

Avni came up and said hesitatingly, 'Hi Aunty.' She might have already felt that something was wrong.

'Hi Avni. Dhruv, make her eat something and drop her back safely. It was nice meeting you, Avni. I am in a hurry right now,' Maa said and left without speaking any further. Avni looked at me.

'Hey, don't mind. Maa is too busy with Hemant Bhaiya's marriage.'

'It's okay. You better join her. I'll leave.'

'You will leave? And go where?'

'Nothing. I will go to Anju's room and then return tonight to Chennai,' she said, without making eye contact with me.

'Avni,' I said, holding her chin and lifting her face. Her eyes had tears.

'She doesn't even want to see me, Dhruv,' Avni broke down.

'Avni, come on. I am sorry for Maa's behaviour but she didn't mean to hurt you.'

Avni didn't say a word. I wiped her tears and held her face.

'I will marry only you and no one else. I promise. Maa loves you so much.'

'I am not good for you, Dhruv,' Avni cried.

'Avni, it's not like that. We just need to have patience,' I said.

Then I saw a call coming in from Maa.

'I will leave. Better be with Aunty. She needs you,' Avni said.

'First, wipe your tears,' I said and got a glass of water for her. Maa called again.

'Now, please wait. I am coming back,' I told Avni.

Alok Mama wanted me to show them the pictures I had clicked at Anjana Bhabhi's house. Maa asked me to serve everyone the snacks that she had got from Patna. After I was done with all this, I immediately went back to the meeting area but Avni was not there. I checked with the receptionist and she said that Avni had already left. I called Avni multiple times but she did not pick up. Damn. I came back to my room where Alok Mama was sitting with the rest of the family members. Maa was showing them photos of a few girls she had chosen for me.

'Are they from a good family? I mean, are they well settled?' Alok Mama asked.

'Yes, Bhaiya. These girls are from very rich families.'

'You have checked, they are non-manglik, right?'

'Yes, Bhaiya. That was the first thing I asked the pandit to check.'

'Yes, Sugandha. It is not safe for non-mangliks to get married to mangliks. Don't make that mistake.'

'I know, Bhaiya. By the way, what happened to Mishra ji's daughter-in-law? Why did they get divorced? It was an arranged marriage, right?'

'Mishra ji's daughter-in-law was having an affair with someone else. Mishra ji caught her red-handed with another guy. Can you imagine? He got a heart attack that same day but he is safe now.'

'Did he not match his son's kundli with the girl's?'

'Their kundli had twenty-four matches, but if the upbringing is not right, what can anyone do?'

'I just want my son to get the right girl.'

'Dhruv is a good kid. He will get a nice girl, Sugandha. Don't worry.'

I was listening to their conversation, but my mind was thinking about Avni. What would she do if I got married to another girl? Would she move on? Is it so easy to move on from the people you love or do people just pretend for the rest of their life that they have moved on? How does it feel to spend your life with a person you don't want to? Will I be able to find a girl like Avni? Will I be able to love any other girl?

Will I be able to forget her? I know many people who did not marry the person they loved. They all look so happy in their social media pictures. But are they really happy or are they just faking it for the camera? Is this what our society is all about?

Haven't we all forgotten our real heritage which LORD RAM and SITA MAA left for us, that LOVE and LOYALTY go hand in hand? Aren't we fooling ourselves? This was not how I thought my life would be. I wanted to marry a girl whom I could love for the rest of my life and be loyal to her. I don't see that happening.

'Dhruv, come here,' Alok Mama called.

'How is this girl?' he asked.

'She is nice for Hemant Bhaiya,' I said rudely.

'Shut up, Dhruv,' Maa said.

'Then, please don't show me any other girl. I am not characterless,' I said.

'Sugandha, is he still meeting that girl, Avni?' Alok Mama asked.

'She came to the hotel, Bhaiya,' Maa said.

'Dhruv, didn't you tell her what your mom said?' Alok Mama asked.

'Papa, please. Don't torture him like that,' Hemant Bhaiya said.

'Alok Bhaiya, did you like Akanksha?' Maa asked.

'Very beautiful. It looks like all girls related to Anjana are beautiful.'

'Yes, Bhaiya. Talk to Anjana's father.'

'Let Hemant's marriage happen. I can talk freely after that.'

I looked at my phone. There was no reply from Avni. I gave her a call, but she did not pick up.

Two days passed. Maa and Dad were still in Hyderabad at my flat. It was really tough for me to talk to Avni. She had somehow got back to normal.

'Hi Avinash,' I told Avni. We were speaking on a call.

'Hi Kamini,' Avni said, referring to me.

She said that she had saved my name on her phone as Kamini, which was her maid's name in Bangalore. I felt really bad after I got to know that. Only people who know Hindi know the reason why.

The IPL was going on. So, we both decided to talk in code language when our parents were nearby.

'So Avinash, how is the weather over there?' I asked.

Weather meant the environment at Avni's house.

'Weather is very hot, Kamini. We need some rain here, very soon.'

Rain meant Avni wanted me to talk to my parents and reply to her ASAP.

'Okay, okay. And how is Thalaiva?' I asked.

Thalaiva meant Avni's dad.

'Thalaiva is not ready to cool down.'

'It would be great if Dhoni gets a super over. What do you say?' I said.

Super over meant I would come to Avni's house to talk again.

'Super over won't work this time, Kamini. Try to understand. He has sent all fielders to the boundary. No chance of a four or six.'

Fielders on the boundary meant shoot-on-sight orders for me.

'It means Thalaiva will win the match this time,' I said.

'As always. No one can stop him, Kamini,' Avni said.

'And how is Mrs Dhoni?' I asked. Maa looked at me.

'Oh. She is also getting on Thalaiva's side these days,' Avni said.

'Is it? I thought she was trustworthy,' I said.

'No one is trustworthy. It's IPL, Kamini. Bidding is going on for the next match once again as the player is hurt.'

Bidding meant marriage proposals.

'It looks like Kohli has to declare his innings.'

Kohli meant I was talking about myself.

'Let us wait, Kamini. RCB will win. Don't worry.'

RCB means love marriage.

'So Avinash, when is Pujara coming on the field?'

It meant, when was Avni going to meet me?

'Oh, Kamini. Coming on the field is not happening soon. Thalaiva has sent players on the boundary for Pujara too.'

It meant there were shoot-on-sight orders for Avni too.

'Oh. Okay. See you on the field soon.'

'Okay. Is there any chance of drinks for me?' Avni said.

Drinks meant she wanted me to say 'I love you'.

'Do you want me to be thrown out of the team? No ways. That's not happening.'

'Get lost then,' she said and disconnected.

Maa looked at me.

'Who is Mrs Dhoni?' she asked.

'Sakshi, Maa. You don't know?'

'And how come Pujara is coming on the field? He is retired hurt, right?' Maa asked.

'Pujara? Who said Pujara? I said, Raina, Maa.' I was finding it hard to breathe because of the stress.

'My sweet Maa,' I said and squeezed her cheeks. She got up and went to the kitchen. I heaved a sigh of relief. I needed to be more careful next time or else I would die in this game of Thalaiva, Pujara and Kohli.

Maa and Dad were going to stay for five more days in Hyderabad. It would be better if the next time I tried Baahubali, Kattappa and Devasena instead of IPL players.

20

One Week Later

I reached Didi's apartment in Delhi and rang the bell. Didi opened the door.

'Oh my god. What an amazing surprise!' Didi said and invited me to enter.

There were a few guests at home. I smiled at them and went inside. I heard someone washing vessels. I went into the kitchen where I saw Jiju washing up. He looked at me and smiled.

'What a surprise!' Jiju said.

'Let me help you, Jiju. Please shift a little and give me a scrubber. I will help you wash up.'

'Are you serious?'

'Yes, Jiju.'

I took a scrubber from him and we both started cleaning the vessels. After that, Jiju prepared ginger tea and pakoras for the guests.

'They are your sister's colleagues,' Jiju said.

'Don't they know that your interior work is going on?'

'Yes. They wanted to see how the work was going on. They will get theirs done by our designer himself. By the way, how's life?'

'Life sucks, Jiju.'

'That is there, but I meant, how bad does it suck right now?'

'Have you ever seen a guy who wants to leave this world and go to the Himalayas? It sucks that bad.'

'Bro, that is the last stage. I am in the second-last stage right now, by the way,' Jiju said.

'Hahaha. That was really funny.'

I took the tea and pakoras out for everyone.

'Girls, that's my brother, Dhruv,' Didi said and introduced me to Kavita, Kalpana and Garima. 'He is a budding writer,' she added.

'Oh wow, a writer! What do you write?' Kavita asked.

'Romance,' I said, without delay.

'Commendable. In today's world, we need romance writers. Our cinema has no real romantic stories.'

'You didn't like *Kabir Singh*?' I asked.

'That was romance?' Kavita said and laughed. 'Just kidding. That was one of the best movies I've seen lately,' she added.

'Exactly. Love is love. Everyone has their own individual story. Preeti also had her own story,' I said.

The guests left after some time. Didi came into the kitchen.

'Who did all this?' Didi asked, looking at the condition of the kitchen.

'Your guests wanted to eat pakoras and have tea. Do you think it could happen without dirtying vessels?' Jiju said.

'But so many, Aadi? Now, you both leave the kitchen,' Didi said and started cleaning the vessels. I wanted to tell them something but I was scared to.

'Why are you checking your phone, Dhruv?' Jiju asked.

'Actually, Avni is waiting outside. She said that she would only come in if you don't have any issues with her.'

'What? That kid is waiting outside in this hot weather? Are you mad, Dhruv?' Didi said and ran to the living room to open the door, but Avni was not there.

'You were busy with your guests, Didi. So I didn't tell you. Avni is waiting downstairs. She told me that she would be there,' I said.

Didi ran down and brought Avni into the flat. Avni was drenched in sweat.

'Avni, are you mad? You should have come in along with Dhruv,' Didi said as Avni sat down.

'No, Didi. I thought you might not want to meet me,' Avni said.

'Avni, I love you more than anyone in my family. Do you get that? Don't ever think that we don't care about you,' Didi said and Avni had tears in her eyes.

Didi wiped Avni's face and asked her to change.

'You are sitting in the AC room and you left her outside, Dhruv. I will send you to jail for this,' Didi said. 'Has she eaten anything?' she added.

'No,' I said.

'And you are eating pakoras in the kitchen?'

'You don't know how much she argues with me, Didi. I messaged her to come and eat pakoras but she refused. Ask her,' I said in my defence.

'Dhruv, she is someone's kid, okay?'

'It's okay, Didi,' Avni said as she came back into the living room.

'Avni, have these pakoras,' Didi said.

All of us went out of the house after some time.

'Do you see how Didi is holding Jiju's hand? You should also,' I told Avni politely.

'You mean, I should hold Jiju's hand?' Avni said.

'Avni, you should hold my hand,' I grunted.

'On the road? No way,' she said.

'Jiju!' I shouted. 'Can you please come back? Let Avni walk with Didi.'

Jiju came back and Avni went to Didi.

'Is she still angry with you?' Jiju asked.

'Very angry. I made her stand outside.'

'Dhruv, Avni is madly in love with you. You know that right?'

'I just know that I cannot live without her.'

'I can see that. Now, do one thing. Do you see the roses over there? Pluck one and give it to her.'

I looked at Jiju quizzically.

'Do as I say,' Jiju insisted.

Then, Jiju turned on his phone camera. I thought he would click our photo when I gave the rose to Avni. I hoped

Avni wouldn't slap me on the road in broad daylight or else it would be the worst photo of my life. I plucked a rose and ran towards Avni. She stared at me as I handed her the rose, keeping one hand on my left cheek. She happily took it and fixed it in her ponytail.

'Thanks,' Avni said. Jiju clicked the shot perfectly.

'Wow, it came out so well,' I said.

'Yes, Avni looks so nice in this pic,' Jiju said.

'Avni is like Shreya. Maybe that is why I fell for Shreya. Never leave Avni, I'm telling you.'

'No Jiju, I won't. Just talk to Maa, please.'

'I will.'

'I brought Avni to Delhi to make her feel that my family loves her. After what Maa did at the hotel, Avni was really upset. So, my first plan was to make her feel good, feel included in our family.'

'I have an idea. Why don't we go to Prithvi's house? Avni can also come.'

'Shreya, can we go to Prithvi's house, if that's okay?' Jiju shouted.

'Do you think this is your bedroom that you can shout so loudly? Look around. Now all the autorickshaw drivers know my name is Shreya. That's what you wanted, right?' Didi said. Avni and I laughed seeing them fight.

'Mrs Shreya, can we go to your brother Prithvi's house if you have no issue with that?' Jiju asked politely this time.

'Sure. Avni, babes, shall we go to my brother Prithvi's house?'

'Babes?' Jiju and I repeated in shock.

We reached Prithvi Bhaiya's house.

'Where is Bhabhi?' I asked.

'I am here, Dhruv ji,' Bhabhi shouted from the kitchen. She was busy cleaning vessels.

Avni sat on a recliner sofa like a princess. I guess my mission to make her feel included in my family was successful so far.

'Avni, would you like to have something?' Prithvi Bhaiya asked.

'Do you have Fanta, Prithvi Bhaiya?' Avni said.

Prithvi Bhaiya looked at me. I smiled at Bhaiya.

'We have Maaza. That's fine?'

'Sure, Bhaiya.'

'Hi babes,' I whispered to Avni when everyone got busy watching the news on TV.

'Don't you dare call me babes!'

'My sister can call you that, but I can't?'

'No. She's my friend.'

'And me?'

'You . . . no.'

'Are you still angry with me?'

'Why would I be angry?' Avni said, sipping her Maaza.

Bhabhi got Avni and Shreya Didi to dress in sarees as we were all visiting the Hanuman Mandir in Connaught Place. Avni had never worn a Banarasi saree before. She looked like a proper North Indian.

There was a huge queue outside the mandir. We stood outside the temple, listening to the *aarti*. When we went inside, we heard chants of 'Jai Siya Ram'. We all sat down along with a pandit who explained why we chant Jai Siya Ram. SIYA stands for MAATA SITA. He said that our traditions teach us that women are always before men. If women in a society are not treated right, such a society can never prosper. For that to happen, men in our society should think, act and live like Lord Ram. I looked at Avni, my Sita, and prayed to Lord Hanuman to always take care of her happiness. We performed a small puja and returned to Prithvi Bhaiya's house.

It was dark already and we had to leave for Chennai. I would drop Avni at Chennai and then I would take a flight to Hyderabad. We bid goodbye to everyone and boarded our flight. Both of us were very tired. So, we slept on the flight. Avni waited at Chennai airport until my flight was ready to take off.

'Avni?' I said. The boarding for my flight had started.

'Yes?'

'Was it you who helped me to get the job, when Didi informed you about my layoff?'

'What?'

'I'm asking—was it you?'

'No, I didn't find a job for you, Dhruv.'

'I know it, Avni. Just tell me the truth.'

'Okay, fine. I spoke to a few people and they told me that there was a vacancy.'

'You could have told me, right?'

'No. Amma says that when you do something with a pure heart, you should not disclose it. So, I told Shreya Didi not to tell you.'

'Shreya Didi didn't tell me.'

'Then who did?'

'She might have told Jiju. He told me,' I said.

Avni patted her forehead. The boarding was about to close. I kissed her forehead.

'Bye Avni,' I said and got up to leave.

'Dhruv!'

I turned around. She kissed my forehead. I kept looking at Avni.

How can she love me so much?

21

A week later, I was in Patna for a puja at Hemant Bhaiya's home before his engagement. Everyone was in a wedding mood except me; everyone was happy except me; everybody was in love, except me. I tried talking to Maa about Avni but she was not ready to listen. Shreya Didi also tried to convince Maa but she was not ready to meet Avni's parents. Maa was behaving as though she did not even want to see Avni's face any more. Our society sucks when it comes to going against old rituals and practices.

'Maa,' I said, as I placed some vessels on the shelf.

'What, Dhruv?' said Maa, who was cutting vegetables.

'Why are you treating Avni like this? It looks like you really hate her.'

'You started again. I don't hate her. She is a nice girl.'

'Then, let me marry her. You will be free of my marriage tension.'

'Dhruv, you don't understand. We don't marry such girls—'

'What do you mean by such girls? Do you know her qualifications? She earns more than your son. She loves me. She'd die for me. People would die for a partner like that.'

'Then let them die. Not my son.'

'Why?'

'You know why.'

'Don't you feel bad treating someone like this? How would she feel, Maa, when you behave like this with her just because a pandit said something?'

'It is not just "something". It is serious. I am not stopping her from marrying. She can marry guys of her choice.'

'She doesn't love them, Maa. She loves me. She wants to marry me.'

'Are you out of your mind? What will I do if anything happens to you?'

'Nothing will happen to me, Maa.'

'Who said so?'

'I am trying to say that you are educated, Maa. Think about it.'

'Exactly and our pandits have set some rules.'

'So, these old rules are more important than a girl's life? What will I do if she does something to herself? Maa, she will blame herself all her life that she chose a guy like me.'

'Dhruv, we are done. I know that I can't beat you in arguments.'

'Do you really want to see me happy?'

Maa glared at me.

'If I am not with her, I won't be happy.'

'Then don't be happy,' Maa said.

'Seriously. This is a joke for you.'

'Nothing is a joke, Dhruv. That girl is not meant for our family. I can't risk your life.'

'Then I know what to do. I will do a court marriage.'

'You dare not do anything like that. I have so many hopes for your marriage. Don't spoil that.'

'And Maa, even I had hoped to get married to a girl who loves me. What about that?'

'I know. I will find a girl from a good family. She will be more beautiful than Avni.'

'Maa, you don't understand. Our way of thinking matches. She has values that are not easy to have. I won't get a girl like her.'

'I will find one for you. Give me some time.'

'No, I won't. I am marrying her and that's final.'

'Why don't you understand?' Maa said.

'What about that girl? What will she do Maa? What will she think about herself, if I leave her because she is a manglik?'

'It happens. People leave people for their betterment only.'

'She will spoil her life, Maa. She is not like every other girl.'

'No girl spoils her life. They find another guy and marry in a few months. Don't teach me.'

'I have told you already, Maa, and that is final. I am marrying her.'

'They have wronged you totally. Dirty family.'

'Maa,' I was outraged.

'Is this how you talk to your mother?' Dad came inside and shouted.

I looked at Dad and then I looked at Maa. I left the kitchen. There was no point anyway. They will do what they feel is right. I couldn't even look at them right now. I had to do something. I had to fight for my love.

22

I did not want to go back to Hyderabad. I was not able to focus on work. So, I spoke to my manager, and was working from Patna.

Amit Mama had come to meet Maa. He and Alok Mama were not speaking to each other for the last one month due to some misunderstanding. So, I think he might have come to collect some information regarding Hemant Bhaiya's wedding and their Hyderabad visit. He was sitting in the living room and talking to Maa. I was sitting in the adjacent room but I could hear everything. Dad wasn't there; he didn't like Amit Mama that much.

'Finally, you came to my house after so many years. It would have been good if you had brought your wife also,' Maa told Amit Mama.

'I will get her some other day, Didi,' Amit Mama replied. 'So, Didi. When are you going to get Dhruv married?' he asked.

'Very soon. If your blessings are with him, he will get married pretty soon.'

'Our blessings are always with him. Did you meet Avni's parents? You told me that you really liked her.'

'No, Amit. Not that girl. I will find a girl who lives in our city. Nowadays, it is good if the boy's in-laws live close by.'

'Why? What happened? I asked about Avni because I thought you had already spoken to her parents. And, let me tell you that you will not get such a nice girl in our entire clan.'

I felt like hugging Amit Mama.

'Yes, I know that, Amit. I also liked her a lot but—'

'But what, Didi?'

'Anyway, leave it. Just let me know if you find a nice girl for Dhruv.'

'Sure, Didi.'

'Hemant and Anjana make a very beautiful couple. I need a girl like Anjana,' Maa said.

'I have heard a few things about that family but I am not sure how far it is true—'

'What have you heard?'

'Nothing special. I will tell you if there is anything you should know, Didi.'

'Okay, Amit. Good girls are not easy to find these days. In our time, most girls were good.'

'Because most of them were not working. Today, girls are going out and doing things that men used to do once upon a time. How do you expect them to be like you when you were young? Most girls want to live and roam around with multiple guys. Even guys are doing the same. I am scared about my son, if he will get a nice girl or not.'

'Amit, tell me one thing. Is it safe to marry manglik girls?' Maa asked.

'I don't even believe in kundli bullshit, Didi. Why are you talking about manglik? I am telling you, please do not fall into this trap. Are you seeing these fraud cases in which a girl's family is imposing on a boy's family just for money and property? Just look for a nice girl from a nice family. This kundli matching is for people who can give their kids to anyone irrespective of their upbringing just because their kundli has matched.'

There was silence for a bit, after which Amit Mama softly asked, 'Is Avni manglik, Didi?'

'Yes.'

'I would suggest, go ahead with her marriage to Dhruv. She is a nice girl, Didi.'

'I understand, Amit, but I am very scared.'

'How can you be against your own son? You know that he likes her so much.'

'Amit, I am not as open-minded as you. If anything happens to my son tomorrow, I will die blaming myself for it.'

'Nothing is going to happen, Didi. Dhruv loves that girl. If this marriage doesn't happen, he'll die blaming you.'

Maa was quiet. I was tearing up, sitting in the other room.

'Didi, instead of just getting our kids married, we need to understand why their decision is correct if they want to marry someone specific. Look Didi, our kids are leaving their city, their parents, going out on their own, cooking their own food and then they are able to find a partner of their own. Do you think they will not be frustrated if we reject their choice? Didi, they have earned this person in their life on their own. We have to respect that.'

'I get your point, Amit, but it all comes down to one question. Will he be safe? I love him a lot, Amit. You know how sensitive and reserved Dhruv is. He is not like other kids.'

'Then what do you want, Didi? This way you will only hurt him and his feelings. I am telling you that he will never be happy.'

'Amit ji, what did I tell you a few weeks back? My wife is not well. Didn't I tell you that?' Dad said as he entered the house.

'What happened, Jija ji? Did I do anything?'

'It would be better if you don't interfere in my family matters,' Dad said.

'But Jija ji, I was just trying to tell Didi that—'

'Please stop. It would be good if you looked at your own family issues. Better focus on your son's marriage than giving advice to my wife.'

'Jija ji, why are you talking about my son now?'

'Then why are you interfering in my son's matters? Did we ask you?' Dad shouted.

'You don't have to shout at me. We can talk like civilized people,' Amit Mama said.

I came out of my room. Maa held Mama ji's hand to control him.

'First, you behave like a civilized person. Now, I don't want any more discussion about my son. Do you get it?' Dad said and went to another room.

Damn, Dad will never stop talking to Amit Mama like this. Their rift will never end.

'Is this why you called me here, Didi? You see, he still talks to me as if I am a nobody.'

'Amit, you know he is short-tempered.'

'No Didi, this is not right. He can't talk to me like this. That is why I don't come here.'

'Mama, I am sorry from Dad's side. He has been like this for years. You know it,' I said.

'I won't come again here. Never ever,' Mama said as he got up to leave.

'It is raining, Mama. Please stay,' I said.

'I will wait outside. I won't sit here,' Mama said and left.

I went to Dad's room. I remember how Dad used to be so chill until a few months back. Now, even I am scared to talk to him.

'Dad?'

'Yes, Dhruv?'

'Nothing, I just want to talk.'

'What do you have to talk about now? Did your Mama leave?'

'Yes, Dad. He left.'

'Good.'

'Dad, you need to control your anger. I can see that you are getting angry a lot these days. Since the last few months, you have been looking very tense and you are getting angry about small things.'

Dad was quiet. He just continued reading his book.

'I understand Maa is not well. She has BP issues but if you continue like this then it will impact your health as well. And I don't want you to have health issues.'

'Look, Dhruv. We are getting old now. All my kids are staying elsewhere. I have to look after my health, her health, her medicines and housework. What do you expect me to do? I am also human. I get frustrated sometimes.'

'You can tell me whatever you need, Dad. I am here for you both.'

'Okay, Dhruv. I got your point. Now go and do your office work.'

'Dad, can you ask Amit Mama to come inside? He is standing outside the door. It is raining.'

'He hasn't left?'

'No, Dad. Can you please talk to him?'

'Okay, I will do it. But Dhruv, will you promise me that you will not bring up Avni again in this house? Look, I don't have a problem if Avni becomes your wife. I just don't want your Maa's health to get impacted. I have no one except her.'

'I understand, Dad. I will never discuss Avni again.'

'I will be the happiest if your Maa accepts Avni as your wife but please don't force her.'

I nodded and left the room. Dad got up and opened the front door.

'Amit,' Dad said. 'Please come inside. I did not mean to insult you in any way and I am sorry if you felt so,' Dad said, folding his hands.

Amit Mama came in. Maa smiled looking at them. I came back to my room. Dad's words echoed in my head. No one understands what I am going through. How is it possible to tell Avni that I can't marry her? She keeps asking me every single day and I put her off, saying that I am trying. But it looks like my family will never accept her. Avni and her memories keep following me everywhere. How will I live without her?

I did not want to talk to Maa and Dad at all about Avni any more. I would never speak to Didi either. Everyone is playing the drama of seeing me happy when they know I am not happy with what they are doing. I feel really disgusted that I was born in a family like this where people only care about themselves. I did not want to talk about marriage any more, did not want to attend any wedding any more and did not want to meet married people any more. I hate all of them. Marriage sucks. Love sucks even more. I was scared to talk to Maa again about Avni because I knew that I might end up hurting her if I said anything rude. The truth was, I really hated seeing my own family members go against my own happiness.

I picked up my phone. There were a lot of messages from Avni. I missed her as I read her messages. I can't even imagine how much I will miss her if she gets married to anyone else, but it is not good to make her wait for no reason. It was better to tell Avni that it would be nice for her to marry someone her parents wanted. I can't fight with my family any more. I dialled Avni's number.

'I will call you in some time. I'm in a meeting, Dhruv.'

Avni disconnected the call. I wonder how she can do her office work with so much stress. I continued working on my book. There was a call from Avni after two hours. I picked it up.

'Sorry, I got an ad hoc meeting with my manager. He is asking me to report back to Bangalore office,' Avni said.

'That is good for you, isn't it? There must be so much stress staying with your parents, right?'

'Why have you really called, Dhruv?'

'Avni, I have to tell you something,' I said, with a heavy heart.

'Tell me, Dhruv.'

'I don't know how to say this but my family is not right for you. I mean, we are not good people, Avni. I should have told you about my family before.'

'What are you saying?'

'I just want you to be happy. I know that in my family, you will never be happy.'

'Did they say anything?'

'No, but I can't keep you waiting like this. It looks like my family doesn't want to see me happy. They are not at all ready to listen to me.'

Avni was silent.

'They don't love you, Avni' I added.

'But you love me, right? That is enough for me. I mean, I am ready to have a court marriage with you,' she said.

'Maa is not well. If I do anything she does not want, her health will further deteriorate. And, I know that I am only giving excuses to you now and then, which is not right.'

'It is okay, Dhruv. I am ready to wait. I am not in a hurry to marry now either. We can marry next year.'

'You told me last week that a guy was coming to see you. Did you meet?'

'He came and met my family.'

'How did things go? I hope he liked you.'

'Dhruv, why are you talking about all this? I want to marry only you. Don't you get it?'

'And I want you to stop thinking about our marriage. I am under a lot of stress, Avni, and I don't think I can take this any more.'

'So, what do you want now? Do you want me to stop calling you, messaging you and meeting you?'

'Maybe.'

'I don't want to hear that, Dhruv. Please be clear. Tell me if you don't want to marry me any more. Did your Maa find a girl for you already?'

'Avni, it would be better if we stopped talking.'

'Is it easy for you to say that? I feel so disgusted with myself right now. I loved you, was truthful to you, and what did I get in return?'

'Avni, as I said, I am in no mood to explain anything. You can think whatever you want.'

'Mood? What the hell do you mean by that? Am I a joke for you that you can tell something one day and something else another day? Have you made a mockery of my life?'

'Avni, calm down, I didn't me—'

'Calm down? I am fighting with my family every day. I tell them that I love you shamelessly and you are telling me to forget you. Are you playing with my life?'

'No, I am not.'

'Yes, you are. First, you told me that you wanted me to marry you and even asked me to have a court marriage. Okay, fine, I did not want to have a court marriage earlier but now I am saying that I am ready to have one with you. Then why are you denying that? What are you trying to do with me?'

'Avni, why are you shouting? I told you to calm down.'

'Do you have something called self-respect or not? How can you even think of talking to me about all this? I will never forgive you for this.'

'Avni, I am sorry. Listen to me first, ple—'

'No, you listen to me. Either you are clear about marrying me or you are clear that you don't want to marry me. Don't you dare play with my life. I will never forgive you for this.'

Avni was sobbing. My heart broke.

'Avni, I am really sorry but I did not mean to hurt you. My family is not listening to me. I can't marry any other girl but I can't keep you waiting forever, right? You also have a life, you also want to enjoy life like other girls, you also want to have a family of your own. Don't you?'

'No, I only want to be with you. I only want to marry you. I only want to have kids with you. I don't want anything else, Dhruv. I am ready to wait. Please don't say that you don't want me any more. Please, Dhruv,' Avni sobbed.

Tears gushed to my eyes too. How could I even speak to her like this? I felt ashamed of myself.

'Avni, Avni, stop crying. How do I make you understand that I also want to marry only you and be with you? But, will you be ready to wait for me?'

'I will.'

'What if we never get married?'

'I don't know. I just want to be with you.'

'Avni, I love you. Please don't think that I want to marry any other girl but I want to see you happy. In my family, you won't be happy. Do you understand this?'

'I will manage, Dhruv. It is okay. I just want to be with you.'

'Avni, you can trust me totally. Don't ever think that I want to leave you. I just want to see you smiling and I thought this is the best for you.'

'No, Dhruv. You can't say that to a girl like me. I have never felt for any other guy like I have felt for you. I can't feel this for any other guy,' she said and started crying again.

'Okay, fine. Stop crying now. Will you?'

'Yes.'

Avni kept crying and I kept silent. Tears were in my eyes too.

'You won't leave me, right, Dhruv?' she asked, sniffling.

'I won't ever leave you, Avni. I promise.'

23

I reached Kolkata. It was my colleague Meghna's wedding reception. She was finally married to the love of her life, Achal. Since I was friends with both of them and I'd already missed their wedding ceremony, I did not want to miss their reception. I looked at the decorations. Meghna and Achal were both from modest means. Meghna was a Bengali and Achal was a Kannadiga. The arrangements at the reception were really grand. People from two different states were trying to converse in English with each other. I could see happy faces everywhere. Love marriages mean happiness after all.

I had met Meghna's mother once when she visited Bangalore but I could not see her in the reception hall. Meghna and Achal waved at me as our eyes met. Meghna looked beautiful, with a heavy dress, jewellery and hands and feet full of mehndi. Achal wore a cream-coloured sherwani. I ran on to the stage with a small gift and got some pictures clicked with them. I could see a different happiness on their face—of relief, of finding that right partner, and of finally living with someone you can love for the rest of your life.

I was sitting in the open area enjoying the fountain and greenery all around. I met Achal and Meghna's parents who greeted me with tight hugs.

'Next marriage is yours. You have to invite us,' Meghna's mom said.

'Sure, Aunty,' I said.

'Okay, Dhruv, we have to receive a few guests. Have a great time and please have something to eat,' Meghna's dad said and left. He looked healthier than the last time I had seen him.

Meghna and Achal were finally done with their reception around 9 p.m.

'Thank you so much for coming. It really means a lot, Dhruv,' they said.

'I am the lucky one to see you both getting married. How does it feel, Achal?'

'Life is not safe any more,' he said. We all laughed.

'Same here,' Meghna said. Achal and I laughed, clapping our hands.

'You both look so beautiful together,' I said.

'She is looking beautiful because I chose that saree for her,' Achal said.

'Excuse me. It is not about the saree. It is about the girl wearing the saree,' Meghna said.

'Girls will never accept the truth,' Achal said. I laughed again. I was so happy to see them that I forgot my own situation, my own love story.

'You both continue. I'll be back, Dad is calling,' Meghna said.

'So, when are you getting married? I am hearing a lot about you lately,' Achal said.

'Maa and Dad are looking for a girl.'

'But Meghna said that you are with a girl.'

'We might not get married, Achal. Indian culture. She is manglik.'

'So what? I mean, yes, I understand, but what did the girl say?'

'Who, Avni? She wants to marry me but Maa is not ready to accept her.'

Meghna arrived with three bowls of ice cream on a tray. 'So, what did I miss?' she asked.

'You told me about that girl, right? Dhruv is not getting married to her,' Achal said, looking at Meghna.

I explained the whole story to both of them.

'Did your families match your kundlis, by the way?' I asked.

'My family did not. Achal's family did but our kundlis did not match,' Meghna said.

'How did you both get married then?' I asked.

'We need two people to agree to get married. We don't need a pandit to convince us to get married, Dhruv,' Meghna said.

'If all girls think like you, this world would be such a beautiful place. By the way, how much dowry did you get for marrying her, Achal?' I asked Achal playfully.

'Bad luck. I had to give her parents dowry to marry her, bro. I was not finding a girl to marry. I had no other option,' Achal said. We all laughed hard.

'Dhruv, Can I give you one piece of advice? Don't run behind any girl. If she wants to really marry you, she will find a way, or else she will give you an excuse,' Achal said.

'I agree. Nowadays, some girls are very smart. All they want is to spend time with a guy for a few years and then refuse him when it comes to marriage. I mean, I really can't believe some girls are doing this,' Meghna said.

'Just tell me one thing. Is Avni beautiful?' Achal asked.

'Let's check that right now. Do one thing, call her. Video call her,' Meghna said.

'Right now?'

'Yes, right now. I will talk to her.'

I made a video call.

'Oh my god. Someone is looking hot,' Avni said.

'Avni, relax. You're on speaker. Meghna and Achal are with me too,' I said.

'Oh no. You should have told me. Okay, wait. I'm coming back,' she said and returned after a few seconds.

'Am I looking pretty now?' she asked as she came back on the call.

'Avni, they can hear you,' I said.

'Hahaha,' Meghna and Achal laughed when I turned the camera towards them. They said hi to Avni.

'Oh my god. She is actually beautiful. How did you get her, Dhruv?' Meghna said.

'Lucky me, can I say?' I said.

'Many, many congratulations to both of you. And I am sorry that I could not come,' Avni said.

'We're seeing you. That is more than enough,' Achal said.

'Avni, don't mind. He is flirting with you now. Before marriage, he used to flirt with me too. That is why I fell for him,' Meghna said. We all laughed.

'When are you calling us for your wedding?' Meghna asked. I fell silent all of a sudden.

'I hope this year. In fact, I want to marry Dhruv as soon as possible. But there are a few issues.'

'Issues will always be there. In fact, issues make us realize whether we really want to be with that one person or not, right?'

'I wish I was with you guys. I need a break badly and I need to be with someone like you. I am really tense,' Avni said.

'We will surely meet soon, Avni, and I must say that Dhruv loves you a lot,' Meghna said.

'And one more thing. You are really beautiful and Dhruv is really handsome. So, please marry him,' Achal said. We all laughed.

'It is my dream to marry him.'

I felt blessed.

'Okay, guys, enjoy and congratulations once again. Hope to meet you soon,' Avni said and disconnected.

'Now, you have seen her. What do you think?' I asked.

'Don't worry. She is a nice girl,' Meghna said.

'That's why I don't want to lose her.'

'She should be worried about losing you too. Love is not a one-sided emotion, Dhruv,' Meghna said.

'Thanks, guys. I'm feeling so nice after coming here. Really,' I said.

After that, the three of us had some food together as we were really hungry. I met Achal's dad and mom once again. I was having a very stress-free and amazing evening after a long time. And I had seen Avni on a video call after so many days. I missed her. I loved her. I wanted to marry her.

I took the flight to Patna the next morning.

'Maa, listen to me once,' I said.

Maa took a deep breath and then released it. She was doing pranayama. Baba Ramdev was on the TV screen.

'Dhruv, focus on your pranayama. We can talk later,' Maa said.

I took a deep breath and released it. Baba Ramdev started talking about marriage. Everyone in the audience opened their eyes, though Maa kept hers shut.

'I don't believe in kundli matching at all. God has given us birth. God will take care of us. There are many people who say that mangliks are not good for marriage. I would suggest you should marry only mangliks. They are the best,' Baba Ramdev said. Maa opened her eyes as she heard that.

'Maa, did you hear that?' I said. 'Come on, Maa, you follow Baba Ramdev. Listen to him at least.'

Maa closed her eyes and took another deep breath.

'Dhruv, haven't I told you this before? You want her to be admitted to the hospital?' Dad had come in.

'Sorry, Dad. I was just asking Maa to listen to Baba Ramdev.'

'Dhruv, am I clear? Don't bring the same topic up in this house,' Dad said and left.

I had never seen him so angry. I don't understand one point. If they all follow Baba Ramdev, then why don't they believe in what he is saying? I ignored Baba Ramdev and focused on Maa. She opened her eyes, met my eyes and closed hers again.

Being in love is a crime in this society.

24

After a month, I was coming back to Hyderabad. Avni had told me that she would come to the airport to pick me up. I was really excited. I was calm and relaxed for the whole flight except when it finally landed. It feels really special when there is someone waiting for you at the airport. After collecting my baggage, I dialled Avni's number but it wasn't ringing. I tried again but it said that the phone was not reachable. I came out but I did not see her at the Arrivals. I dialled her number again but the call was not connecting. There was hardly any charge left in my battery and my phone finally switched off. Damn. *Where is she?* I took out a power bank and started charging my phone. I looked around once again when I saw someone waving at me. It was Anju, Avni's college friend and roommate. I hurried towards her with my luggage.

'Hi Anju. Long time since we met. Where is Avni?' I said, smiling.

'Hi Dhruv. Yes, long time,' she said.

'Where is Avni?' I repeated.

'Can we go to the cab first? I'll tell you,' she said, in a tense tone.

Why did Anju sound worried?

'Avni's phone is switched off. Is she all right?' I asked as we walked towards the cab pick-up point.

'Dhruv, actually I wanted to tell you that—'

'What happened, Anju? Where is Avni? Why are you so tense?'

I was getting nervous now. Why was Anju not saying anything?

'Dhruv, I just wanted to tell you that Avni loved you.'

'Why are you saying that *she loved me*?'

'Dhruv actually . . .?'

'Anju, will you stop creating this suspense? Now, you are really scaring me. She is okay, right? Please tell me.'

'No Dhruv. She is not,' Anju said.

'What happened? Where is she?'

'She is in the hospital.'

'What? But why? What happened?'

'Nothing. First, please relax and wipe that sweat off your face. It's not so bad.'

'So, she is all right. Correct?'

'Yes, she is. Just a little food poisoning,' Anju said. I felt relieved that Avni was okay.

'But what did she eat?'

'As you know, she has been with me for the last month but yesterday, she ate something from outside. Generally, she does not do that. She was not well after she reached my flat. She vomited a lot. I took her to the hospital where the doctor told her that she had food poisoning. Also, Avni has become very weak, Dhruv. She is not eating properly. The doctor scolded me, thinking that I was her sister. He asked her to be admitted for a day.'

'Oh no. So, she really is in the hospital?'

'Yes. I will drop you to your room. You can freshen up and then come to the hospital.'

'No, Anju. I will come with you to the hospital now. I am okay.'

'But Avni won't be okay. She told me to tell you to get some rest and then you can come in the afternoon.'

'Who is she? The prime minister?' I said, angrily.

'Oh my god. Driver bhaiya, please take us to the hospital,' Anju said.

'Anju, can I tell you something? Please don't mind,' I said.

'Yes, Dhruv. Tell me.'

'Please don't make me scared like this about Avni again.'

'I'm really sorry. I didn't realize that even today, guys get so emotional about their girl.'

'I am not emotional, Anju. But when it comes to Avni, I get most emotional,' I said.

'I can understand. I wished someone loved me too just like you love her.'

'You will also find someone when the time is right.'

Anju looked at her watch and then at my watch.

'Isn't the time right?' Anju asked. I smiled at her sense of humour.

'Dhruv, do you really love Avni?'

'Of course I do. Why are you asking me that?'

'Because Avni loves you a lot. She cannot live without you.'

I looked at Anju and then I looked outside. The weather had turned cloudy. We reached the hospital in half an hour and went to Avni's ward. It was a small one where another patient was admitted.

'Hi Ms Avni,' I said. Avni was shocked to see me. She tried to get up from the bed.

'It's okay. Relax,' I said and took out a rose from my pocket. I had kept it there before getting on the flight.

'This is for you,' I said.

'Dhruv, what are you doing? This is a hospital,' Avni said, looking at the other patient—an old man staring at us.

'Sorry, Uncle. He is little mad,' Avni told the old man.

'No, Uncle, I am totally mad,' I said.

'Hahaha. Good girls make good guys mad,' Uncle said.

'Thanks, Uncle,' I said and handed the rose to Avni.

'I won't take it. Anju is right here. Have some shame,' Avni said.

'Anju, will you take my rose?' I said.

'Any time,' Anju said and took the rose.

'Now, are you happy?' I asked Avni.

'Very happy. You have to do drama everywhere you go, right?' Avni said.

'Yes, because life without drama is boring,' I said.

'Have you eatcn anything?' I added.

'Yes, I had soup.'

'You are the most beautiful patient I have ever seen,' I said. 'But why are you not eating properly? The doctor said that you are really not well.'

'I just don't feel like eating these days. There is too much office work, Dhruv. I have to work night shifts. Tomorrow, I have to leave for Chennai. Dad is not okay.'

'Work will always be there and tell your manager that you cannot do the night shift,' I said.

'You guys are so cute,' Anju said.

'Anju, are you recording us on your phone?' Avni said.

'Yes, your kids need to see the romance of their parents in the hospital,' Anju said. Uncle and I laughed. The nurse came in.

'Who is laughing so loudly?' she asked.

'That guy,' Anju said, pointing towards me.

'Sir. You should leave now. Visiting hours are over,' the nurse said, looking at me.

'But we are family,' I said.

'Ma'am, you can come and stay with the patient in the night. Gents are not allowed,' the nurse said.

Avni nudged me after the nurse left.

'Happy now? I told you,' Avni said.

'It's okay, Avni. I will get your clothes at night. Tomorrow, they will discharge you anyway. I spoke to the nurse,' Anju said.

'Dhruv, please drop her home,' Avni said.

'Of course, now she has my rose. So, technically she is my half-girlfriend.'

The old uncle laughed so loudly that the entire room echoed. Anju and I ran out of the ward before the nurse could come and scold us again.

We reached Anju's flat in the afternoon. She paused at the entrance.

'Anju, I heard you and Avni when you were talking. I was outside Avni's ward,' I said.

'What did you hear?' Anju asked.

'I heard Avni saying she didn't want you to let me come inside your flat,' I said.

Anju looked at me.

'Even I want to ask you so many questions, Dhruv,' Anju said, as she opened the door of her flat. She asked me to come inside.

I sat down on a chair. Anju was standing.

'Did you tell Avni that you cannot marry her?' Anju said immediately.

'Oh come on, Anju. That was nothing.'

'Nothing? Do you know what is happening to Avni these days? Do you know what she is going through?'

'What do you mean?'

'Avni is not fine, Dhruv. She is not telling you anything and she is forcing me also to hide it from you.'

'I did not get you.'

'How do I make you understand, Dhruv, that this girl loves you more than anything? You have no idea about it.'

'I know it.'

'You don't know anything, Dhruv. If you knew, you wouldn't have said all those things to her.'

'Why did you say that she is not fine, Anju?'

'When a girl loves a guy so much that she is ready to go against her own parents, despite being their only child, do you know how much that guy means to her? And then, if that guy tells her that he cannot marry her, do you have any idea how that girl feels?'

'Anju, what happened to Avni?'

'Dhruv, Avni has not been fine for the last few weeks. She is not in the hospital because of some food poisoning. She's there because of you.'

'Me?'

'She has been running behind doctors for the last few weeks, Dhruv. I am the one who is taking her to the doctors.'

'For what, Anju? Tell me.'

'Panic attacks. Depression. Anxiety and what not. She is going mad, Dhruv.'

'Mad? What are you saying?'

'Yes, Dhruv. She loved you for so many years but you and your family are treating her as though she is a piece of shit. Do you know how much she slapped herself last night? I have never seen her like that. She got back-to-back panic attacks in the last one week. Yesterday night, it was so serious that I had to rush her to the doctor.'

'Why did she not tell me?'

'She has not even informed her parents. She is living here because she cannot take these medicines at her home. Doctors have said that she should not take any stress or else her condition will only get worse.'

'Why didn't Avni ever tell me all this?'

'She won't tell you. She only tells me. Do you know her relatives told her that you will leave her just like most guys do? But she said, "Dhruv is not like that. Dhruv loves me." They said everything a girl should never hear in her whole life but still, she was taking your side. You don't know, Dhruv, how much you mean to her, but what did she get from you in return?'

'I did not know her relatives treated her like this, Anju.'

'Because she never told you. Because she will never tell you. Because she cares about you. Do you know how disgusted she felt about herself, how much she cried that whole night, how much I tried to console her that you won't leave her at any cost? But all her patience, her trust broke that day when you told her that you cannot marry her. She broke that day. Since then, I got to know about her condition. She loved you for so many years. She loved you since college and what did she get?'

'No, Anju. She did not love me since college.'

'Because she never told you, right? You have no idea how happy she was when you met her in Goa. She was crying on the phone when she called me and told me about you. She did not let me sleep that whole night. When she returned to Bangalore from Pratap's marriage, she showed me all your photos. Do you know that she has kept your things, small gifts, including the papers which have your handwriting? She has kept everything safe with her. In college, on your birthday every year, she would buy a gift but she would never give it to you. She would say, "What if Dhruv likes someone else? He won't like it." From your pen cap to your used notebooks, everything means so much to her. And still, you are telling her that you will leave her?'

'I just told Avni that my family is not ready even today, Anju. I did not know that one sentence of mine could break Avni like this.'

'Do you know, every time you spoke to her during college days, even once in a week or once in a month, she would be so happy for the rest of the day saying, "Dhruv spoke to me today. Dhruv gave me this. Dhruv gave me that. Dhruv said he likes to spend time with me. Dhruv said he missed me."'

'How do you know all this, Anju?'

'Because Avni has told me all this. Do you want any more proof? Look around. You will see the proof.'

I fell silent for a moment. I looked around. The last time I came to Anju's flat, I did not have a good look at her room. The room was neat and all the shelves were full of stylish new items. And then I saw a shelf which had old diaries and a few old boxes. It was weird. On one side, there was only new stuff and on the other, an entire shelf was full of old stuff.

My eyes fell on a jacket on that shelf which looked familiar. I felt that I had seen it somewhere before. I walked to the shelf and looked at the jacket again. I tried to recall where I had seen it. It was the same jacket I had given Avni on the last day of our college, as it was cold, and I had forgotten to take it back. Her bus left early and I could not even meet her to tell her goodbye on our last day.

I wondered why this jacket was lying in Anju's house and why Avni had kept it so safely. There were many diaries. I felt tempted to open each one and read them to know what was written inside. I picked up one diary from the top and flipped the pages.

Every page of the diary started with the name Dhruv. I turned the pages, as I was getting impatient. On every page, Avni had written how she felt after meeting me each day. On a few pages, she had written how much she missed me when I bunked college or could not meet her. I was shocked. She had mentioned in a few pages how she would pray every night after our placement, that I would get an offer from the same company as she did. I could not believe my eyes.

I turned a page.

Dhruv, I don't know if I will ever show you this diary. Maybe I will never be able to tell you how much you mean to me, Dhruv. Yours and only Yours, Avni.

I turned to the next page.

Dhruv, I did not like it when you spoke to that dumb girl, Swati, who keeps hitting on you. I am really jealous of her.

In all the pages, it looked as if Avni was talking to me as she had written my name everywhere. I turned another page.

Today, we fought. I felt that I had lost you. I came back home and cried a lot, could not eat anything. I won't eat until you talk to me again. I missed you, Dhruv. So, I said sorry to you even if it was your mistake this time. I love you, Dhruv. Will you love me, Dhruv? You won't leave me alone in this world, right Dhruv? Avni only belongs to Dhruv, today, tomorrow, and forever.

My eyes fell on a door that led to the bedroom. I could see a lot of photos hanging on the wall inside. I looked closer. I entered the room, and I was shocked. There were photos of me, from the college days where I was standing, laughing, dancing. I had never taken these pictures if I remembered correctly. Then who took them? Did Avni click my pics without telling me all the time? I recalled Pratap's marriage where he showed me random pics with Avni from college days too.

The girl whom I was asking a day before to leave, the girl whom my Maa thinks is not safe for me, the girl whom everyone thinks is not good for my life has loved me for so many years without even telling me—and this is how I behave with her? Am I just supposed to throw her out of my life and marry another girl? How will she even live without me, if I leave her like this for no reason? She won't tell me but I know she will never love anyone again.

'So, you saw it?' Anju said.

'She never told me, Anju,' I said and broke into tears.

'Avni is like that only, Dhruv. You know, there were times when you did not talk to her in college because you both had fought. She would come to me and cry the whole night. And then she would write in her diary. I told her so many times that she should share her feelings with you but she said, "What if he doesn't love me?" She did not want to lose you. I felt it was weird. I mean, everyone should say if they love someone or how else would people get to know?'

'Only I can understand what she means by that,' I said.

'Maybe. I don't know when I will get a guy who will propose to me and give me flowers like this,' Anju said, looking at the rose I had given her. I smiled and felt a little better.

'You are so beautiful. How come no one has proposed to you?'

'Sometimes, being beautiful means that you get to meet only guys who want to flirt with you.'

'It's not like that. Being in love is not easy. You are safe, I must say. Look, how much Avni and I are struggling.'

'But still you are not giving up.'

'After seeing all this, do you think I can ever leave her?'

'You should have seen her flat in Bangalore. A room was dedicated to your photos hung on the wall. Avni loves you a lot, Dhruv. I mean, I can only request you not to leave her. No girl or no guy dies if someone leaves them, but certainly, they are not the same person any more if that happens.'

'I won't leave her, Anju.'

'You won't believe that all these years, I felt that her love story was just a fairy tale but it was not. She cannot live without you, Dhruv. She won't tell you. That is why I am telling you.'

25

Two Weeks Later

It was Avni's birthday, and I was stuck with my office work. Technically, it was my birthday too. I mean, as per the Hindu calendar, today was supposed to be my birthday. That's why Avni wanted me to be in Chennai at any cost. My manager, Murali, suddenly informed me that there was an important meeting with our onshore team in the US. Damn. I told Avni that I would come down to her house and wish her a happy birthday. I switched on the laptop. The meeting was supposed to start exactly at midnight. If it were just thirty minutes later, I would have managed to go to Avni's house, wish her and come back. However, after I got Murali's message, I informed Avni that we wouldn't be able to meet each other.

She said, 'It's fine. We can meet tomorrow.'

I was angry and upset, feeling really bad about my fate. I had come to Chennai a day before with so many plans. It was

11.55 p.m. when I got a message from Murali. He informed me that the meeting had been cancelled. I cursed him. Why did he do this to me? He had spoilt the whole thing. Now, the only way to wish Avni was through a video call.

Avni's house was just fifteen minutes from my apartment. So, I really wanted to wish her happy birthday, in person exactly at midnight. I know, it was childish of me to behave like that but I liked being childish these days. It was 11.58 p.m. when I checked my network. We can't even trust our phone network when we have bad fate. It was 11.59 p.m. when I dialled Avni on a video call. She picked up the phone immediately. We looked at each other but we didn't say a word. She was probably waiting to wish me before I wished her happy birthday. It was midnight when we both said happy birthday to each other.

'I'm sorry I couldn't come to meet you,' I said.

'It's fine. I'm glad you called,' she said.

'My manager spoilt the whole thing.'

'Are you in the meeting? Can you just keep your laptop on mute for a few seconds and come out on the balcony?'

'The meeting is cancelled, Avni,' I said.

'Your meeting is cancelled?'

'Yes.'

'Okay, fine. Come to the balcony, please.'

'But why?' I asked, when I suddenly noticed something. A parking board appeared behind Avni in the video call. A similar parking board was close to my apartment's exit.

'Avni, are you here?' I asked.

'Yes. Now will you come out?' she said.

When I came to the balcony, she was waving at me. I waved back. She sent me a flying kiss. She had parked her Scooty at the side and was holding her helmet in her left hand.

'Why did you come here, idiot? It's so late!' I said, still speaking to her on the video call.

'Now, don't scold me on my birthday. Come down fast. Cut the cake and I will leave.'

I dressed up in a few seconds and ran downstairs. Avni was wearing a maroon salwar and churidar. She had her specs on, which she mostly wears at work. She looked so cute. She smiled when she saw me. I felt like scolding her for coming at this time.

I wanted to hug her but she resisted, keeping one hand distance from me and making sure no one could see us.

This girl is so scared all the time but she would still do these silly things.

'Are you mad to come out alone at this time?' I said.

'Yes. If you had come to wish me, I wouldn't have had to come here,' she said, removing her specs as though she was going to scold me more.

'It is not safe to come out at this time,' I said.

'Dhruv, please cut the cake. I have to leave soon,' she said jumping up and down.

She picked up the cake hanging on her Scooty handle and kept it on the seat. Lighting two candles that illuminated her face, Avni started singing 'Happy Birthday'. We both blew the candles at the same time.

Some dogs barked from a distance. They were also celebrating our birthday.

'Oh no, will they bite?' Avni said, listening to the dogs.

'I told you not to come at this time—'

'Happy birthday, Dhruv Mehta,' she said and gave me a piece of cake. I hugged her.

'Leave me, leave me,' Avni said, as I pasted a portion of the cake on her cheek.

'Happy birthday to the cutest girl I know. Always be happy like this,' I said.

She wiped her face with her dupatta.

'Okay, I'm leaving,' she said, in a hurry.

'Wait here,' I said and ran inside the apartment.

I took the bike keys of a guy who was a student. He lived next door to my flat and I had often helped him with his college projects. Now, it was his turn for *guru dakshina*. I came down. Avni had both hands on her waist and was standing on the other side of the road, throwing an attitude as if I had made her wait for an hour.

'Stop throwing attitude and start your Scooty,' I said.

'Wait. Let me take a selfie. You also put on your helmet,' she said as she did the same and sat on her Scooty.

We took a selfie, a birthday selfie in helmets, a memory for a lifetime. Girls always want memories and more memories.

'Let's go now. I will drop you and then come back,' I said, starting my bike.

'Dhruv, you can stay. I can go alone. I am fine,' she said.

'But just now you asked me to wear the helmet.'

'That was for the selfie. See, the photo looks so cute,' she said and showed me the selfie.

Of course, she was looking cute and I was looking like a roadside loafer chasing this cute girl. Girls never care how the boy looks when they take a selfie. They just make sure that they look cute and then they declare the whole pic as cute.

'You stay here, I'm telling you it's okay,' she said again.

'Will you stop arguing with me? It's my birthday too,' I said.

I told her not to honk on the empty road but she was in the mood. She was honking on the empty road and then the obvious thing happened. All the dogs on the streets started chasing her. She was in the front, the dogs were behind her and I was behind the dogs. It was funny and scary at the same time. We somehow sped off and got rid of the dogs. I laughed at Avni when I reached her house. I said bye to her and immediately came back to my room. And then we spoke to each other on a video call.

'Thanks for making this birthday a little special. I wasn't expecting this,' I said.

'I know, you are hopeless,' she said, yawning.

'Yes, I am. I agree.'

'Thank god I don't have a manager like Murali.'

'Even if you had, these managers won't disturb girls like you.'

'Why?'

'Men will be men, Avni!'

'Avni, Avni, is it you?' I could hear her mom shouting from the other room.

'Okay, I will hang up now. Amma is awake. You are coming tomorrow to my home. You promised me,' she said and disconnected.

I realized I was twenty-six years old but whenever I was with Avni, I felt like a teenager again. I had heard of girls leaving the guy they loved and marrying another guy for their social status. Maybe because there are only a few girls like Avni who are trustworthy. Maybe it's a girl's innocence and trustworthiness that keeps a guy loyal to her. With Avni, life felt so complete. I wanted to live once again for her. Just a year ago, I was asking myself why we are born and what makes life worth living. A year ago, I hadn't met Avni. I did not know if I would meet her ever again. But now, I have got all my answers. I want to live for her, I want to see her smile, I want to keep her happy, I want to bear her tantrums. With her, I feel I am the same twenty-year-old Dhruv. Now, I know why people want to be in love. They want to care for someone genuinely. They want to have a purpose in life. And love gives you that purpose, which is to live for someone else.

The Next Day

'Avni, I am really scared to come to your house. Don't you think it's too risky for me? Will your uncles beat me?' I asked.

'What are you even saying? Dhruv, people do so much in love. You can't do this much?'

'Avni, I love you. I can't live without you but I can't die for you, my baby.'

'You won't have to die for me, stop being so dramatic! I am trying to introduce you to my family and you're shying away.'

'Okay, fine, I'll come but make sure I sit next to the door. If something is fishy, I'll run away immediately. And please keep the main gate wide open,' I said.

Avni laughed.

'Is this a joke for you? My heart is beating at the speed of a bullet train.'

'Just relax and be there on time. Okay?'

'Okay, fine.'

'Good boy. I'll see you soon.'

I had slept for two hours last night. The rest of the night, I was planning my escape from Avni's house in case things got out of hand.

Shall I book a sniper who can be in another building keeping a watch on me? Yes, that was one of the many thoughts that had crossed my mind. *Shall I wear shorts? I can run faster in that.*

I had thought of all the possible scenarios.

I reached Avni's house. Avni's uncles had folded their dhotis up to their knees. They then unfolded them all at the same time, when they saw me. And guess what? *Where did Avni make me sit?* Right in the middle of all these people. I swear on my mom's mom, I have never been so scared in my entire life. Avni's uncles looked at me and I looked at the main gate. It was kept open. I felt safe. Avni looked at me from the kitchen. Today, she was wearing an off-white churidar salwar suit.

'Avni, keep your distance from me as much as possible,' I mumbled, as she brought me a glass of water.

All her uncles, who were really healthy-looking, were staring at me as though I was going to pass a bill in the Parliament. I faked a smile at them, turning my head from extreme left to extreme right. Something was cooking in the kitchen.

Then Avni came towards me. This girl was walking up to me as though her entire family wasn't sitting there. She was courageous. She sat beside me.

'Dhruv, can you come to the kitchen, please?' she mumbled in my ear and left.

Everyone looked at me. Going into the kitchen was like inviting trouble for myself but I had to be courageous today. I silently got up, adjusted my shirt and stood up straight, but my legs were shivering with fear.

Relax, Dhruv, take a deep breath.

'Why did you call me, Avni? Do you know how risky it is for me to come here?'

'Amma told me to put some masala in this curry. I forgot what she said. Can you help me?'

'What? You don't know what your mom said? Are you serious?'

'Amma and appa have gone to the neighbour's home. It's already late. Do something, please.'

'Call her, Avni. How would I know which masala to put?'

'Amma left her phone here,' Avni said, making a puppy face.

'Look, I will put the masala of my choice. Are you okay with that?'

'Just make it taste nice.'

'Okay. Move aside.'

For the next twenty minutes, I kept asking Avni for all the masalas needed to make the aloo paneer tasty.

'When did South Indians start eating aloo paneer?' I asked.

'Dad loves it and now all my uncles love it.'

We waited for the dish to get ready. Meanwhile, Avni stood in one corner away from me as though she was scared of me.

'Where is my birthday gift?' I asked.

'I called you here. Is it not enough?'

'Wow, Avni. You call me here on my birthday and make me cook food for you. I don't think any other guy could have gotten a better gift.'

Avni giggled and said, 'Don't expect too much from me. You have no idea, I have not slept the whole night.'

'Why?'

'Just thinking about how I'll propose to you.'

'What? Propose to me?'

'I never proposed to you like other girls do.'

'There's no need to be so dramatic.'

'But I want drama. So, close your eyes.'

'Avni, relax.'

'Dhruv, close your eyes.'

'What? Why?'

'Just do it, na.'

'What if when I open them again, you put red chilli powder in them?'

'Bad joke. Now close your eyes, fast!'

'Fine.' I closed my eyes. Meanwhile, god only knows how the curry was turning out to be.

'Now, open your eyes,' Avni said.

There was a tulsi leaf in her hands.

'Will you marry me, Dhruv?' Avni asked.

I took the tulsi from her hands, put it in my pocket and hugged her.

'You are so romantic,' I said.

It sounded like someone was walking to the kitchen. Avni pushed me aside and moved to a corner.

'You are so unromantic,' I said.

No one came inside the kitchen. The curry was ready. Avni liked it.

'Avni, listen na.'

'Yeah?'

'I helped you cook, right? Won't you say anything?'

'Yes. Thank you.'

'Just thanks?'

'Then what else do you want?'

'Can I squeeze your cheeks and you promise you won't scream?'

'Okay, fine. What's with you boys? Why do you have to pinch our cheeks? Appa often does that to amma.'

'Is it? How romantic.'

'Yes, and I have caught them many times. But Dad stops when he sees me.'

I guffawed and Avni shushed me.

'Dhruv, lower your volume.'

I pinched Avni's cheeks. It gave me immense happiness. Aunty suddenly came inside the kitchen. Thank god she did not see me do that.

'That one, Avni,' I said, pointing towards a masala bottle.

'What is Dhruv doing here?' Aunty asked. I turned to her.

Aunty too looked cute today. She was wearing specs. No wonder Uncle pinches her cheeks.

'He helped me with the curry,' Avni said. Aunty tasted it. She said something in Tamil.

'Dhruv, what did you put?' Aunty asked.

'Just added laung and daal-cheeni. And ginger-garlic paste.'

'But I did not have all this in the kitchen,' Aunty said.

'I got it from the nearby shop,' Avni said.

Aunty looked impressed. Her daughter looked upset, seeing her mom impressed by me.

'Dhruv,' Aunty said.

'Yes, Aunty,' I said.

'Sorry for speaking rudely to you that day, beta. Avni's dad was angry about what had happened. So, just to save you from his anger, I spoke angrily to you.'

'It's okay, Aunty. All men are the same,' I said.

'That is true,' Aunty said.

We heard someone coming into the kitchen.

'Surjamukhi!' Uncle said and was about to hug his wife when Aunty pushed him aside. Avni and I stood frozen. We did not know how to react. In fact, we were surprised to hear Uncle calling Aunty . . . *Surjamukhi?* Aunty glared at Uncle. She might have been feeling shy.

'What are you both doing here?' Uncle asked me.

'I was helping Avni, Uncle,' I said.

'I was helping Dhruv, Appa,' Avni said.

Uncle looked confused. Even I was confused. Uncle tasted the curry.

'It's nice,' he said.

'Dhruv made it,' Aunty said, without making eye contact with me and Avni.

'Salt is a little too much,' Uncle clarified and left the kitchen.

These men are always angry with their daughter's boyfriend.

'Surjamukhi? Amma? How romantic? Since when has this been going on?' Avni asked her mom.

I couldn't control myself and burst out laughing. Aunty ran out of the kitchen out of shyness. Avni and I high-fived each other.

'Surjamukhi!' We both repeated and then high-fived again.

'Your dad is so romantic. I didn't know that,' I said.

'He's in a good mood today, hahahahaha. Okay, listen. My cousin's marriage talks are going to happen today,' Avni said.

'In your house?'

'Yes. They don't have a nice house. So, they wanted the boy's family to come here.'

'But what if the boy chooses you instead of her?'

'Shut up.'

'Good, because in all South Indian movies, it happens. Remember *Roja*?'

'Dhruv, focus. You just help me with serving food and cold drinks. Am I asking too much from you?'

'Yes, of course, you are asking so much from me. But it is better than sitting in the flat, doing nothing. I am loving it.'

'Great.'

We heard a few people talking at the entrance. Avni's cousin's family had arrived. They all looked humble and were very polite. The girl's father touched Avni's dad's feet with tears in his eyes.

'You are our family,' Uncle said and hugged him. Avni's uncles greeted the girl's family with great respect.

After some time, the boy's family arrived. The guy was good-looking. The girl's father and mother rushed to the gate to welcome them into the house. Avni asked me to serve them water.

I followed my future wife's orders instantly. It feels nice to be a part of such ceremonies. Avni's mom didn't look too happy seeing me doing that. Avni's dad glared at me as I handed him a glass of water. My legs started shivering after that. Somehow, I continued serving water to everyone and came running back to the kitchen.

'Your dad is no less than Amrish Puri,' I said.

Avni giggled and told me to shut up so she could hear everything that was happening outside where everyone was seated and talking. The talks continued for another hour. It was boring but the best part was that I got time to spend with the girl I love.

When would my parents come and ask for this girl's hand for me? When will I feel complete? Avni wore a *gajra* in her hair and the smell enveloped me. It was so enchanting that I felt like announcing, 'Listen, guys, I have decided to marry Avni and she has decided to marry me. Come for our wedding.'

But I knew that they would beat me up. So, I controlled myself. Just then, I heard people laughing. Avni peeped out of the kitchen.

'The girl's father and the boy's father are hugging each other,' Avni mumbled.

'Is the marriage fixed?' I asked.

'Mostly yes,' Avni said.

I couldn't help it and came out of the kitchen to see the full scene. The boy's mother asked the girl to take a bite of a sweet from her hand. The boy smiled as the girl did that.

'Wow. They asked for dowry?' I muttered.

'No, Dhruv. No dowry.'

'Wow. Arranged marriage without dowry?'

'What do you mean? We don't take dowry any more.'

'But why? I will take it,' I said.

'How much?' Avni asked.

'Just one kiss before office every day.'

'How shameless.'

'Only for you.'

Both the girl's and the boy's families left soon. There were only Avni's uncles and her parents, and me, standing in the corridor of her house. I stood in a corner as Avni had asked me to wait. She told me that she would pack food for me as I had not eaten. I was getting late as my return flight was in a few hours.

'Didi, go inside,' Avni's Mama, Raghunandan said.

Avni's mom looked at me and then at Raghu Uncle.

'But Raghu,' Aunty said. She looked tense.

'Please go inside, Didi,' he repeated.

Aunty went inside.

'Why did you come here, rascal?' Raghu Uncle said, looking at me.

'Today is Avni's birthday, Uncle. She invited me here,' I said in a scared tone.

'See Jiju. He is again using our daughter's name. He is fooling us even now. He is going to use our daughter and then leave her like other guys,' Raghu Uncle said, looking at Avni's dad.

'I did not get you, Raghu Uncle,' I said.

'Don't try to act smart. I know guys like you. Why don't your parents come and talk to us? If they are not ready to get our daughter married to you, then why are you fooling her?'

'Uncle, I am not fooling Avni. I have told her everything,' I said.

'What have you told her? That you cannot marry her.'

I kept quiet. I had no answer.

'I know these guys, Jiju. They need to be treated nicely with slippers,' Raghu Uncle said.

I stood there without uttering a word. I did not want to create a scene.

'Close the gate,' Raghu Uncle told his brother. I waited quietly where I was.

'Now tell me. Will you dare to meet our daughter again?' Raghu Uncle said, holding my collar.

'Leave it. Leave it right now, I say,' Avni screamed, as she came out of the kitchen.

'Leave it, I say!' she screamed again.

Raghu Uncle did not leave my collar.

'How dare you touch him? How dare you? He is alone. So, you can do anything to him? Who the hell are you?' Avni screamed at Raghu Uncle.

'Avni,' her dad interrupted.

'No, Appa. How dare they touch him? He has come here because I called him. He is a simple guy who has been in love with me since college but never told me. Every time I was late for home from college or missed the college bus, he would miss his own bus and drop me safely home before going to his. His parents would be worried about him but he always told me that if I reached home late, my parents would be worried. He gave me all the love and respect that a girl can only dream of. He waited for eight years for me, Appa. He did not stop loving me for a single day. Which guy will do that today, Appa? Please tell me. He told me today that he is scared to come here but I told him to come. For my happiness, he just came here so that I don't get hurt. His family is against me, Appa, but still he came to my city to meet me. He is fighting with his family for me, Appa. Can't you see this? Look at him, Appa. Will a guy like him make a fool of me? And all of you made a mockery of him as though he is a nobody. He is fighting with every single family member for your daughter, Appa. And you all are judging him, insulting him, threatening him. Is this how he is supposed to be treated?' Avni said.

I had tears in my eyes and I tried to control them.

'You will ask for help from us when he will ruin your life,' Raghu Uncle said.

'No, he will not. You are ruining my life by interfering in it. Who told you to interfere in my matters? Did I ask you, Uncle?'

Raghu Uncle's brother came forward to hit me this time.

'You dare not touch him, I'm telling you!' Avni shouted.

Raghu Uncle's brother stopped.

'Dhruv, leave from here,' Avni said.

'Avni, what are you saying? I won't leave you like this.'

'Dhruv. They don't care about you. They don't care about me. The only thing they care about is their society. Goddamn it. They only want their community to be happy by ruining our lives. They don't want to see us happy. Please leave, Dhruv. Please. I beg you. Oh my god. They insulted you like this. I am sorry, Dhruv,' Avni broke into tears.

'Raghu, step back,' Avni's dad said.

'I am sorry, Dhruv,' Avni's dad said and calmed Avni down. Aunty came running to us.

'Didn't I tell you not to do this? He is a genuine guy, Raghu,' Aunty said.

More tears sprang up in my eyes. Maybe I was missing my Maa. I felt her in Aunty's voice.

'I am just asking you to get them married. People are spreading stories, Didi,' Raghu Uncle said.

'Then let them. It is our problem. Not yours,' Avni shouted.

'If this is how your daughter talks to us, we will never come here again,' Raghu Uncle said.

'No, Raghu. I apologize for her behaviour,' Avni's dad said and made Raghu Uncle sit down.

'I will marry her, Uncle. I give my word to you,' I said, looking at Raghu Uncle.

'When will you marry her, kid? Look at her. No girl in our entire family is as good as her but still people are talking about her character,' Raghu Uncle said.

'Soon, Uncle. Please give me some more time,' I said.

'Okay, fine. But if anything happens to our daughter, I will be the first to meet you.'

I nodded.

'I didn't mean to disrespect you, Dhruv. I just love this girl a lot. We all do. She is innocent. She cannot hear one word against you. And we still don't know if you are the right guy for her.'

'He is the *right guy* for me. He will always be,' Avni said.

'Then we are happy that things are clear. And I apologize for my behaviour, Avni. We all love you,' Raghu Uncle said.

Avni calmed down. Her uncle asked me to have food with them. After that, they dropped me off safely at the airport. Avni came along with them. She was still scared. I told her not to worry and returned to Hyderabad. I realized how much Avni loved me. She fought with everyone for me. Which girl does that in today's world? Most girls will just leave the guy and forget him. Avni once more proved that love is not just about spending good times but about standing with each other in tough times.

26

Eight days later, I got an email from my manager. I had to travel to the US in a week. It was good news. In one way, Maa would not be worried about my marriage if I was not around. She wouldn't talk about it for a month at least, as we would be in different time zones.

I reached Texas, and I must say that Bala's Didi, Shanti, who lives in Texas, saved my life or else I would have had to struggle for food, shelter and transportation. Her twins, Anuj and Dhanush, became my stressbusters in a single day. They were just six years old. It felt nice to take the kids for an evening walk and talk to them about whatever I felt. I spoke to them about their school life and they were in depression already. I asked them why. They said that they both had fallen in love with the same girl, who was an American. I had never laughed so much listening to anyone's love story; it was also the most complicated. Since Dhanush was older by five minutes, he was asking Anuj to sacrifice Lindsey, the girl, for him. Anuj was not ready to forget Lindsey.

They did not seem interested in my love life. They said that Indian girls were boring. I laughed really hard after listening to that and asked them why. Anuj said that Indian girls don't give free hugs whereas US girls give free hugs and kisses. I laughed even harder after that. Dhanush told me not to inform Shanti Didi that they get kisses from girls or else she would send them to Bala Mama's house in India. I promised them that I wouldn't say anything to her. I was feeling better staying with two lovers who were fighting over Lindsey, day and night.

At night, I would tell Avni all this and she would laugh listening to their love issues. The workload was heavier here, and my US manager's cabin was right beside me. He would always keep a close eye on me. My stress would be relieved after meeting Dhanush and Anuj.

On my first weekend in Texas, I met the hottest girl on the planet—Miss Lindsey. I was literally laughing looking at her. She was the cutest girl I had ever seen and I fell in love with her instantly. Yes, it was love at first sight. I immediately called Avni who was going to sleep as it was night in India and told her all about Lindsey.

'Avni, I have found a new girl for myself. Hope you don't mind.'

'Who is that unlucky girl, Dhruv Mehta?'

'Her name is Lindsey, but I cannot marry her.'

'Why?'

'She is just six years old and Anuj and Dhanush are already in love with her. They would throw me out of their house if they find out about my feelings.'

Avni laughed.

'Three boys have fallen in love with the same girl. I have never heard such a story,' Avni clapped, laughing out loud.

I asked Shanti Didi if Lindsey had a sister. Shanti Didi said that she had a twin sister but she had a crush on another guy whose name was Mohan. My head was spinning after hearing this. Six-year-old kids were falling in love here. I wish Avni and I had been born here. Our love story would have been so simple. No kundli matching, no *gothra* matching and no manglik fights. Here, people just fall in love and get married.

Avni missed me a lot though she knew how much fun I was having here with Bala's nephews and their girlfriend. I am ashamed to even use the term 'girlfriend' for Lindsey. She was just six years old.

I told Avni that if she could come here, I would be the happiest person on earth. Avni told me that she would have to travel to Texas after three months once she moved to Bangalore. She said she would meet Lindsey personally and fight with her for stealing her boyfriend. I laughed on hearing that.

Maa would be really tired at night and busy in the morning. There was no other time for us to interact. So, the topic of my marriage was on hold for some time, which was good for me and Avni.

Hemant Bhaiya's wedding date was finally out and he was getting married a week before I was to travel back to India.

A day before Hemant Bhaiya's wedding, I called him. Everyone from my family was in Hyderabad as the marriage was happening there.

'Hi Hemant Bhaiya,' I said.

'Hi, my sweetest brother.'

'Many, many congratulations in advance, Bhaiya. I am so happy for you and Anjana Bhabhi. You both make a great couple.'

'We just did not meet each other like you and Avni did.'

'Sometimes, good love stories like yours take time, Bhaiya.'

'I hope Anjana falls in love with me.'

'Of course, she will. You are so sweet. Which girl won't love you?'

'Thanks, Dhruv. I must tell you something. You are coming after a week, right?'

'Yes. I'm so sorry I cannot attend your wedding. I had no option.'

'I can understand. But Aunty is trying to set you up with a girl. She was talking to Dad and planning to call you to Patna. But she wants to get your *roka* done soon. So, please be careful. Aunty is very serious this time. I have heard that you have stopped arguing with her. She was telling Dad.'

'Yes, you know that doctors have told me not to give her any sort of tension. Her reports are not good even now, Bhaiya. Anyway, my love story looks like a total waste of time now. I tried so much but no one is ready to understand. In fact, a family is coming to meet Avni tomorrow. If everything goes well, her parents are ready to fix her marriage tomorrow. I am tense already. I couldn't sleep for the last few days.'

'What? But you told her parents to wait, right?'

'Yes, but for how long? I asked Maa to call her parents but she won't budge. What do you expect Avni's parents to do?'

'I hope that guy rejects her.'

'I will get to know tomorrow, Bhaiya.'

'Relax. Once you are in Patna, we will do something. I will make sure your roka does not happen with this girl. Meanwhile, you try to make sure Avni's marriage does not happen with that guy.'

'I am in the US. What can I do?'

'There is always a way, Dhruv. Do something.'

'I really love Maa, Bhaiya. I can't take a risk by giving her stress due to my marriage.'

'I will do something. Don't worry. It is on me now.'

'Please, Bhaiya. I trust only you.'

'Oh come on. You have helped me so much with Anjana.'

'Hahaha. Is it? Now, my love story is in your hands, Bhaiya.'

'Don't worry. We will do something.'

'Congratulations once again, Bhaiya.'

A Week Later

I reached India. My flight from Texas to Delhi was on time. I took another flight from Delhi to Hyderabad. I felt tired and jet-lagged. Avni had told me that she was shifting to Bangalore tonight. She would start going to her office from the day after tomorrow. It would take an entire day to set up her room in the new flat in Bangalore.

I yawned but I wanted to hear her voice. I had twenty-one missed calls from her already. My battery was low, so I did not switch my phone on.

'Hi Dhruv ji. Welcome back to Bharat,' Avni said as she picked up my call.

'Dhruv ji? Oh my god. I love it. In one month, I've changed from Dhruv to Dhruv ji. If I had stayed for one more month in the US, what would you have called me then?'

'Haha. Very funny. I would have called you Swami,' Avni said.

'Hahahahaha, how are you?'

'I am tired and frustrated. There is so much packing to do and I have not even seen your face. Can we do a video call?' Avni said.

'But I am not looking good right now. Is that okay?'

'I just want to see your face. Switch on the camera.'

'Hello princess,' I said as I switched on the camera.

'Oh my god. Dhruv ji has grown a beard.'

'Yes, and why are you in such a nice dress? Looks like you are going out.'

'No. Just came back. Need to change. When are you coming to Bangalore?'

'Avni, there is a sudden change of plans. Maa has asked me to come to Patna. She wants to see me.'

'Dhruv, is it to meet a girl?' Avni asked.

'Shall I lie or tell the truth?'

'Truth, please.'

'Hemant Bhaiya told me that Maa wants me to meet a girl but Maa told me that she is not well. So, technically, I am meeting a girl there. And you know my answer.'

'Then why do you have to go?'

'Avni.'

'Okay, I got it.'

'Don't worry. I will come back in a week.'

'A week? When will we meet then? Today is Wednesday. I thought we would meet this weekend.'

'I just booked my ticket to Patna. My return ticket is not yet done. I promise I will try to be back by the weekend. I have given you the contacts of a few friends. You can call them if you need any help in Bangalore.'

'Okay, fine.'

'Are you mad at me?'

'No, I am just . . . I just miss you, Dhruv.'

'I miss you too. I'll see you faster than you can blink your eyes.'

Avni chuckled. Just then, I saw that Maa was calling me.

'Okay. Maa is calling, Avni. I will talk to you later. Bye.'

'I love you,' Avni said, sending me a flying kiss.

I sent her one back and received Maa's call.

'You did not call me,' Maa said.

'How are you now? How is your health?'

'Not well. I want to see my son.'

'I am coming tomorrow. And I have got a lot of gifts for you and chocolates for the kids.'

'Whose kids?'

'I mean, Amit and Alok Mama's kids, Maa.'

'What gift did you buy for me?' Maa asked.

'I am bringing a lot of sarees for you.'

'Sarees!'

If I tell Maa that Avni chose all these sarees for her, Maa's excitement will go away.

'Okay, Maa. See you tomorrow. Please don't be late to the airport,' I said and cut the call.

Please, god. I do not want to get married to anybody else.

27

The next day

I landed in Patna. Maa smiled and waved at me when she saw me at the airport exit.

'Where's Dad?' I asked.

'He didn't want to pay the parking charges. So, he is waiting for us in the car outside.'

'Your husband will never change, Maa,' I said.

'Not in this life, I guess,' Maa said. I laughed.

We walked a few metres when I saw Dad. He was busy arguing with the parking guy. I immediately ran and touched Dad's feet. The parking guy got busy with another driver.

'Why can't you pay them?' I asked Dad.

'I haven't used their parking. I won't pay. They loot us,' Dad said.

Maa and I looked at each other and smiled. I gave twenty rupees to the parking guy, behind my Dad's back.

'You have a lot of money to waste, right?' Dad said as I sat in the front seat. 'I saw you,' he added.

'I'm sorry. I won't repeat it. Now, please. Let's go home. I am hungry.'

Avni was calling me. It was a video call. I did not answer.

'I'll call later. Maa and Dad are here', I messaged.

I saw two new flyovers on the way. The roads had gotten wider; no wonder there was less crowd compared to my last visit. The government was doing great work towards the development of the city. Dad showed me the Lord Shiva Mandir in Khajpura, which had been renovated. We stopped at Hanuman Mandir on Bailey Road. Dad and Maa went inside to perform a small puja. Maa told me to wait outside. I forgot my hunger as I heard the aarti inside the temple. I took the *prasadam* after the puja. We reached home in twenty minutes.

I immediately took a cold shower. It felt relaxing. After the shower, I had my favourite food; Maa had cooked poori and aloo paneer. After lunch, I went to my room and opened my laptop. I had to call my college gang. Sandeep, Dilip and Sunil were in Patna. There was no better time to meet them. I needed their suggestions before meeting this girl, Ritu. In the car, Maa finally told me about meeting a girl's family, just as Hemant Bhaiya had informed me. I called Sandeep and told him I was in Patna.

'What are you all doing together at Sandeep's house?' I asked. 'Bala, Raj? You too? When the hell did you come here?'

'Sandeep was after us for a long time. And there was no better time than this to meet. Dilip was getting engaged,' Raj said.

'When did this happen?' I asked.

'Day before yesterday,' Bala said.

'Congratulations, Dilip,' I said.

'Thanks, buddy. You're not invited,' he said. We all laughed.

'When did you arrive in Patna?' Raj asked me.

'Just now. Just touched down,' I replied.

'Did the pilot drop you straight into your bedroom?' Dilip teased, sparking laughter all around. Their banter was as predictable as ever.

'I really want to meet you all face-to-face, guys,' I said.

'But we're not so keen on meeting you,' Raj retorted.

'It always seems like you've got a bone to pick with me,' I replied, feeling slightly defensive.

'This time, it's all of us,' Sandeep interrupted.

'What did I do now?' I asked, shooting a glare at Bala on the screen. That guy was the worst at keeping secrets.

'You didn't tell us that you have a girl in your life.'

'Let's catch up first,' I suggested.

'But first, tell us when we're meeting your bride-to-be,' they all said together.

'She's not my bride-to-be, and I'm not getting married,' I clarified.

'Then what's the point of meeting you?' Sandeep said, provoking another round of laughter.

'We also heard her relatives were going to beat you. Why would you want to marry into that family, Dhruv?' Sunil interjected.

'I'll explain everything, guys, but right now I need your help,' I pleaded.

'First, we want to speak to your bride-to-be,' Raj insisted.

'All right, I'll let you talk to her. Happy now?' I said.

'Come over to my place,' Sandeep suggested.

'Not here, man,' Bala objected.

'Let's meet at the same Z Café where we used to hang out,' I proposed.

'We'll be there in an hour,' they confirmed.

I arrived at Z Café, where we exchanged warm hugs. Raj gave me an especially tight embrace, as we hadn't seen each other in six months—since he got married.

'Okay, guys. So, I am meeting a girl for a proposal tomorrow,' I said. Everyone's eyes popped out.

'But just now, you said you'd let us talk to your bride-to-be, and now you're saying you're meeting a different girl. What is going on, bro?' Dilip questioned.

'Well, there's a bit of an issue. Maa doesn't approve of my so-called bride-to-be. Maa wants me to meet this girl, Ritu, but I am going to refuse this marriage,' I confessed.

'Then why meet her?' Sandeep reasoned.

'Good point,' Dilip chimed in.

'Just to keep Maa's word. My bride-to-be advised me to listen to Maa if I want Maa to listen to me,' I elaborated.

'It's all very confusing,' Raj remarked.

'Are you guys free tomorrow?' I inquired.

'Sorry, I'm busy,' Sandeep declined.

'We are too. We're all going to the Mahavir temple,' Dilip informed.

'Mom's organized a puja there,' Sandeep added.

'Perfect, even I am coming there,' I decided.

'What? Why?' Raj questioned.

'Maa mentioned the girl's family wanted to meet me at the temple. They live close to the temple,' I explained.

'Be careful with your mom. What if she marries you off to Ritu tomorrow? Then we'll be laughing at your fate,' Raj teased, prompting laughter all around.

'I'm already nervous. Please don't scare me any more. I just want you all to be there for me tomorrow,' I pleaded.

'What exactly are we supposed to do?' Raj inquired.

'I'm really scared, guys. I plan to reject the proposal. If the girl's family does something to me, I need you guys to have my back. You know how unpredictable people can be,' I confided.

'We've got your back,' they assured me.

'Love you, guys,' I said.

'But when do we get to meet your bride-to-be? Can we at least see her photo? We should know who we're risking our lives for tomorrow,' Raj insisted, and everyone nodded in agreement.

Men will always be men.

'I promise I'll show you her photo tomorrow. I swear on Dilip,' I declared, placing my hand on Dilip's head.

'Hey, how dare you make a false oath on my head?' Dilip protested.

'He's been doing this since college,' Raj chuckled.

'At least tell us if she's beautiful,' Sandeep said.

This guy only has one concern in life: he wants every girl to be beautiful.

'Yes, stunningly beautiful,' I assured them.

'How did you find her?' Raj asked.

'Through Google Maps,' I joked, eliciting laughter from everyone.

'Love. Ever heard of it?' I replied clearly.

'Has anyone loved as passionately as I have?' Sandeep boasted.

'How could anyone top your love story, bro? You fell for every girl in college,' Dilip quipped, prompting more laughter.

'So, you guys will be there tomorrow?' I confirmed, as our cold drinks arrived.

'Yes,' they all confirmed, raising their glasses in agreement.

I reached home. Maa told me what to say to Ritu the next day. I'd never met a potential marriage partner in person before, and I was feeling incredibly nervous. I wanted motivation. I took out my phone and dialled Avni.

'Avni,' I began as soon as she answered.

'You're calling me after four hours since you landed,' she chided.

'Avni, I'm meeting Ritu tomorrow at the temple.'

'And what do you want me to do about it? Marry her right there in the temple. Why did you even call me?' she retorted.

'Avni, please. I need your help. I'm getting nervous,' I admitted.

'Yes, and I'm thrilled to hear about your marriage plans,' she replied sarcastically.

'I called for some encouragement from you,' I pleaded.

'Go to hell and I am cutting the call. I have a meeting now.'

'Avni, can I ask you one thing?'

'Hmmm.'

'Look, I can't say anything to Maa. Dad will kill me. So, the only option is that I run away from here. Will that be fine? The girl won't feel I was rude to her, right? She won't die of suicide, right, if I do this?'

'Oh wow. Are you SRK, that she will kill herself?'

'Avni, why are you talking like this?'

'First, you both don't know each other and you have already started caring for her. No doubt, if she turns out to be more beautiful than me, you will marry her.'

'I asked for your advice. Not a lecture.'

'How nice. You are asking your own girlfriend to tell you what to do? Do you have any shame?'

'So, I can run away, right?'

'No, that will disturb your Maa even more. Just take a deep breath and go.'

I took a deep breath.

'And make sure you recite the Hanuman Chalisa before you go. Make it a daily habit,' she added.

'What?' I exclaimed.

'I hope Lord Hanuman keeps you single for me,' she declared.

'Avni, I don't understand anything,' I admitted.

'Dhruv, I have no clue how guys talk to a girl. I'm just saying whatever pops into my head. You have any idea how nervous I am?' she confessed.

'You are taking your medicines, right?'

'Yes.'

'Okay, I will hang up now. Maa is calling me.'

'Dhruv?'

'Hmmm?'

'Please don't dress up too nicely tomorrow.'

My sweet girl.

I called Hemant Bhaiya immediately.

'Hi Bhaiya. I am in Patna.'

'Hey Dhruv. That is nice, man. Welcome back!'

'Bhaiya, when are you coming to meet me? I have to go and meet Ritu. Can you please come?'

'Oh yes. I totally forgot, Dhruv. I am out of station. Anjana wanted to visit a few places. Here, talk to her.'

'Hi Dhruv ji!' Anjana Bhabhi sounded happy. Bliss, that's what married life sounded like, especially with the one you love.

'Hi Bhabhi.'

'Don't worry. You love Avni, right? Everything will be fine. I've to go cook now, we'll talk later. All the best.'

The Next Day

'Just follow my car', I messaged my college gang on the WhatsApp group. I was nervous.

'What time are you leaving?' Sandeep called immediately.

'Sharp 9 a.m. Over and out,' I said.

'Roger that,' Sandeep said.

'You sound like you are on a mission. That's my boy.'

'Yes bro, but it would have been nice if we had seen Bhabhi's photo. It will give us motivation.'

'Sandeep, when will you change, bro?' I said and cut the call.

Maa, Dad and I left to meet the girl's family at 9 a.m. I was feeling a bit relaxed because my friends were following my car. They were my support. My last hope. Another thought was bothering me. It feels embarrassing if a girl rejects you. You can't live with that. And I was scared that if Ritu rejected me, these boys would laugh at me for the rest of my life. But that's fine. I have Avni in my life. I don't care.

I kept turning behind, to see if these guys were following me or not. Sandeep's mom was coming to the temple later in her own car; she was going to be there by 10:30 a.m. It was good for me or else these guys wouldn't have come to save me. They are idiots but they are useful. We need friends like these.

Suddenly Bala called me.

'Macha, stop the car,' he said.

'But why?'

'Change in the plan.'

'Don't tell me that you have to go somewhere else now?'

'Just stop the car,' he said.

I asked Maa to tell Dad to stop the car.

'No. We are already late. The girl's family will be there any time,' Maa said.

'Bro, Maa is not allowing me to stop the car,' I said.

'Guys, Aunty is not allowing him to stop the car,' Bala said.

'What are you saying, Bala? *Start to stop?*'

'Wait, macha. I am nervous,' Bala said.

'Dhruv. Just tell your Mom that you want to pee,' Sandeep said taking the phone from Bala.

I looked at Maa and thought twice. In my whole life, I had never stopped a car for a pee. It's disgusting to pee on the street. Even though she was my Maa, I was a grown-up now. How could I tell my Maa that I wanted to pee? It would sound so bad.

'Did you tell her?' Sandeep shouted on the call.

'I am telling her. Will you wait, please?' I mumbled.

I looked at Maa. She glared at me.

'Maa, I want to pee,' I said, keeping all my self-respect aside.

'Stop the car,' Maa said, patting Dad's shoulder.

The boys on the call hoorayed. The car stopped. I immediately came out of the car and looked behind. The idiots had already stopped their car and got out. They were standing in a circle as if they were planning a rocket launch at NASA. Sandeep came running towards me.

'Do you want me to break up your marriage with Ritu?' he asked.

'Yes, of course.'

'Then I have to get in your car.'

'Okay, fine.'

'I want to sit in the middle,' he said.

'Do what you want.'

Sandeep sat between me and Maa.

'How come Sandeep is here?' Maa asked.

'I came to Patna a few days back, Aunty. I am going to the temple to pray for a good girl for my marriage by walking there,' he said.

'Yes, Maa,' I added.

'Then what are you doing in our car?' Maa asked.

'Hehe. I am tired of walking, Aunty,' Sandeep said. Dad started the car. Raj started the car behind.

'Did you pee, Dhruv?' Maa asked.

'Maa, please. Sandeep is here,' I said.

'What's wrong with that?' she said.

'Hehehe. Peeing is good for health. You should pee most of the time, Dhruv,' Sandeep said.

'Wow,' Dad said.

'Thanks, Uncle,' Sandeep said.

'Will you stop talking about peeing and focus on my marriage? Now, I actually feel like peeing, out of marriage pressure.'

'Control, bro. Let me talk. And please don't pee on me. I don't like it,' Sandeep said.

He turned towards Maa and whispered something in her ear. I was confused. Maa whispered something back to him in his ear.

'Bro, no one can save you from this marriage,' Sandeep told me in my ears.

'What the h—,' I stopped myself. 'Please don't say things like that, Sandeep,' I begged him.

'Uncle, can you please stop the car? I want to pee,' Sandeep said. Dad turned around and glared at him.

'I drank a lot of water, Uncle. Sorry. Next time, I will pee in the house,' he said, smiling.

Dad stopped the car. Sandeep got out. Dad started the car. My head was spinning, thinking of what was going to happen. What if I ended up losing Avni today?

I cannot leave her. I cannot do this. I will not be able to live without her. What do I do?

'Maa,' I said.

'Yes, Dhruv?'

'Maa, can I talk to Ritu alone for a few minutes? Will you please ask her?'

'Okay, fine. I will call and tell her.'

Maa looked at me. She understood I was really nervous.

We reached the temple. Dad got out of the car. Now, my heart was thudding in my chest.

'Dhruv, you remember what you have to say, right? Ritu is in the common puja room in the mandir,' Maa said.

I got out and ran to the puja room. Ritu was standing near the window facing away from me. It was dark. I couldn't see her face.

'Hi Ritu. How are you?'

'Hi Dhruv,' she replied in a low tone.

'Ritu, I wanted you to know something about me. I cannot say this to Maa because she is not well, and the doctor has told me not to stress her. So, I want to tell you this.'

I took a deep breath and continued, 'Ritu, I have been a very simple guy all my life. I was never like those guys who would party, enjoy, impress girls and all. Maybe because I belonged to a middle-class family. My dad had very little money, and he had to educate three of us. It was not easy for him. So, when I went to Bangalore, he would send a little money to me, and with that little money, a guy like me could not afford what other guys could. So, in college, I used to stay away from other guys because of how I looked or dressed. I started living even more reservedly. I was boring too, you know. So, nobody found me interesting enough to spend time with me.

Now, you can understand what sort of a guy I was—broken, alone, a guy who also wanted to talk to someone about how he felt, how he also wanted to enjoy life, how he also wanted to wear good clothes but could not. So, I started living alone, having my food alone, I would talk to no one in the hostel because I was always scared that other guys would ask me, "Why do you wear the same T-shirt every day?" "Why don't you wear different T-shirts on different days?" "Why do you wear the same T-shirt for going out also?" I would not be able to explain to them my situation, my dad's situation. No one would understand. Instead, they would laugh at me. So, even in the hostel, I used to be in my room, alone. I would avoid meeting people. The less you meet people, the less you get hurt.

And you know, one day I met this girl, Avni, through a common friend, Pratap. Avni used to spend time with a guy like me; she would listen to my boring talks for hours, and she was okay with me wearing the same T-shirt to college every day. You know, she never asked me why I didn't wear different T-shirts on different days. So, I felt comfortable with her. I could be myself with her. I could talk to her about anything. You know, Ritu, during lunch, I never used to have money to buy food. Dad told me that he could only manage my breakfast and dinner. So, I used to spend my lunchtime alone until Avni finished her lunch with her friends. When she would come, I used to tell her that I was also done with my lunch. She used to ask me what I had for lunch, and I would tell her that I had paneer and aloo paratha. I also kept a tiffin box with me in case Avni checked my bag. One day, Avni met me in the morning and asked me what I had brought for lunch; she told me to show her my tiffin box. I said I would show her at lunchtime, but she insisted. I did not show her my tiffin box. She forcibly checked it that day. It was empty, and Avni understood everything. She knew that I was lying to her every day. You know what she did? From the next day, Avni would bring two lunch boxes, one for me and one for her. That was the first day I had lunch in college. Avni would make sure that she ate her lunch with me since then.

Tell me, Ritu, can a guy stop himself from falling in love with a girl like her, who never questioned him about anything? You know, I had started liking her already, but when I got to know that she was from a rich family, I started avoiding her. I did not want her to be with someone like me or else people would make fun of her. For a month, I did not meet her. But I always missed her, wanted to meet her, wanted to see her face, talk to her. One day, she met me, and she told me that she hated me because I was avoiding her. She told me that if she did not meet me for a single day, she would not feel nice. She told me that she missed me. You know, I never thought that anyone could miss a guy like me. Then, I told her the real reason I was avoiding her. You know what Avni said? She said she did not know what she would do if I was not in her life. So, she told me never to avoid her again. After that, we became very good friends.

I have never told this to anyone, but I am telling you, Ritu. If today I have been able to believe that even a middle-class boy like me can be important to someone, it is because of Avni. If today I feel that if you are a nice person, people will talk to you irrespective of your status, it is because of Avni. If I believe that no matter what clothes you wear, people can still be nice to you, it is because of Avni. She gave me the hope that I could also live just like every other guy, she made me realize that I was also important in this world, that I was not a nobody, that it is okay to be not okay, it is okay to come from a middle-class family, it is okay to wear the same T-shirt every single day, it is okay to have less money. You know, Ritu, now nothing looks good if Avni is not there. Life looks so empty without her. If Avni is not there in my life, Ritu, I don't know what I will do. I love only Avni, today, tomorrow and forever. I belong only to her.'

I had tears in my eyes after I finished talking. I kept standing there when I heard Ritu sobbing. Then she stepped ahead, and that's when I saw her face. I could not believe it.

'Avni?'

I fell on my knees and broke down. It felt like, all of a sudden, someone had fixed my whole world. I kept crying for some time before I controlled myself and looked at Avni. I stood up.

'You love me so much, Mr Dhruv Mehta?' Avni asked, with tears in her eyes.

'You cannot even imagine, Avni Mehta, how much I love you,' I said and we both hugged each other. We kept hugging for some time and cried our hearts out. I don't know why we both were crying. Maybe, we were just relieved that we could live our lives with each other now.

'So, I am Avni Mehta, is it?'

'I am ready to become Dhruv Mathur if you have a problem with that.'

Avni smiled.

'Everyone is standing outside, Dhruv,' Avni muttered.

I turned around. Avni's parents, her relatives, my parents, Shreya Didi, Aadi Jiju, Prithvi Bhaiya and Bhabhi, all had tears in their eyes. I took my hands off Avni, wondering if her uncles would beat me again.

'I am sorry, Uncle,' I said, looking at Raghu Uncle, when he came inside the room and hugged me tightly.

'I am sorry, kid. I am so sorry for judging you,' he said, looking straight into my eyes.

'So, can I hug Avni again, Uncle?' I asked.

Everyone laughed with their tears shimmering in their eyes.

'I love you both so much,' Avni's mom said.

'Uncle, you don't love me?' I asked Avni's dad.

'I love you more than Avni, kid. Finally, one more North Indian like me will steal a South Indian,' Uncle said.

We all laughed again. The puja room was echoing with laughter.

'Hi Dhruv,' someone said from behind me. When I turned around, it was Aditi. I was shocked. She was with a guy.

'Hi Dhruv, Rohit here,' he said.

'Rohit? Rohit, your—'

'Yes,' Aditi smiled shyly and held his hand. 'Avni helped us,' she said when I looked at Avni.

'Dilwale dulhaniya le jayenge?' Another voice came from behind. This time, it was Hemant Bhaiya along with Anjana Bhabhi.

'Now, that is a surprise,' I said and hugged them.

Sandeep and the rest of my friends met Avni. They all were shocked when they realized that Avni was the same girl who used to come to see my theatre show in college alone. Our elders had left for home after they performed a small puja for both families. We all sat down in the temple and discussed our college days.

'Now, will you tell me how Maa agreed to our marriage?' I asked Shreya Didi.

'Hemant told Maa everything a day before his marriage,' Didi said.

'I don't understand,' I said.

'When Hemant's marriage got fixed with Anjana, Alok Mama did not tell Maa the fact that Anjana is also a manglik. Alok Mama knew that if Maa learnt about this, she would create a big drama in Hemant's marriage. So, he preferred not to tell Maa.'

'But why would Maa create drama in Hemant Bhaiya's marriage?'

'Because Alok Mama had told Maa to find another girl instead of Avni because she is a manglik.'

'I am confused. If he did not want me to marry Avni, then why would he want Hemant Bhaiya to marry Anjana Bhabhi?'

'He got to know that Avni is a manglik way before Hemant got the proposal from Anjana's family, Dhruv. He had no idea that his own son would get a similar proposal. When people fall into the same situation, they think differently. Alok Mama is very selfish.'

'Didi, relax. He is my dad, and your Mama!' Hemant Bhaiya pouted.

'Okay, I am sorry. I shouldn't have said that.' She continued, 'Where was I?'

'Alok Mama got Anjana Bhabhi's proposal,' I recited.

'Yes. Alok Mama did not want to reject Anjana's proposal at any cost,' Didi said.

'After all, she is from such a nice family,' Hemant Bhaiya interrupted.

'Either you talk or let me talk,' Didi told Hemant Bhaiya. We laughed.

'Hemant, let her talk, bro. She did not allow me to open my mouth for so many years. Who the hell are you?' Jiju said.

'What did you say?' Didi asked Jiju.

'I said who the hell am I, dear?' Jiju said, folding his hands.

'Yes. So, Hemant did not want to lose Anjana just because she was a manglik. So, he asked Alok Mama to let the marriage happen as Anjana's family had no issue with it. Even Mama ji just wanted a nice girl in his family. So, he checked with a famous astrologer who revealed that it is completely normal for a manglik and a non-manglik to get married. In fact, that astrologer's own parents had a love marriage and they were manglik and non-manglik but they never faced any issues in their thirty-five years of marriage.'

'What did Maa do when she got to know all this?' I asked.

'What do women usually do?' Jiju interrupted.

'Fight,' I said.

'Right. That's what your Maa did,' Jiju said. We laughed.

'Yes, So Maa fought with Alok Mama after knowing all this. She said that because of him she had almost lost a nice girl like Avni,' Didi said.

'Then?'

'Hemant Bhaiya informed Maa that a guy was coming to see Avni the next day. So, Maa could not wait. The next minute, she dialled Avni's number and spoke to her parents. She asked Avni and her family if they could come to Hyderabad. Avni was already so happy to know that she got a call from Maa. She agreed to come to Hyderabad the next day. Her parents had to attend a ceremony. So, they could not come.'

'After that, what happened, Didi?' I asked.

'The next day, we all reached Anju's house before Avni arrived. Maa saw the gifts Avni used to buy on your birthdays, read Avni's diary and saw your jacket which Avni had kept safely in Anju's house. Anju explained the whole story to all of us. When Avni reached, Maa greeted her with a tight hug. In fact, Maa invited Avni to attend Hemant's wedding. So, Avni joined us there where Maa introduced her to everyone.'

'Wow. Avni, you never told me all this,' I said.

'There is no point telling you anything. You don't do anything anyway, idiot,' Avni said and the room echoed with raucous laughter.

'I'm glad that you told me one day before my marriage, Dhruv, that a guy's family was coming to see Avni. I was feeling scared that if I didn't tell the truth about Anjana to your Maa, I would lose a bhabhi like Avni,' Hemant Bhaiya confessed.

'But we did not tell your Maa another secret, Dhruv. If Hemant's revelation wouldn't have worked, we were planning to tell Maa that—' Jiju said.

'What? What secret?' I asked.

'Aadi, what are you doing?' Didi said.

'Let me speak, Shreya. Your Maa is not here anyway.'

'Will you please tell me now?' I asked.

'At the time of our wedding, I changed my kundli because one of us was manglik and one was non-manglik. So, just to make sure your Maa did not create a scene in our marriage, I did that,' Jiju said.

'Oh my god,' we all said in sync with our mouths wide open.

'Thank god you did not tell Maa this,' I said.

'How could I, Dhruv? You know how Mummy ji is,' Jiju laughed. 'Forget about your Maa, Dhruv. I had not told this secret even to your sister until last week. She was thinking all these years that our kundli matched.'

'He's a big liar,' Didi said.

'Darling, all is fair in love and war,' Jiju declared.

I got a call from Dad's number but it was Maa on the call.

'Hi Maa,' I said.

'Give the phone to your Jiju,' she said. I handed the phone over to him.

'Hi Maa,' Jiju said.

'I heard your story. You lied to me? Come home and I'll show you,' Maa said and cut the call.

'Oh no. How did she get to know about my story?' Jiju asked.

'Oh no. I was on a call with Aunty and I forgot to disconnect. She heard everything,' Avni said.

Jiju was sweating already.

'Relax, Aadi. Maa will just beat you up. That's all,' Didi said.

'She will beat you too, Shreya,' Jiju said.

'But just now you said that I did not know this for all these years. So, enjoy alone,' Didi said playfully.

'I'll never stop being scared of your mother. I am not going home, your mom is scary,' Jiju said.

We all laughed.

'Avni, you still haven't cut Maa's call on your phone. You will get all of us beaten,' I said. Avni disconnected the call.

'Avni, you did this to me?' Jiju said.

'I am sorry, Jiju,' Avni said.

All of us laughed and then left. We reached home in an hour. Jiju entered the house last. He was pretending to be normal.

'Hi Aadi beta,' Jiju's mom called out.

'Mom, you are here? How? When? Why?' Jiju said as he saw his own mom.

'I can understand that you lied to Shreya's mom for all these years. But you lied to me as well? What do you think of yourself?' Aunty said angrily. All of us were shocked.

'Mom, relax. Let me explain,' Jiju said.

'No Mummy ji, don't relax. He did not even tell me this for so many years,' Didi interrupted.

'Exactly, he thinks he can do anything,' Aunty said. She had brought out a spatula from the kitchen and proceeded to beat Jiju.

'No Mom, please,' Jiju ran around the room. Aunty ran behind him.

'Jiju left! Jiju right!' I shouted, guiding him to save his bum from Aunty's spatula.

'Beat him, Mummy ji. Beat him!' Didi screamed.

'Save him, Dhruv,' Avni said.

'Relax, let me enjoy this,' I said.

Finally, Jiju was caught and got his ass beaten by his mother.

'Welcome home, Avni. Sorry, in this house, we all are a little crazy,' Maa said and hugged Avni.

'It's okay, Aunty. I will manage just like Shreya Didi managed with Aadi Jiju,' Avni said.

'Now, you have to call me Mummy, not Aunty,' Maa said to Avni.

'And now you have to call me Aadi, not Jiju,' Jiju told Avni.

'You better call him Bhaiya,' Maa told Avni. We all held our stomachs and laughed out loud.

'Maa, I have to tell you something,' I said.

'What, Dhruv?'

'Shreya Didi is expecting a baby,' I said.

'Are you serious? You made my day, Dhruv,' Maa had tears in her eyes as she hugged Shreya Didi and Aadi Jiju.

Avni and I got married a month later. Maa loves Avni, no less than she loves Shreya Didi. Now, Avni keeps running in the house shouting 'Mummy, Mummy' because I keep pinching her cheeks the whole day. And Maa keeps running behind me, forcing me to stop pinching Avni's cheeks. But I don't care. Now, Avni is mine forever.

Acknowledgements

I am happy you picked my second book after the success of my first novel, *She Stood by Me*. You, the readers, have been a huge support for me in the last five years.

For *The Right Guy*, every person and every experience I had are the reasons this book is in your hands right now. Still, I would like to thank a few people in particular whom I don't want to miss expressing my gratitude for:

My parents, Ashok Kumar Gupta and Pushpa Lata Gupta, who have been my role models throughout my life. My dad is the pillar of my life, and my mom is the foundation of that pillar. My dad has always been an inspiration to me whenever I needed one. My mom is the reason I am creative; she herself is also a creative person in the field of embroidery.

Abhishek and Aparna, the protagonists of *She Stood by Me*, have been a huge support for me throughout the writing process. Without their constant support, frequent calls and motivating words, writing the second novel would not have been this easy. Didi reviewed the book multiple times and gave me valuable suggestions that added more humour to the story. Thank you, Didi. Thank you, Jiju.

My elder brother, Praveen Kumar, has been always there to assist me day and night, offering his expert advice, encouraging me constantly and creating doodles for the book cover. Bhaiya is a sketch artist himself.

My bestie, Raj Kiran, for being the ray of hope among my entire circle of friends who don't read books—except for Raj. I began giving him the starting chapters as sample, and that is when he started guiding me. His initial suggestions were incredibly helpful, and I cannot thank him enough for that.

Ankit Jha, for being in touch with me during the writing of my second novel and for believing in me.

My best friend, Sangeet Kumar, who has been with me all the time. Despite not being an avid reader, he always had valuable suggestions when I needed to add drama to the story. His inputs helped me develop the characters better than I could have alone.

I would also like to thank Deepak Ujala, who consistently showed his belief that I could write the second novel. Thanks for your trust.

Last but not least, I would like to extend my gratitude to the amazing team at Penguin India, who invested their valuable time and elevated the whole story. They have remarkable patience with me, for which I am deeply grateful. They are truly sweet and talented.

Scan QR code to access the
Penguin Random House India website